Praise for Quan Barry's

When I'm Gone, Look for Me in the East

"A peaceful and edifying story that can be endlessly mined for deeper meaning. . . . *When I'm Gone, Look for Me in the East* is a journey worth taking. The writing is simple but powerful, like a proverb."
—The Rumpus

"There's much to savor in Barry's descriptions of Buddhist scripture, rites and concepts. . . . Barry, who visited Mongolia in 2008, imbues the book with all the wondrous detail of the best observational writers. . . . [She] exposes overlooked places and history in a world where, against all odds, there is always something new under the desert sun."
—*Los Angeles Times*

"Faith and brotherhood are at the heart of Quan Barry's compelling new novel."
—PopSugar

"Utterly original, a unique immersion in history, philosophy, religion, the nature of time, and the clash of old and new happening all over our world. . . . An award-winning poet, Barry shapes transparent, simple language into images that are lyrical and haunting. . . . *When I'm Gone, Look for Me in the East* is a story of much magic and many miracles—a startling, yet gentle, book."
—*Washington Independent Review of Books*

"A dreamlike and lyrical journey steeped in the tenets of Tibetan Buddhism."
—*Kirkus Reviews* (starred review)

"The expansive imagination of Massachusetts-raised Quan Barry knows no bounds. . . . Barry explores large questions about Buddhist philosophy and faith in general while painting a lush portrait of the Mongolian terrain."
—WBUR

"An imaginative tour de force. . . . Evincing the same dazzling talents that won high critical praise for *We Ride Upon Sticks*, Barry vastly expands readers' horizons, both geographical and metaphysical."
—*Booklist* (starred review)

QUAN BARRY

When I'm Gone, Look for Me in the East

Born in Saigon and raised in Massachusetts, Quan Barry is the author of the novels *She Weeps Each Time You're Born* and *We Ride Upon Sticks* (winner of the ALA Alex Award) and four books of poetry, including *Water Puppets* (winner of the AWP Donald Hall Prize for Poetry and a PEN Open Book Award finalist). Barry's first play, *The Mytilenean Debate*, premiered in the spring of 2022. She is the Lorraine Hansberry Professor of English at the University of Wisconsin–Madison.

ALSO BY QUAN BARRY

Fiction

We Ride Upon Sticks

She Weeps Each Time You're Born

Poetry

Loose Strife

Water Puppets

Controvertibles

Asylum

Plays

The Mytilenean Debate

When I'm Gone,

Look for Me in the East

When I'm Gone, Look for Me in the East

QUAN BARRY

Vintage Contemporaries
Vintage Books
A Division of Penguin Random House LLC
New York

FIRST VINTAGE CONTEMPORARIES EDITION 2023

Copyright © 2022 by Quan Barry

All rights reserved. Published in the United States by Vintage Books, a division of Penguin Random House LLC, New York, and distributed in Canada by Penguin Random House Canada Limited, Toronto. Originally published in hardcover in the United States by Pantheon Books, a division of Penguin Random House LLC, New York, in 2022.

Vintage is a registered trademark and Vintage Contemporaries and colophon are trademarks of Penguin Random House LLC.

This is a work of fiction. Names, characters, places, and incidents either are the product of the author's imagination or are used fictitiously. Any resemblance to actual persons, living or dead, events, or locales is entirely coincidental.

Grateful acknowledgment is made to HarperCollins Publishers for permission to reprint excerpts from *Essential Tibetan Buddhism* by Robert A. F. Thurman. Copyright © 1995 by Robert A. F. Thurman. Reprinted by permission of HarperCollins Publishers.

The Library of Congress has cataloged the Pantheon edition as follows:
Name: Barry, Quan, author.
Title: When I'm gone, look for me in the East / Quan Barry.
Description: First edition. | New York : Pantheon Books, 2022.
Identifiers: LCCN 2021028160 (print) | LCCN 2021028161 (ebook)
Classification: LCC PS3602.A838 W48 2022 (print) | LCC PS3602.A838 (ebook) | DDC 813/.6—dc23
LC record available at https://lccn.loc.gov/2021028160
LC ebook record available at https://lccn.loc.gov/2021028161

Vintage Contemporaries Trade Paperback ISBN: 978-0-525-56544-4
eBook ISBN: 978-1-5247-4812-8

Book design by Anna B. Knighton
Map and compass art by Rodica Prato
Buddhist symbols by kathykonkle/DigitalVision/Getty Images

vintagebooks.com

Printed in the United States of America
1st Printing

For the sangha

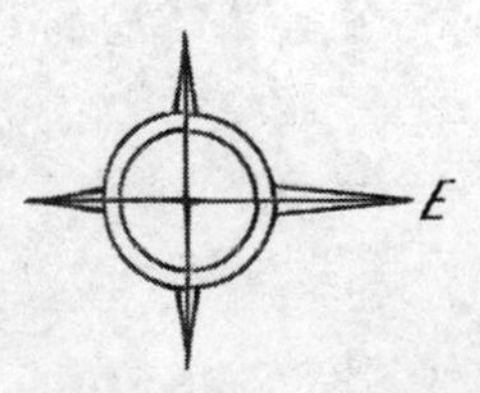

RUSSIA
KAZAKHSTAN
Khövsgöl
Lake
God
Mountain
Altai Mountains
MONGOLIA
KARAKORUM
ULAANBAATAR
E
Gobi
Desert
INNER
MONGOLIA
CHINA

CONTENTS

With homage, homage, homage I bow down!
Offering praises, I pay homage!
Who praises, who is praised?
When will I understand that we are like
Water poured in water, butter poured in fire?

Either You Get to Ulaanbaatar by Sundown or You Don't

Listen Without Distraction

Outside the post office in Bor-Urt, a handful of men clump around a pool table, its felt top sun-ravaged and mangy, the men's faces weathered from living in a world without trees. When I step outside they stare, each man a finger in a fist, and the one slumped in the ratty camping chair at the head of the table is the thumb. I glance at the digital watch the Rinpoche hands me last night, its plastic band already cracked, the thing used. I know it is a necessity, that I must have it for the places I am to journey to in my search that must not fail. Nevertheless I feel like one of the wild horses foreign researchers shoot down with arrow guns, the animal succumbing so that the researcher can fix the radio collar around its neck, the collar eventually becoming a part of the body. After just a few hours in the July light, the skin around my wrist is already somewhat paler than the rest of me, though like the planets and the summer sun, nothing is permanent.

It is ten in the morning. The main road through Bor-Urt periodically billows with dust as a breeze blows through town. The men stare at me and then look away. Someone spits in the dirt. Hidden in the folds of my robe there is a bag filled with more *tögrög* than they can earn in six months or even a year if the winter is harsh. Normally they would be out on the grasslands, out watching their flocks or herding them in for one of the two daily milkings, but today they drive the many kilometers into Bor-Urt on their motorbikes to bring their wives in to do the shopping. The men huddle idly around the table as men often do as they wait for women. Men with time on their hands, looking to establish their status among their kind.

I step out of the post office, and their faces fall. I am not what they want. I am a novice of the Yatuugiin Gol monastery, a monk who lives in the shadow of the sleeping volcano. As it is mid-morning, the mail truck I am to ride to Ulaanbaatar on the first stage of my journey is not scheduled to arrive for hours. Thirteen hundred years ago Shantideva tells us the only source of happiness in the universe is the cherishing of the other. Silently I approach the table and nod.

Brother, booms the one enthroned in the camping chair. He is sitting with his legs spread wide, a toothpick in his fingers as he works at his teeth. Something in the lackadaisical arrangement of his limbs reminds me of Mun, Mun's long black hair often loose like a horse's mane. I only play for money, the man says.

A good policy, I say. I lay ₮2,000 on the table.

Ten minutes later and I can tell the others do not know who to root for—the one who sits outside the post office each day looking to deprive the local herdsmen of their money or me, a young monk from Yatuu Gol in his simple red robe. My body wavers like a flame in the summer heat. On the faded table the balls roll and crack like stars.

In the Universe's Eternal Calendar, It Is Always Now

Now there is only the black ball remaining for me to sink, the thing a hole rumbling in space. At the other end of the table my opponent draws heavily on the cigarette he lights after I sink three in a row. He stands smoking with the toothpick still wedged in his teeth, eyeing the two balls he has left on the table. The angle of my final shot is not an easy one. Earlier the second ball I pocket is a spectacular combination shot, the men all gasping as it rolls in. As there is no chalk, I rub the tip of my stick in the dirt. My opponent is breathing hard. It is proving to be an exciting game. Should he lose there is no reason for him to hang his head. Oddly enough, a loss could be good for business. Once word gets out, normally reticent herdsmen might begin to saunter up and lay down their hard-earned *tögrög,* thinking he is beatable. I wonder if he has a wife and children. I wonder why he chooses a life in town, the town consisting of a few hundred people and a series of dusty buildings constructed in the blocky Russian style, when every beautiful thing is far from here.

I clear my mind and lean in, the stick an extension of my body. In the silence Övöö's two favorite sayings come to me—the world is what we make it, and a man's dreams are the most real part of him. My grandfather with his thick limp, his broken teeth, his eyes forever scanning the horizon. I draw my arm back and send the universe scattering.

The cue ball goes spinning erratically off the eight, a comet colliding with an asteroid. Collectively we watch the white ball roll toward a pocket. Life is suffering. Everywhere mercy and the power of mercy. I exhale and the cue ball falls in. The men cheer. My opponent smiles.

Very nice game, he says. Because I am a monk, as a formality he offers me back my ₮2,000, but I bow and he stuffs the bill in his shirt.

Brother, how do you play so well, someone asks. I do not tell him the truth, that this is my first game ever. I think of Mun, my brother with his hair braided down to his shoulders in the old style worn by the horsemen of Chinggis Khaan. If I close my eyes I can see one of Mun's braids skimming the table as he bends down to survey a shot. Each day at Yatuu Gol's morning *puja,* in my mind's eye Mun on his golden cushion silently reminding me we are all Chinggis Khaan's wandering descendants, every last one of us.

I turn toward my questioner. Even under his hat the work of years in the summer sun is obvious. I imagine the simple life this man leads out on the grasslands, the smell of sheep and the milk hardening on the roof, but nothing is ever simple. Once you are bitten by a snake, you become cautious of rope. I tell the man an approximation of the truth.

In another life, I say.

Then I walk to the community center and the town's one larch tree and I plant myself beneath it with nothing but a bag of money and a half-written letter wrapped up in the folds of my robe and wait for my destiny to claim me. Listen closely: today may be the year 2015, the month July, but in the universe's eternal calendar, it is always now. What every moment of sentience for the past twenty-three years teaches me. There is one thing and one thing only: suffering and the end of suffering. This is the true journey. Everything else is bait. I place myself on the earth with the intention of rising up rooted like a tree.

When the Only Hope Is a Boat and There Is No Boat

The moon is already rising hours before sundown when my opponent staggers up the road and motions for me to follow. Both pool sticks are gripped in his hands, the toothpick still clenched between his teeth. Prior to this moment I am sitting all day in the lotus position under the larch tree, trying to conquer the feeling spreading in my chest, a feeling like being carried away by a swollen river, the water like a series of hands dragging you into the turbid cold. For the past several hours my heart alternately beating *the mail truck arrives* and then *the mail truck does not arrive*. But I think of the Rinpoche back in the monastery at Yatuu Gol, my teacher a man well into his eighties. How he entrusts me with this task, his digital watch periodically beeping on my wrist. How I am only fifteen kilometers from the sleeping volcano and already I am stuck.

Such is the life of the grasslands. There are few paved highways here. With travel there is never any certainty. Journeys that should only take hours stretch on into days or longer. The grasslands are rife with lands where no car ventures. From Bor-Urt the mail truck that arrives in town once a week is the only scheduled way out, and today it has yet to appear. Though the sun is still well above the horizon, already the moon begins its nightly climb. To be defeated before I even begin. Inside me the watery feeling starts to take root, solidify, ice curdling on the surface of a river, my eyes rimed like glass on a winter day. I move deeper within myself, occupying as little space as possible.

My opponent waits for me to rise. Does he know how important it is that I get to Ulaanbaatar's Gandan Tegchenling Monastery before sundown tomorrow? The Buddha says *when the only hope is a boat and there is no boat, I will be the boat.* I watch as my opponent spits the toothpick into the dirt. There is nothing else for me to do but follow. My heart falls silent. Destiny is letting yourself go where you are meant to go even when your mind says otherwise.

I Am Not on the Edge of a Forest

My opponent leads me along the one dusty road through Bor-Urt to the other side of town. He walks silently ahead, his eyes locked on the ground as if deep in prayer. Each time he moves, the small burlap sack slung over his shoulder clatters with a sound like old bones. In each hand he grasps a pool stick which he carries like a spear. An aura of violence surrounds him—some of it past, some of it yet to manifest. The way he walks with a swagger, his shoulders muscled like a horse.

Despite his aggressive emanations, something about this man's presence comforts me. I begin to feel hopeful, a boat lifting off rocks as the tide rises. But then I remember the pitfalls of such feelings. Hope makes it difficult to accept things as they are when things as they are seem unacceptable. Hope is about projection, about living in a time to come. Doubt is one of the six mental afflictions and the near cousin of hope. To combat it, I must always remember where I am. On the edge of a forest, the sun would just now be falling into the tops of the trees, a spectacular sight. But at this moment I am not on the edge of a forest.

Instead, we turn and enter a neighborhood of *ger*. The structures look alien, like objects from outer space. I am used to *ger* dotting the grasslands, gray smoke spiraling from their iron stovepipes, their impermanence an absolute. One day you pass them and the next day they're gone, a trampled circle left behind in a vast sea of grass. But here within the borders of a town riddled with square concrete buildings, the *ger* look extraterrestrial, a flock of peculiar animals penned in for the night.

Evening. Bor-Urt. A pool hustler. Emerging stars. Just last night the Rinpoche at Yatuu Gol asking me to make this journey. This is what life brings. I bow my head and accept.

For the sake of every sentient being who exists both now and in the thought realms of past and future, I must help find an ancient light, what we call a *tulku*. A *tulku* is the reincarnation of an enlightened teacher. This *tulku* chooses to be born again here in Mongolia under our eternal blue sky. While this being is not the reincarnation of the Dalai Lama Himself, who lives in exile in Dharamshala, this particular *tulku* is destined to help carry on our faith through these troubled times. My mission: to lend my strength where needed in the search for this reincarnation. Last night I stand in the Rinpoche's cramped room, his bed piled high with prayer books, so many that he sleeps on a woven mat on the floor. When he requests that I lend my strength to the search, I know he is not referring to any physical gifts I may have but to my spirit, my indomitable patience, which is remarked on by others time and again, this rock that anchors me in this world. I tell him I am ready to add whatever light I may possess to the task. I bow in a manner that I hope conveys that I am aware of the trust being placed in me.

Then it happens. The Rinpoche offers me a bag filled with *tögrög*. For the journey, he says. Outside, the sound of Yatuu Gol's only rooster informing the world of his existence. For the first time, the Rinpoche bows to me in a manner that goes beyond convention. Something in the length of time he holds the bow, the angle of his back. I am stunned. The world trembles. This elderly monk who survives the purges by remaining hidden for decades and is now singlehandedly resurrecting the faith in a five-hundred-square-kilometer radius is bowing to me. He is bowing to me as an equal. When he stands back up, I accept the bag of money with both hands, and press it to my forehead. It is the most money I am ever to hold. May this *tögrög* bring only blessings into the world.

As Is Tradition, This Door Faces South

When we arrive, a blue light is flickering under the threshold. My opponent pushes open the wooden door. Come, he says impatiently, ducking his head. I enter with hands folded.

Now that I count myself among the monks at Yatuu Gol, I stand just inside the door for a moment and marvel. It is a long time since I find myself in a Mongolian *ger*. When the need arises, a *ger* can be packed up and loaded onto a truck or cart within a few hours. This *ger* is typical, no more than nine meters at its widest, much like the one I grow up in as a child. Electrical cords snake over the floor, a parquet plastic sheeting covered with worn rugs. Because we are in town, a thick orange power cord runs up one of the two central pillars that supports the roof. The cord continues on out the *toono* that opens at the top. Around the *toono* the wooden slats that make up the roof fit into a circular ring, the slats painted a fiery orange and radiating out from the center of the roof like rays of light. I imagine the power cord must plug into an electrical box somewhere outside, possibly a box the whole neighborhood shares. When my twin and I are children out on the grasslands, our *ger* is electrified by both a generator and solar energy, a small panel winking in the sun just outside the door.

As is tradition, this door faces south. A cast-iron stove sits in the middle of the room. Next to the stove there's a small table, some wooden stools for guests to sit. Several large chests are pushed up against the walls. Much of the interior furniture is painted red, orange, and yellow, and covered with intricate designs. Two small beds face each other on opposite sides of the *ger*. Memories of long nights on the steppe sweep over me. If a family has many children, they might place felt mattresses down on the floor each night. Growing up, Mun and I stuff our pillows with old clothes that are out of season. Since the age of eight, I live in a monastery, but anytime I find myself in a *ger,* I remember my first self. There is nothing like the sense of home to open one's heart to all things. And here above it all a blue flag hangs from the skylight—a nod to Tengri, the Eternal Blue Sky, our people's first god.

There Are Times When We Must Walk Toward the Darkest Dark

Because of the light from a television in the corner, it takes my eyes a moment to adjust. The sound on the TV is off, but through the blizzard of staticky snow I can make out four western women sitting with shiny triangular glasses in their hands, the women sipping daintily. Then I see her. Down on her haunches in front of the stove. A little girl, probably no more than ten, the girl throwing dried dung in the fire, the flames brightening. When she sees my opponent, the girl jumps up and wraps her arms around his waist. For the briefest of moments, his aura wavers. The way the moon sometimes dons a halo, its skin as if smudged with light. He licks his fingers and wipes a dark smudge from the child's face.

You're off to Ulaanbaatar, the little girl says as my opponent carefully props the pool sticks in the corner by the altar. In the honored place next to a shot glass and an empty bottle of vodka, a young woman poses unsmiling in her best jacket, the Eiffel Tower in the background, though the cityscape is just a photographer's backdrop.

It takes me a moment to realize the child is talking to me. I wonder how she knows my destination. Perhaps earlier today someone in the post office tells my opponent who somehow whispers it to her just now. I wonder if the girl knows what lies ahead of me. If I am up to the task. If I have anything to offer.

Yes, Littlest Sister, I say.

Tonight, she says.

Yes, Littlest Sister, I repeat.

Okay, she says. First let's eat.

There is something about this girl. I know that to travel on the same path as this child and her guardian places me on a road toward darkness. I envision a ruin atop a hill, a circle of stones gleaming in the moonlight, and within this ruin, I know there is a place waiting for me. All the same I must continue on. Despite the vows I swear of highest integrity, there are times when we must walk toward the darkest dark, not because we believe in the dawn to follow, but because the darkest dark is simply the world as it is in that instant. This is what we must take refuge in. The truth of every moment, the way things are and not as we wish them to be. I am not to act in a manner that may bring shame on my brotherhood. I am simply to witness and be present to whatever is.

My opponent lays the burlap sack down on the floor. A clattering of bones, then the eight ball rolls out, a sudden hole in the darkness. The girl stuffs it back in with her foot.

The Tail of a White Mongol Sheep

Happily, the *guriltai shul* is made with mutton and not beef, which I actually prefer. I have had little to eat, only a sliver of hardened *aaruul* I carry with me from Yatuu Gol. Vegetables can at times be a luxury in a nomadic culture, the people never in one spot long enough to harvest a crop, but this soup is thick with turnips. Because most of Mongolia's traditional dishes involve meat, I and the monks in this region eat it regularly. Still, it is not something we do lightly. Before I take a single bite, I intone the mantra of clairvoyance as a blessing:

Um badma üshnikha vimali khum pad

With these powerful words, I purify the environment and wish the one born of an animal womb a higher rebirth in their next incarnation. Even His Holiness in exile down in Dharamshala is known to partake of the flesh of animals. Many years ago He feels sluggish and western doctors cannot fix Him. Then the Oracle says He must replenish His body with the energy of the spirit, and when He eats the tail of a white Mongol sheep cooked in a traditional broth, He is whole again, the tail of the sheep of Mongolia renowned for its fattiness.

My opponent sits tearing at his bowl of food, his eyes locked on the snowy television. The girl does not eat with us but kneels by the stove poking at the flames. Next to a pile of dried dung there is a plastic bowl full of cold ashes. I do not know how to make sense of what happens next, though I try and hide my astonishment. Is it an act of mortification, an attempt to erase the self? The girl puts down her stick and takes a deep breath. She holds it in, her chest fully expanded. Without warning she shoves both her hands in the ash and rubs the grime over her face. There is nothing playful in her movements. A sooty cloud clouds the air. When she's done, she exhales. My opponent throws her a rag. The girl looks at him and smiles, wiping her hands, her teeth like little moons in the dark.

Rock 'n' Roll

It is now well past ten o'clock. The summer sun is finally bedded and the sky filled with night. Across the table my opponent puts his bowl down a third time and points at it with his finger. With her newly blackened face the little girl scoops it up and hurries to the doorway where she refills the bowl from the plastic barrel filled with *airag*. When she lifts the lid, I can smell the sourness from across the room. In Mongolia's central provinces, a house without fermented mare's milk is not a home. Though technically an intoxicant, which the Five Precepts counsel Buddhists to avoid, it is not unusual for monks to drink *airag*.

I am still on my first bowl. It is a long time since I drink *airag*. From house to house, the taste is unchanged—the way the bubbles tingle at the back of the throat, how the head seems to loosen on the neck. The sourness can make the eyes water if you are not used to it. A western monk from Australia who is currently on retreat at Yatuu Gol describes it as tasting like a mixture of champagne and unsweetened yogurt.

Outside, a truck rumbles up out front. Because it does not have its lights on, at first I think it is thunder rolling through the skies. But then I hear a car door open and slam shut. Two men push the door open and enter without knocking. Each grabs a bowl from a shelf. One of the men looks at me and then looks at my opponent, the question forming in his eyes. Why is there a monk here? *When the only hope is a boat and there is no boat, I will be the boat.*

On the television, fuzzy images of a man and a woman wrestling in a western bed, the sheets crisp like a field of snow. I wonder what these people are expecting from me, then I stop wondering. It is out of my hands. Together the five of us sit and watch the television. I wonder if this is the kind of thing Mun watches in his apartment in the capital. On-screen one of the women walks into a room filled entirely with shoes.

The girl stands up and shuts the television off. She collects the men's bowls and then she and my opponent slip on their *deel,* the man's tattered along the bottom. Nights on the grasslands the temperature can drop a full twenty degrees even now in the throes of summer. Ready, she asks.

Rock 'n' roll, I say in English. Once it is out of my mouth, I realize this is a favorite saying of my brother, a tiny fire gleaming in Mun's eyes.

One of the strange men bows to me. I can tell by the uneven way he dips his shoulders while keeping his eyes on my face that he is jesting, that he thinks my robes are just a show. I want to tell him I am simply a reflection like the moon on water, but I remain silent. As I rise from the table I bow my head, thinking of the animal spirit I consume. *I will liberate those not liberated.*

The girl with her blackened face is the first out the door.

The Man's Patterns Are Inside

Only three people fit in the cab, so the second man opens the gate at the back. I boost myself up. There is no roof, the walls wooden slats built like an animal pen so that the air can stream through. The truck is mid-sized and obviously used to transport livestock. The warped wooden floor is wet perhaps from being rinsed, though here and there I can still see dark clumps of their droppings. Despite the openness of the truck bed, everywhere the smell of animals; in a few spots what looks like blood maps the floor. Just as the man is about to close the gate, the girl appears, her eyes flashing. The man lifts her up and she walks to where I am squatting behind the cab. Her footsteps boom on the wood. The cab is missing its back window, a piece of dirty canvas taped in its place. Through it I can clearly hear one of the men singing. His song is an old tale about a beautiful horse that refuses to take a lover. The song's bawdy lyrics cut through the darkness in sharp contrast to the beauty of its melody.

Hold on, says a voice through the window, and the truck starts to move. The girl takes my hand. There is something protective in the way she holds it.

We drive with the headlights off, just the glow of the moon to illuminate our way. Sometime in the next few weeks it should be full, a face shadowing us in the sky. We drive past the post office and the now-abandoned pool table like an empty garden plot, then on past the larch tree in the middle of town. Through the flimsy canvas I can see a shadow pass the driver a bottle. Tell me a story, the girl says. Something about this child reminds me of the adage: the man's patterns are inside, the snake's outside. All the same I honor her request.

I think of my brother Mun walking the streets of Ulaanbaatar hundreds of kilometers away, his mind full of strange words and images, a library for me to draw on. Because she is not tall enough for the wind to find her in the leeward side of the cab, all the way across the grasslands the child remains standing.

The Earth and Sky Never Meet

Listen without distraction, I say. I can feel her grip tighten on my hand. In the sky the moon hangs like an ear.

The earth and sky never meet, but the children of men do, I say. Once there are three brothers. They live in a *ger* by a bend in the Singing River.

Does the river sing all the time, day and night, asks the little girl. I can tell it is no idle question, that nothing I say is being taken lightly.

No, I say. It only sings to those with the patience to hear it. I wait a spell for her to respond to this, but when she does not speak, I continue.

One winter the brothers' animals die one by one until all they are left with is an old blind mare. When all the other animals are gone, the old mare no longer sleeps outside. Each night she hobbles into the *ger,* her big wet eyes like moons. One night Oldest Son goes to ladle a cup of *airag* out of the barrel by the door. Suddenly the *ger* fills with the sound of the wooden ladle scraping the bottom, the sound like a fish hook dragged over rocks. In the morning when the sun rises Oldest Son and Second Brother tell their third brother, Simpleton, that they are going out beyond the grasslands to make their fortune in the world, only to return when they are rich. From the doorway Simpleton watches them disappear over the horizon.

On the grasslands, winter drags on. In the larder there is less and less to eat. Your brothers are not coming back, says the old mare one snowy night, her eyes wet as eggs.

You don't know that, says Simpleton brightly.

The old mare sighs. Then drink of my milk, says the animal, and

Simpleton gets down on his knees and reaches up for the shriveled teat with his mouth.

Spring comes and goes. Summer burns the grasslands. Then it is fall. Each night Simpleton curls under the old mare's belly, the outline of her ribs like the staves in a barrel as he drinks his fill, the animal's milk perfectly sour yet fizzy, as if it ferments into *airag* right there in her teat.

Your brothers are not coming back, says the old mare. Do you know it now?

Yes, says Simpleton, and after he packs up the few things he cares about in this world—a lucky anklebone, a scrap from his mother's dress—he and the old mare walk side by side out of the grasslands following the Singing River.

It's easy for him to find his brothers because the river tells him where to go, says the little girl.

Yes, I say. In the truck's cab two of the men are playing cards. All around us the grasslands lie dark as an ocean. Each night as they lie down to sleep, the river sings to Simpleton and the old mare, I say, telling them which way to head. Within a month the two find his brothers sleeping in a cave. Then Simpleton informs Oldest Son and Second Brother that he comes to join them so they might go forth together to make their fortune in the world. His brothers laugh.

It is harder to make one's fortune in the world than we could ever imagine, says Second Brother. How can you help us when you walk beside your horse as if it is your equal?

She is my equal, says Simpleton. And how I may help you that is not for me to say, he says. But let us go. And so they go.

The girl is looking at the sky. I am not sure if she is listening. Quickly I relate how Simpleton's honesty and compassion to various animals he and his brothers encounter along the road are paid back in full when all three brothers are charged with an impossible task by a magician. With the help of his animal friends, Simpleton marries the Khaan's daughter and comes into possession of a herd of ten thousand. Because he is a kind man, he gives to his brothers the older sisters of his wife.

I finish my story, secretly relieved to find my way to a suitable ending. For a long time my only reward is the night's silence.

Weaving Like a Dancer to Emphasize His Point

Finally the girl looks at me. How do you know that tale?

I tell her the truth but simplified. My brother reads a lot, I say.

She nods. That's a nice story, she says. It tells us how we ought to live.

Yes, I say.

Only thing is, we don't live like that, she says. I watch her eyes in the dark night of her face. Stories about good people doing bad are the best kind, she says. Don't you think?

I don't know any stories like that, I say.

How come, she asks. She slits her eyes as if she suspects me of dishonesty. If you don't know about evil, how can you know anything about good?

I contemplate this. All around us the grasslands like the Singing River chirring in the dark. Currently at Yatuu Gol, I am a novice. Eleven vows tie me to this way of life. In two months' time, on the day of my ordination, I am scheduled to take the full 253 vows that forever pledge me to this tradition, the vows falling into five categories beginning with the Four Defeats and ending with Misdeeds. At least five fully ordained monks are required to perform the ceremony. That evening in celebration, I and the other newly ordained monks are expected to sit upon the cold earth in the main courtyard of Yatuu Gol. Like the generations that precede us, we must sit in the lotus position with our legs folded like pairs of wings as we wait for the Rinpoche to begin by asking us any question he likes based on the Collected Topics. Once we are called forth, we are to rise for debate two by two, one to defend his position, the other to question the soundness of his reasoning. Each questioner stamping the earth with his foot and clapping his hands, his prayer beads hanging from his arm, moving his body rhythmically through space, weaving like a dancer to emphasize his point, all night long the stars tracking their light through the heavens the way snails leave a bright path on stone.

But as this night is quickly approaching, the question haunts me: am I up to it? Am I ready to defend the Collected Topics? Is my knowledge of the very subtle consciousness sufficient? Am I able to explain how this consciousness is similar to but different from the Christian concept of the soul? What if I am asked to remember how my own body's indestructible drop forms when the egg and sperm collide? Here I am, unable to deliver a simple story of good and evil to a child—me, a being who lives the past fifteen years cloistered behind monastery walls. What do I know of life? And am I ready to give up the pleasures of living when I know so little of experience?

Overhead the moon sits in the sky, familiar yet distant. Up until now in my life, I am never more than a few hundred kilometers from the place of my birth, the moon always questing at the same angles through the night. Secretly I am relieved to be here in the back of this truck on my way to wherever the universe may lead. Just once I want to see the moon from a different angle. I want to drink deeply of this world with both hands before I renounce it.

I place a hand on my chest and feel the letter I have yet to finish writing tucked in my robe next to my heart. At Yatuu Gol we believe the natural state of the mind is one of luminosity and bliss. May this path I am on return me to this state of pure light free of doubt!

The girl lets go of my other hand. For a moment bathed in the moonlight she looks like an old man.

The truck comes to a stop. I look down. My palm is black with soot and in the darkness it seems to disappear.

We Can Smell the Milk Turning

The driver appears at the back of the truck. He begins fumbling with the latch to open the tailgate, but the thing seems to be stuck. My traveling companion puts both hands over her ears. The man nods, keeps working at it in a quieter manner. Finally the thing comes loose and the door opens. The little girl jumps down without help. I sit on the edge of the truck and ease myself out. My opponent and the second man pull dark masks over their faces. I can still recognize them by their size and shape. The driver climbs into the truck bed. He finds what he is looking for and slides a metal ramp down out of the back until it touches the ground.

For a moment the five of us stand in the moonlight, the little girl with her face blackened with soot. Sadly I know why we are here. This is not the first time I ride across the grasslands to watch someone take ownership of something that does not belong to him. When Mun and I are seven years old, my brother wakes me in the middle of a summer night much like this. We ride our horses an hour west until we come to a *ger* where a young widower lives alone with a few animals. Everyone knows the man is a thief, that after the slow death of his wife in childbirth he now milks healthier animals that do not belong to him and sells the milk in town. I remember how Mun and I arrive at the man's *ger* and find it unattended, the man out raiding the bounty of his neighbors. Inside his *ger* we can smell the milk turning, the whole roof covered with blocks of it. That night Mun steals a radio which he later trades for some old VHS tapes of American movies. I remember there is what looks to be a prayer book lying on a table. Take it, says Mun, but I can't even bring myself to unroll it just to see what it says.

The girl is good at her job. Soundlessly she opens the first pen. When she enters, a silent jolt of electricity seems to ripple through the flock, the sheep connected to one another. The animals huddle together along the edge of the enclosure, their legs folded underneath them as they lie sleeping, the ground as if littered with clouds.

Seemingly effortlessly, the girl manages to cull an animal away from the others. She leads it out of the pen. The girl is a professional. Even in the dark she selects an animal that should fetch a good price but is not the pride and glory of the flock. An animal that is not remarkable, that is not singular enough to be missed. In some ways I am this sheep. In a few hours when the sun rises on Yatuu Gol, is there anyone among my cohort of young novices who might notice my absence at first ablution? I watch the sheep walk up the ramp into the back of the truck. It does not hesitate. It simply trusts.

Karma Simply Means "Action"

Mun and I are never caught for our transgression which in a way is worse than if we are. Early the next day at breakfast Övöö asks why the flanks of our horses glisten with sweat. Mun tells our grandfather that as it is the full wolf moon only the night before, the animals must be possessed by dreams of riding over the grasslands as part of the Khaan's Mongol horde. Most days any mention of Chinggis Khaan makes our grandfather smile, but not that day. That day Övöö shakes his head. Somehow his toothless mouth appears more sunken. Like spoons unable to taste the flavor of soup, he says, are the fools who cannot see truth. He leaves it at that. Our father also says nothing. It is the worst rebuke. As if they are conceding that we are incorrigible, not worthy of correcting. After my morning chores I do a hundred full-body prostrations out in the emptiness of the grasslands. From atop his horse Mun watches as I press my face into the earth over and over. My face covered with bug bites, as each time I move, the grass comes alive.

If I perform a hundred prostrations that time just for accompanying my brother out to the house of a lonely thief, how many must I do now as we rob an innocent family of their livelihood?

What Mun would say: nobody is innocent.

When she is finished, the girl closes the pen, then walks up the ramp into the back of the truck. Silently I follow her up the plank. She is my shepherd and I am her sheep. In Sanskrit, karma simply means "action." In its truest sense, it is the law of cause and effect, but is anything that simple? Tomorrow in Ulaanbaatar, I and the others charged by His Holiness the Dalai Lama must start the search for the rebirth of one of the oldest lights in the Tibetan Buddhist world, a being destined to help carry on the ancient truths in a world that seeks to destroy the ancient truths. If the path to finding the one born to bring wisdom to millions requires that I be present at this act of thieving, am I wrong to do so?

The girl looks at me and smiles. The half-finished letter hidden next to my heart feels as if it is burning. Somehow this is the way to Ulaanbaatar. At Yatuu Gol, the Chinese philosophy known as Daoism is not something we study, but even I know the opening line of Lao Tzu's *Tao Te Ching.* I find myself thinking of it as we float through the night. *The Way that can be readily named is not the Way.*

You're Just Stuck Is All

Within minutes the sheep somehow wedges the shaggy triangle of its head in between two wooden slats. From where I am sitting I can see that by simply tilting its head sideways it could extricate itself. In the darkness I hear the sound of urine hitting the floor, a small cloud of steam rising between the creature's back legs. It is a long time since I deal with animals, the moony fear that pervades their eyes. I look to the girl and nod toward where the sheep is stuck. She shrugs. Maybe it feels safer that way, she says, and stays where she is. I look at the animal and have to agree. Something in its body seems more relaxed, as if the animal is resigned to whatever may lie before it.

Through the darkness the truck bumps and jolts over the grasslands. I imagine it is like riding in a boat, the waves a series of green hills, though I do not know how to swim and have yet to encounter a large body of water.

The girl lifts the canvas and pokes her head into the cab to speak with the driver. Inside I can see a red ember glowing, what in English Mun calls the cherry, the sound of the cigarette burning like meat frying. The girl leans back out. Listen, at the fourth house we need you to keep watch, she says. Okay?

The child looks directly at me. There is something in her eyes, an unnatural orange, a fire I am familiar with. Yes, I think, she walks this earth many times before. She is one of the lost. Hers is an ancient energy working its way up out of some previous darkness. Perhaps even now some wrathful deity is yoked to her journey, some ferocious god attempting to steer her toward the light. Don't worry, she says, as she rides upright over the grasslands like a little prince. We won't make you do it if you don't want to.

Why is that, I say.

The girl spits on the floor. Maybe you play pool like someone from the city, she says, but I know you're a real monk. She points to the sheep with its head trapped among the slats. You're just stuck is all, she says.

Something catches in my chest. I get down on my knees and do ten half prostrations right there in the back of the truck. With each one I can feel the wet floorboards though I am unsure if it is water or something else. When I finish, I remain on my knees.

I have to get to Ulaanbaatar by sundown tomorrow, I say.

Either you get to Ulaanbaatar or you don't, she says, her tone of voice as if this is the most obvious truth in existence. Sometimes you don't sound like a holy man, she adds.

What do I sound like, I say, but she doesn't respond. Instead, she walks off to the far corner of the truck where the sheep stands trapped among the wooden slats. Gently the girl angles the creature's neck and frees it, but within minutes, the animal's head is trapped again.

The Answer Presents Itself to Me

Mischievously the moon floats in and out of the clouds. I wonder how often this band of thieves goes raiding, why they don't wait for the new moon and total dark. Just then the clouds part, flooding the world with light, and the answer presents itself to me. In the total dark, people are more vigilant. They hold tighter to what is dearest to them. When the moon's light is present, their grip is not as tight.

Now in the flickering darkness the driver is careful to keep the wheels in the deep tire tracks worn in the grass by countless vehicles over time, which in Mongolia are the equivalent of highways. Out here we are hundreds of kilometers from paved roads. If we deviate from the ruts, anyone could follow our tracks.

Then the truck shifts into a lower gear. Slowly we climb a small hill. When we crest, the next *ger* presents itself in the middle of a vast emptiness. In the moonlight I can see twenty or more kilometers in every direction. As I stand in the truck bed looking out over the cab, it is as if the whole world belongs only to me. The distances are staggering. It could take you an hour to drive to a spot on the edge of the horizon, yet that spot feels like it's just within reach. This is what it means to live on the steppe. There are no walls between you and nature. You *are* nature.

Fifteen minutes later we coast up to a pen where at night the animals are kept away from the jaws of wolves. The tailgate comes down easier this time. Things go smoothly. Soundlessly the little girl jumps out. I follow. Soon there are two adolescents, one male, one female, making their way shyly up the ramp like newlyweds. Quickly the animals move to the corner where the other is still trapped among the boards. Already they are a family.

At the third house I don't get out of the truck. Within minutes an older female drifts up the gangway. The old ewe makes straight for me and lets out a small bleat. I hold my hand out. The skin of my palm grows moist from the muggy breath steaming out her nostrils. I try to imagine what she's thinking. She keeps nibbling my fingers even after she realizes my hand is empty.

Our Auras Hovering in the Air as We Move

Now we are in the deepest part of the night, the sky dark as an old well. I remember the sound of my heart thundering in my ears the night Mun and I ride home after stealing the radio from the widower. All the way home the muscle storming in my chest. This time, my heart lies still, but I am not fooled by its silence.

It takes an hour to get to the fourth *ger.* Once again the driver cuts the engine. We roll noiselessly for another few hundred meters before coming to a stop. The girl takes a deep breath in through her mouth and pushes it out through her nose. I wonder if she does this to quiet her mind, or if it's just a habit.

After her, I slip out of the truck and wrap my robe around my shoulders. Even in the limited moonlight the breath visibly issues out of our bodies, our auras hovering in the air as we move. The three men pull the masks over their faces. We are still fifty meters from the homestead. It is a large operation consisting of a series of *ger,* the smallest one larger than the one my opponent and the little girl call home. The *ger* are positioned to form a U. In the center are multiple pens, though there are so many they stretch beyond the safety of the half circle.

My opponent taps the little girl on the shoulder and makes a signal with his hand. The child then turns to me. Remember, she whispers, if you see anything, whistle. I neither agree nor shake my head, but she doesn't seem to notice. The four of us fan out behind her.

The first pen is farthest from the *ger.* There must be a hundred animals behind the wire. What is it about the child that keeps them from panicking? Easily she cuts through the flock, culling three before closing the gate. When they're out, she hands them off to my opponent, who runs them back up to the truck. The rest of us move on.

At the next pen just as the girl is unhooking the gate my wrist beeps the hour two times, to my ears the sound like a shotgun. We freeze in our tracks. I stop breathing. A lifetime passes. I remind myself there is no liberation apart from the Triple Gem; to access it we must move beyond fear. Fortunately, we are far enough from the nearest *ger* and the wind is blowing away from us, away from where the family lies sleeping. From the way he balls his hands, I know the second man in our group wants to hit me, but he is too far away. After another minute of standing still, the girl opens the pen and makes her selections. This time it is the driver who disappears into the night with the animals.

The Light We Carry Inside Us Can Never Be Extinguished

The final pen lies just a meter or two from a small *ger* where flour is probably stored along with dried milk, maybe a motorbike or two. I am the one closest to it, the one farthest from the truck. Something about where I am standing, how close I am to the door, makes me wonder about my purpose here tonight. I can hear the sound of my brother giggling as we ride over the grasslands, the radio cinched in his *deel*. He doesn't need me. The widower is gone as expected. My role that night is to witness, to add yet another black mark on the growing list of Mun's misdeeds, to show the world that despite our being brothers, I am the grass and he is the horse, opposites in every way.

Already the girl is rummaging among the animals, deciding who might be taken without notice. I focus on the darkness around me and put the thought of what I am doing here from my mind.

The girl is yet to choose one when I hear the sound of a bullet sliding into a chamber. The only person to ever point a weapon at me is my brother, and in turn he is the only person I ever train a weapon on.

The boy is standing in the shadows, his face painted a shade of black that matches his *deel*. Most likely he is standing there all night, a sentinel to whom time is meaningless. I can only see the whites around his pupils; when he blinks he momentarily disappears off the earth.

In the limited light I feel the boy searching for my weakest spot. With a pull of the trigger, I could be blasted out of this world. A soft wind blows at my back as if ushering me forward. And just like that, all is lost. My heart now thundering in my chest, a warhorse marauding across the steppes. All the years of training, of learning to live a dispassionate life, gone at the sound of a gun. Am I not one who believes that the light we carry inside us can never be extinguished? Then why, in this moment of thresholds, do I find myself clinging to existence, my whole being desirous that the insignificant person that is me be allowed to continue?

I feel the wind's hand marshaling me on. No test of faith could be more crystalline. I am taught to believe that when we renounce the physical world, we gain everlasting peace. A rich man spends his life chained to securing his treasure, but when he finally loses it to robbers, he is suddenly free to live. Now when total renunciation is offered to me, everything looks different. I wait for the state of what is called clear light mind to arise, the highest state of consciousness that precedes death. It is our belief that earthly existence clouds the mind's naturally radiant state of light and pure bliss, causing humanity to live with the illusion that all phenomena are permanent. And so we suffer.

I feel the boy's gun trained on my chest. I think of the indestructible drop that resides in the center of my heart chakra, this drop composed of the red drop from my father and the white drop of my mother. How at the moment of death, this drop splits apart, releasing my very subtle consciousness, the spark at the center of every sentient being, back into the universe.

Then the moon comes out from behind a cloud and saves my life. Somewhere in the everlasting tree that is the universe there is another me living this same life. In that universe the moon does not arrive in time.

When One Hunts the Wolf

His mother refuses to tie my hands, but the boy insists. She stands shining a flashlight in the doorway, a pair of rubber boots on her feet, as the boy leads me into the room. The woman is tired, a fatigue that goes beyond the hour of the night, her fingers clutching the latticed *qana* as if the *ger* walls are holding her up. Conversely the boy is filled with energy, a hunter galvanized by blood. Once we are inside, I hold my wrists out to him, a small offering, but he shakes his head and wrenches my arms behind me. For a child of about twelve, there is such strength in his grip as he binds my hands with an extension cord. The boy makes a double knot. I realize my mistake. What I think is energy is anger.

In the center of the room the grandmother is blowing into the stove as she tries to get the flame to catch. The *ger* is large, its one room big enough to accommodate several families, but from the look of things only adults sleep here. Two teenaged girls run in, one in western-style pajamas, the other in a yellow *deel.* When I see the girl in the yellow *deel,* her long black hair coiled around her head in a traditional style, my face burns hotter. I lock my eyes on the floor, which is layered with fine rugs, the top rug patterned with small blue flowers.

See, says the boy. He walks over to a small radio set lying on a table. He turns a dial on the radio while still holding his gun. It isn't a wolf, he says.

Is this necessary, says the grandmother.

He's a thief, the boy says.

The girl in the yellow *deel* looks at me. I imagine my face is the same color as my robe, the top of my shaved head crimson with shame. I recognize him, the girl says. My hands are beginning to numb. I wish for a hole where I might crawl in and be swallowed up straight to the underworld, that I might be instantly reincarnated as the fly that lives in the wet dung of the yak. He's from Yatuu Gol, she says. He likes to eat western candy bars.

No, yawns her sister. The monk you're talking about lives in the capital now after ruining that girl. The way she says it, the flatness of her intonation, as if she is merely describing an episode on the television. I do not contest her version of events though what she says is not entirely accurate. Unfortunately there is more truth in what she says than not. Even when robed, my brother is not shy about knowing women. I can only imagine what adventures he is up to in Ulaanbaatar.

Mun is my twin, I say in a soft voice. And yes, he now lives in the city.

And where are you headed, asks the grandmother. She remains squatting by the stove, her steel-gray hair falling past her waist.

I am among the lost, I say. I wonder what the Rinpoche would think to see me kneeling here on the floor of a rich man, the Rinpoche's watch still faithfully keeping time on my wrist.

The boy manages to raise someone on the radio. He rests his gun across his shoulders. In the firelight I can see it is a Russian rifle from the days when the Soviet Union is our nation's friend. Earlier outside when I hear the sound of the hammer cocking, I look over and see him standing in the shadows, his face lined like a man's. Stealing livestock in Mongolia is among the oldest of crimes. Though it is extremely rare, people sometimes kill when defending their animals. But the moon comes out from behind a cloud and the boy sees my robe. In the moonlight, confusion clouds his face. In the new Mongolia, the killing of a monk is among the worst crimes. I can see the boy working out the equation in his head as the little girl with the blackened face slips away into the night. This is how I am meant to serve. When one hunts the wolf, one needs the blood of the sheep to light the way to the pit. Yes. I do what I am brought along to do.

I get caught so that others might go free. The little girl is right. I am like that sheep with its head stuck in the truck's slats. Either you get to Ulaanbaatar or you don't, she says. Even now in my darkest hour I must keep believing in the truth of her statement. Either I arrive at Ulaanbaatar's Gandan Tegchenling Monastery by sundown tomorrow or I don't. I must maintain thinking like a holy man or I am only one more being among the desperate.

It Is a Fair Exchange

Why are you stealing animals, says the mother. Is it because you know we are without a man?

I look around the room. The boy puts the radio down. Painfully the skin above his eyes furrows as he looks at his mother. On the altar there is a handkerchief covering a portrait. My heart skips. These people are observing the first forty-nine days of mourning.

There is a darkness in my blood, I say.

Just like your brother, says the girl in the yellow *deel.* I look at the floor. I remember this girl from one afternoon of *gurem,* her black hair flashing in the sunlight.

I and my fellow monks at Yatuu Gol belong to *Sharyn Shashin,* the Religion of the Yellow. Most likely the local people do not know the difference between the Gelug School of Tibetan Buddhism and the many forms of Buddhism in the world. This girl probably doesn't know that, unlike the monks of the Theravada tradition, who live mostly in Southeast Asia, their robes a brilliant saffron orange, the monks of all four schools of Tibetan Buddhism do not go begging for alms. In the Theravadic world, early mornings a river of monks streams out at first light, wooden bowls around their necks, the local people coming forward with offerings. Conversely, in the remote regions where Tibetan Buddhists live, the practice of begging for food is impractical given the emptiness of the landscape.

Among this family, most likely only the grandmother knows the full story of how, beginning in 1924, Buddhism is all but wiped out during Mongolia's communist epoch, though even this elderly woman is probably not alive during the first purges. Just before the millennium when the Rinpoche reestablishes Yatuu Gol after the fall of the Soviet Union, he quickly reinstitutes the practice of *gurem*. Thanks to *gurem,* we monks travel to people's homes where we pray that the family may be free from hunger, thirst, and illness, and in return, the people make us offerings of food and money. Because Yatuu Gol is so isolated, Mongolia a country twice the size of the American state of Texas but with only three million inhabitants, we cannot practice *gurem* often. Mostly we go out to visit the lay community during the Mongolian summer, when the flocks are at their fattest. We cannot deny the people a chance to improve their karma by giving to the disciples of Buddha. It is a fair exchange. Bringing us into their homes reminds the people to be virtuous. Seeing the laity prostrating themselves before us reminds us that we have much to live up to.

Somehow at the end of a day of *gurem,* Mun always returns to the monastery with a few candy bars tucked in the folds of his robe. Unlike him, I dread *gurem.* I recoil from it not because of the long walk out to some isolated homestead, the grasslands shadeless and teeming with flies, nor for the taking of food from simple people who have little to give. No, I dread these prayer offerings in people's homes because of girls like this, this girl in the yellow *deel* with the black coils of her hair shining. There are no women at Yatuu Gol. Outside Ulaanbaatar, Buddhist nuns are still a rarity. And so *gurem* brings me into contact with a part of life I am discovering for the first time. How after a day of *gurem* during the interminable trek back to Yatuu Gol, the monastery nestled in the shadow of the sleeping volcano, some young woman's radiant face always stays tucked away inside me in a room whose existence I do not allow myself to acknowledge.

Sometimes Faith Is the Only Medicine

An hour passes. In another, the summer sun begins to dawn in the eternal blue sky. In the corner by the radio, the boy falls asleep sitting up, his rifle lying at his feet like a beloved pet. His sisters are curled together on one of the brightly painted chests that serve as beds. In sleep the girl with her hair in coils murmurs softly to herself as though singing. Their mother lies among the floor pillows, her forehead creased with what I now know is sorrow, behind her closed eyes her pupils racing back and forth. At Yatuu Gol at this dark hour I would be waking for first salutations in the room I share with eight others, everywhere the red wooden shutters of the monastery thrown open to the cold summer air.

Then someone is untying my hands. I feel the blood course back into my veins. When I turn to look the grandmother signals for me to remain silent. Wordlessly she scrambles over to the altar and lifts the handkerchief, revealing a man in his mid-thirties as he poses with a shiny new motorbike. She looks at me with hope. I am familiar with such looks. During the summer when Mun and I first enter the monastery, a woman gazes on the Rinpoche in this same manner as she holds her sick infant out to him along the road to Bor-Urt. The child looks to be in its final hours. The Rinpoche leans in and places his palm on its forehead. Sometimes faith is the only medicine available. Then the woman smiles and backs away bowing, confident that, with the Rinpoche's blessing, the child is guaranteed to return to this earth in a higher state.

I rub my hands together, the skin marked from the extension cord. The old woman points at the picture. I nod and crawl toward her. I wonder how old she is, if she is indeed old enough to remember the purges, the time when the communists destroy the monasteries, the monks driven out into the winter snows to die. It comforts me to think that like our brothers the Tibetans, we Mongolians manage to hold on to our faith through dark times. The histories of our two nations are intertwined, as it is the descendants of Chinggis Khaan who help establish Buddhism in Tibet. The whole world knows of His Holiness, the 14th Dalai Lama. Few know that the title Dalai Lama is a compound of the Mongolian word for "ocean" and the Tibetan word for "teacher," each of the fourteen dalai lamas an Ocean of Compassion.

I take the stick of incense the old woman holds out to me and light it in a candle. Then I clap my palms together and bow my head three times. With folded hands I beseech the Buddha of All Directions to shine the lamp of His being for all bewildered in the gloom of misery. Gently I place the burning stick in a small bowl filled with ash. The smoke spires up off the tip and fills the room. The girl with the beautiful hair is now unmistakably singing in her sleep though it is not a song I know.

Silently I push a small chest out of the way. The old woman moves a stool. Together we proceed in unison, our bodies heaving up and down, back and forth like pendulums. Despite her age she moves through the poses with agility. By the time the police arrive in a battered truck, we have each done more than fifty prostrations. I feel a bruise on the verge of taking root on my forehead as over and over in my guilt I press my face hard into the floor. Conversely, the old woman remains unmarked, without flaw.

Through Either Action or Inaction, One Must Learn to Forgive

The whole family stands outside in the last dregs of night as I am led to the truck. The boy says I should ride in the back, but the officer patiently explains that sometimes criminals jump out, the truck jouncing over the grasslands for hours before the officer even notices. At the very least the boy insists that I be handcuffed. Silently the officer complies, though later when we are out of sight he removes them. The way the officer moves, as if he is walking through waist-high water, the thinness of his arms and legs in sharp contrast to his stomach which hangs on his front like something strapped to his body. It is easy to see that I am not what the officer is expecting when the boy radios of catching an animal wrangler. Despite this, I sense a strange elation in this officer of the law, a joy he is trying to keep hidden. Perhaps he is tickled at the novelty of catching a monk animal wrangling and the unbelievable tale he can tell others.

Now at the end of this strange night, the girl with the beautiful hair tilts her head and looks at me. I allow myself to return her gaze. Her skin is clear as freshly planed wood, her eyes large. Because I do not look at women often, I can only guess if she is a few years younger than I am, or if she is a teenager. I wonder when she looks at me if she sees my brother, the insouciant monk who hides chocolate in his robes and enjoys the company of women, or if she understands that my brother and I are separate planets, each with our own atmosphere, our own natural wonders.

Chimegee, says the girl's grandmother. She points into the *ger. Tsai.* The girl sighs and disappears through the door. When she comes back she strides up to where I am standing by the truck and holds it out to me. I look to the officer, but the man nods and I realize she is offering it to me. As my wrists are cuffed, I take it with both hands and bow my head. I can see that the seal is broken and the bottle reused as is customary, but I bow again all the same. As she hands me the milk tea, our fingers touch. *Bayarlalaa,* I say. Thank you, sister. What I want to say: *Chimegee, may this suffering in me serve to awaken all hearts.*

Then the officer holds the passenger door open. Just over his shoulder I glimpse the pen filled with sheep that the little girl with the sooty face is pillaging only hours before. For the various ways one hurts oneself through either action or inaction, one must learn to forgive the self. Though we are still an hour from dawn, somehow the sheep's wool looks rosy. Perhaps it is only my need in this dark hour to look for signs of hope that color the world so. I get in the truck and the officer gently closes the door. I can feel the animals' big wet eyes on me long after we pull out of sight.

The Membrane Covering My Face Translucent as Milk

Even after we crest the first hill the officer doesn't slow the truck. We seem to pick up speed as he takes both hands off the wheel and leans over to unlock my cuffs. Once I am free, I bow to him and rub my wrists. I am keenly aware of being awake for more than twenty-four hours. Today at Yatuu Gol the children are riding in for their weekly lessons, the herders sending their sons into the monastery to learn the ancient script, each family wanting one child capable of reading the old prayer books on solemn occasions.

The officer uncaps his thermos and takes a long drink. When he finishes, he offers me some, but I shake my head. From where I am sitting I can smell the sourness. It is barely four in the morning and he is drinking *airag,* but the truth is the entire thermos might have the same alcohol content as one western beer. I'm Noyon, he says. I take a closer look, but there is nothing princely about him. Now that we are away from the family, Noyon seems to be in a better mood.

I'm Chuluun, I say.

I know, he says. You're the stone and your brother's the vicious dog.

I don't say anything as I'm not surprised. In Mongolia we are not named for the sound of our names but for their meanings. Often rather than tempt the gods by gracing a child with a beautiful moniker, parents give the baby an unpleasant one. Perhaps this is why my father names my twin Muunokhoi after a savage animal and me for a rock. Twenty-three years ago Mun and I are born in the year after the Soviet Union loses its grip on Mongolia. Instantly, news of our births ripples through the five hundred square kilometers surrounding the volcano. Of course Noyon knows who I am. Twenty-three years ago when I am born he must be right here in sight of Yatuu Gol.

Through the headlights, Noyon scans the landscape, perhaps looking for a familiar butte, a rock which indicates the way. I look away from him and up into the sky. Though the world is still more dark than not, two black specks are circling on the winds. Cinereous vultures, the largest true birds of prey in the world. I watch the birds funneling up into the sky as they climb the thermal currents. Watching them, I think of the English word *cleave,* one of the first English words I learn from flipping through the monastery's only copy of the King James Bible. The way *cleave* has two meanings which mean exactly the opposite of each other. "To cling with ardor" or "to divide as with a knife." This is the way I sometimes feel about Mun. That I cannot stand to be with him and at the same time ever since he leaves Yatuu Gol I feel an emptiness in my chest.

Ever since I can remember I know the story of how we re-enter the world. The way the stars in the Black Tortoise blaze red the week leading up to our birth much the way a comet fires up the night at the birth of Chinggis Khaan eight hundred years ago. How after three nights of burning pain Mun's appearance at first light explains everything, the midwife pointing to the birthmark on his neck, the woman disregarding the strange white membrane veiling his face. This is the reason why this birth is so difficult, she says, wiping the waxy skin with a rag. See?

I picture my father leaning in, his eyes filling with wonder. The midwife angles the baby in her arms so that he can get a better look. It's shaped like a piece of fire, she says. Aav stares a long time at the dark blue splotch on his firstborn child. Finally he smiles and nods. Then my mother's stomach clenches again, and I appear in the world also as if sheeted, the membrane covering my face translucent as milk so that my father once again takes a knife and makes two slits for my nose and mouth until the midwife can peel back without injury what is essentially a living skin. As the midwife and our father tend to the tissue shrouding our newborn faces, our mother takes her last breath in this world and we become a household of men. My father, Övöö, and Mun and me. The story of the cauls shrouding our faces makes people believe we are old beings though at the time there are no holy men in Mongolia to come and discover us. During the first year of our lives the local people claim that the smoke rises out of our chimney in a straight line all the way up to heaven, the smoke like a white finger, the wind never carrying it away, as if someone is pointing down at us from an unfathomable height.

How Are Your Animals Fattening This Season?

In the sky the vultures are gone. All around us the grasslands are starting to wake. Within the hour we pass a flock being driven out to pasture by a small girl on horseback. Noyon beeps the horn and holds his hand out the window. The little girl watches us drive past. For a moment she spurs her horse and races along beside us.

Noyon wants to talk. It is obvious that he is settling in for a long drive, his belly rising and falling more slowly as he sinks farther and farther into his seat. How are your animals fattening this season, I say, one of many traditional topics of conversation.

It's a good spring, he says, which can mean almost anything.

Noyon, I say. Please forgive me. I am awake many hours.

He nods. When you wake, we'll talk of how the Rinpoche hears of the fickleness of the mail truck, he says, and how I am searching for you at his request. He takes another pull from his thermos. This animal-wrangling business happens because you need a ride, no, he says, but if you're truly a thief, you should tell me now. He looks at me and winks. Just do whatever the Rinpoche is sending you to do, he says, adding, *boltugai,* may it be so.

I remain silent, close my eyes, and empty my mind. For every act, there is a consequence; for every consequence, a source. Earlier tonight I perform among the wickedest of actions, animal wrangling, yet through a series of chance connections, I am allowed to walk free. May I always be mindful of each little mercy lavished on me. And when mercy is not given, may I accept its opposite with equal grace.

Noyon pushes a cassette tape into the deck. The sound of whistling fills the cab, the music like a river flowing out of icy mountains.

He-Who-Is-Always-Hooded

Quickly I fall asleep. From the emptiness within, the dream world arises. In many ways, it is just as real as this world, maybe more so. How I dream of him every night for the past year. The folds of his scarlet robe pulled down over his head. Just his mouth is visible, a wry smile playing on his lips. The six syllables of the jewel-in-the-lotus mantra fill the air, though the figure's mouth never moves. A chorus of voices intones the words, sending the skies rumbling, the sound of throat singing like thunder and sunlight.

Sometimes he is standing at the edge of the steppes. Sometimes he is sitting in the lotus position by a river created by the snow-melt far off in the Altai Mountains. Other times he is stationed in the middle of a *ger* next to a grove of larch trees. I name him He-Who-Is-Always-Hooded, this reincarnation I am going in search of. He-Who-Is-Always-Hooded stands holding the *ger's* center pole. The pole is topped by a wooden ring with slots spaced all around it so that when you insert the slats that support the roof it looks like a star. Orange and yellow rays shooting out in a perfect fiery circle.

In the dream I never ask why he comes, if he is strong enough to shoulder the faith. I never ask why he travels here to the land of the eternal blue sky. Even Mun knows enough to let him be, my brother the heathen who worships only the memory of Chinggis Khaan and the empire of the thirteenth and fourteenth centuries when Mongolia is the center of the universe. Mun who wears his long hair braided in one of the traditional styles as if he can go back to that period of time and be somebody of importance, a leader of men.

Each time I wake I wonder if Mun has the same dream. If the same figure comes to my brother in the night wherever he is far from the shadow of Yatuu Gol, the caldera sleeping peacefully under a mantle of frost even in summer. I wonder if Mun bolts upright under the flickering sodium streetlamps of the capital and feels uneasy at the thought of this robed figure who is beckoning us to find him, or if in the blue-gray dawn my twin feels something stirring in his chest, a sensation forgotten in the course of this past year, the jewel-in-the-lotus mantra filling the horizon. *Om mani padme hum. Om mani padme hum.* Sometimes I like to imagine that a calmness settles over my brother before he falls back asleep, a tranquility that lingers when he rises in the morning.

I have no doubt that Mun knows I am on my way. Not only are we brothers, we are twins, the same thin membrane covering our faces at birth. Because of it, I can see into my brother's mind and he into mine, our experiences passing between us like books in a library. When the Rinpoche tasks me with this journey, I know he is charging both of us with it—my brother with the strength of the flesh and me with the strength of the spirit, together the two of us indomitable.

Why Do We Need to Believe Our Lives Must Add Up to Some Grand Narrative?

The sun is somewhat higher in the sky. I open my eyes. Outside the truck's window the grasslands float as though they have no end. There are no lands more beautiful than this anywhere on earth. I imagine this is what the world looks like in the first verdant days of its birth. The endless blue skies, rolling green hills, wholeness.

Where are we going, I ask Noyon. Already the shadowy outline of Yatuu Gol rising up out of the earth is falling into memory.

Ulaanbaatar, of course, says Noyon. It is obvious he is pleased to have an excuse to drive to the capital. I am glad my pitiful existence can be of use to someone.

When the only hope is a boat and there is no boat, I will be the boat. I close my eyes and settle in for the three hours it takes us to travel there. This is neither a beginning nor an end. If all life on earth is one chapter in the story of the universe, each cosmic night four billion years long, then am I allowed to write a page in the tale of existence, am I to be granted a single word? Does the story even matter or is the witnessing enough, the being aware of each moment of beauty and hardship along the path? And why do we need to believe our lives must add up to some grand narrative, and what happens when we stop believing this?

On my wrist, the Rinpoche's watch sounds the hour.

The Stone and the Vicious Dog

In the Light He Shines and Glints

This time the landscape is sand, the world a never-ending dune in the heart of the Gobi. Everything in flux, everything impermanent. In the nearby cliffs the exposed bones of dinosaurs bleaching in the white heat. The lidless eye of the sun beats down on my shoulder, the skin of my body as dissoluble as limestone. Two cinereous vultures circle overhead. The way their species is named for ashes, what is transitory. Though they soar above at a great distance, I know these two as if we are intimates. Unlike all other birds in existence, these two have no feet, their bodies forever airborne, forever unable to land.

He is standing on the tallest dune, sand the color of turmeric. This time He-Who-Is-Always-Hooded wears no clothing. Instead his whole body resplendent with seashells, bits of coral stuck to his skin as if he is a creature of the sea. In the light he shines and glints like a weapon. The six syllables of the jewel-in-the-lotus mantra fill the air. *Om mani padme hum.* I know what he wants, why this figure appears every night in my dreams for the past year. He smiles and points to the east. His fingers wink with mother-of-pearl, arms studded with the silver coins of sand dollars. His body so radiant I lose him in the desert glare just as I am beginning to understand the path he chooses for me.

It can take innumerable lifetimes to wake up from this dream we call life. When awakening finally occurs, one often wakes up laughing. I open my eyes, but as always no laughter comes. Am I ever to find my way into the one radiant moment that is all things?

How Quickly Things Change

I am lying on a mattress in a western-style bed, the thing so soft I am afraid to move lest it break. This is what it must feel like to float along in a soap bubble or to be the wind itself, the air like hands holding you up. I wonder what it is about this way of sleeping that westerners prefer. To me, despite the ethereal softness, I feel like one of the dead, a body whose ties to the earth are severed so that I feel nothing, am nothing.

Though he tries to hide it, I can tell Mun is embarrassed. He lies on the floor in a patch of dawn that comes angling through the window. When I enter his apartment an hour ago, I see my brother's mind in the chaos of books and DVDs, posters of foreign films. I lie directly under one of four men in dark suits and sunglasses walking down a street, each with a gun in hand. Upon my arrival, the bed is unmade and piled with clothes and dishes, the thing no more than a glorified shelf. On the floor at the foot of the bed is a nest of blankets and pillows, the traditional *leitur* stuffed with straw.

From a young age, I imagine my brother sleeping in a western-style bed, the mattress soft as a cloud of newly shorn wool. Winter nights when we are children it is all he talks about, the two of us lying on opposite ends of the *leitur* in the dark. Someday I'm getting away from all this, the child Mun says in my memory. This morning I try not to laugh as Mun's sheepishness seeps into my waking mind. He may no longer be a herder, but he still sleeps like one.

How quickly things change. Yesterday waking at Yatuu Gol in the shadow of the volcano, and today I am waking a world away in the capital. What never changes: emptiness, no-self, impermanence. It is only a little more than an hour ago that Noyon the friendly police officer and I drive through the heart of Ulaanbaatar, turning a corner in the dawn light to find my brother standing on the street out in front of his building and wearing what he calls a hoodie, my twin rubbing his arms to keep warm. When I get out of the car, there is no hug between us. I know Mun would be there waiting for me and he knows it too.

It's early, he grumbles.

At Yatuu Gol, morning *puja* begins at 5:00 a.m., I say brightly, a fact my twin knows as well as anyone. Mun scowls and our reunion is complete. Mostly we prefer to communicate verbally, especially in front of others. People can sense when we are wordlessly sharing thoughts though they do not know what is happening—our father says he can feel a tingling rippling between us. Since childhood, we practice various ways to keep each other out of our mind, to hold and maintain secrets.

Before heading out on the long drive back to the grasslands, Noyon gets out of the car and does one full-body prostration at my brother's feet. Mun looks exasperated. Nevertheless, he clasps Noyon's outstretched hands in his own, raising them to his forehead and giving them a squeeze. Then my brother turns and leads me into the building.

A Hungry Man Who Remembers the Taste of Food

I sit up in bed and stretch my arms. In the past twenty-four hours I have only this hour of sleep and what I am able to manage on the drive here. It is enough as I am accustomed to existing on little. Mun is sitting upright among his lair of blankets. Already he has a cigarette going, the cherry burning hungrily. I can't believe you're down for this, he says. He runs a finger through his toes as if looking for sand. Instantly I know he also awakens from the same recurring dream of a mysterious figure among the dunes and bejeweled in the treasure of the seas, a figure calling us to find him.

Mun lights another cigarette off the end of the first one. It's unbelievable, he says, how after everything that happens, you still think being a reincarnation is a good thing.

I'm not the Redeemer Who Sounds the Conch in the Darkness, I remind him.

My brother purses his lips and blows a smoke ring my way. Together we watch it rise toward the ceiling. Deftly he begins to braid his hair while still holding the cigarette between his fingers. Neither am I, he says. He waves a hand around the shabby room. Open your eyes, he adds.

It is more than a year since I last see my twin. His hair now hangs past his shoulders, his face adorned with a patchy beard thickest around his mouth. As he braids his hair into two plaits, he reminds me of a young Chinggis Khaan, his face slightly pinched as if he is hearing something with which he does not agree.

It's hot in the cramped apartment, and it's only a little past seven o'clock. The toilet is down the hall and shared by everyone on the floor. In a corner there's a hot plate and a water spigot but no sink, just a red plastic bucket. Mun stretches and stands up. I can see the birthmark staining his neck, the flames sharp as knives. In Mongolia and throughout Asia, many of us are born with the Mongolian blue spot. Generally it is found on the backside, the skin mottled as if bruised, babies born with blue spots on their rumps, their bodies as if tattooed with maps. Most blue spots disappear before the age of five, but not Mun's. To me it looks like a hand grasping for something just out of reach. It is the kind of mark where one can see in it what one wants to see, a test of the perceiver. Come on, he says. We got a lot to do.

Then we can count on your help. I intone this silently. I do not put my request into actual words, as if merely thinking it might somehow soften my desperation.

Mun slaps his naked belly with both hands. I remember this habit of his from Yatuu Gol. On days when his anger is at its sharpest he slaps himself until the skin turns pink, a small conflagration burning around each pupil. I live in the real world, he says out loud. He slaps himself again only harder. I gotta make a living.

I already know what my brother is thinking. I try to hide my disappointment. We are twins, genetically identical in every way. Up until this moment I am hoping the bond between us is enough for him to aid me in this quest I am tasked with. Instead, I pull my bag of *tögrög* out from where I keep it hidden in the folds of my robe. Mun eyes it like a hungry man who remembers the taste of food. Still, he does not say yes. A wall of fire rages between us. Something deeper is needed to get him to agree. But for the moment I do not know what that something is.

Conrad

The fire inside my brother burns lower but does not go out entirely. You wanna come with me today, he asks. Mongolian is one of the world's old tongues, the ancient script like eagle tracks in snow. The sound of the language is almost unchanged since the time Chinggis Khaan shapes the earth and establishes what would become his magnificent court in Karakorum. Or you gonna stay here and pray for the whole world, my brother says, the language in his mouth strangely modern, as if a foreigner is speaking a slang-heavy idiom but somehow in Mongolian. He brings me a bowl of water from the spigot. Bits of dust float on the surface.

Tonight I am to meet the rest of the search party at Gandan Tegchenling Monastery. To walk through the monastery gates alone without my twin by my side is to doom our search before it even begins. We need him and his ancient wisdom even if he no longer counts himself among the faithful. All right, I say, today I'm yours. I bow my head and accept the water. I kneel and begin my ablution. I wash my face and feet, breathing as deeply as I can. When done, I dress. In Tibetan Buddhism, our triple robe is different from our brothers' who follow other traditions. Of the numerous Buddhist sects, our clothes are the most colorful; some even describe our attire as flamboyant. Older Mongolian lamas often wear the traditional *deel* sewn in scarlet fabric or gold brocade; wearing the long-sleeved *deel* keeps one warm in winter. As it is summer, I choose to wear the Tibetan *banzal,* a long full maroon skirt, with a short-sleeved *dongog* that can be either yellow or red. In winter, I wear long sleeves, but for now I wrap an *orhimj* in such a way that my left shoulder is covered by this scarlet shawl while my right arm is bare. In the days of the Buddha, the robes of a monk are made from cast-off fabric, cloth that is sewn together from rags that are stained, perhaps with blood, or used to shroud corpses. Today we use mostly new fabric, though in keeping with tradition, there is always one small section of used material somewhere on our robes. Lastly, I slip on my sandals, my only pair of shoes.

Mun wriggles into a pair of long plaid shorts and a T-shirt with a picture of a baby in a swimming pool paddling after a piece of money. On his feet he wears some type of western sneaker that looks flimsy and is laced in such a way he never needs to tie them. He grabs an already bulging backpack and stuffs a few items in it. The white cord from his earbuds snakes down his shirt to a tiny silver MP3 player that clips on his shorts. I recognize it from his days at the monastery. Many of the monks at Yatuu Gol have similar devices. We may be monks, but we are not hermits living isolated lives in mountaintop caves. Some novices even have iPhones.

Ready, he asks. He takes a hat off a hook, a gray fedora much like the kind herdsmen wear out on the grasslands. As my twin now knows from his interactions with tourists, fedoras are also popular with young urbanites in the west. Mun scans the room. I let him feel my disappointment about his refusal to help, but I don't mention it out loud. We must play the game as we learn to play it and as life demands. To act as if we do not share an inner life, that we cannot read each other's thoughts, which we discover time and again makes others uneasy.

I too glance around the apartment. I wonder how long it takes him to accumulate the trappings of this new life. I myself am my own planet. Everything I need is right here—on my body, in my heart, in my mind. As I think this I sense Mun's agitation. Tonight the journey I set out on from the gates of Gandan Tegchenling does not sit well with him. He wants no part in it. To him, the idea of branding another as a *tulku,* a reincarnated being, is abhorrent. He knows better than anyone the subsequent responsibility of such a naming. I wonder if there is something else my brother, the Redeemer Who

Sounds the Conch in the Darkness, is not telling me. I am your servant always, I say.

Cut it out, he says, swiping a pair of keys off a hook.

I follow him out into the hallway and watch as he locks the door. By the stairwell he leans over and tucks a key on a ledge up high above a grimy window. The sunlight is filled with dust, tiny motes swirling haphazardly. I think of the billion-billion-armed universe that contains every sentient being. For the millionth time in my life I am glad I am not the Redeemer Who Sounds the Conch in the Darkness. Instead, I am the Servant to the Redeemer Who Sounds the Conch in the Darkness. Mine is only an honorary title. My neck is perfect and unmarred. May it never be otherwise!

It is only then that I notice. As he reaches up to tuck the key on the ledge. The script running down the inner forearm of his right arm. The script dark green and in English, the letters tattooed in a simple font. IT IS WRITTEN I BE LOYAL TO THE NIGHTMARE OF MY CHOICE.

My twin sees me staring. Conrad, he says, adjusting the earbuds in his ears. *Heart of Darkness.* You should read it sometime.

I feel as if the world tilts, as if I might slide out of existence. Together and apart we walk down the stairs.

O Possessor of the Eye of Omnipotence—
Look Upon Us With Compassion!

Today, the first week of July, Ulaanbaatar is full of foreignness. Every physical characteristic. Brown eyes, green eyes, eyes blue as wolves'. Skin from palest ivory to deep-brown sand. This is my first time in the capital. I also feel foreign, my red robe like a flag, but nobody pays me any mind. Mun lives on a small side street in a maze of streets, this the heart of the district that caters to tourists. There are internet cafés and hostels and tour agents, places to rent motorbikes, places to do laundry. In the shop windows there are foods packaged in bright colors, things I would not even recognize as food except for Mun's memories of eating them.

We pass women with long black hair, their bodies thin, their faces Chinese, cheekbones chiseled as if eroded by the wind. In the same block we pass women who look like our mother in the photographs on our childhood altar, their bodies thick and stout with the ruddy complexion of most Mongolians, their cheeks flushed with blood. It is the influence of the Silk Road, for the last millennium people from all over the world flocking here and interbreeding. A man who looks like a white Russian walks by with a woman dark as India, the two of them speaking Mongolian.

Like Chinggis Khaan, Mun positions himself in the center of the world. Sükhbaatar is Ulaanbaatar's central governmental district, the place of commerce and tourism. Ulaanbaatar is a city of just over a million, almost half the population of the country. More and more young people are leaving the steppe. Earlier this morning as I drive into the city with Noyon, we pass neighborhoods composed entirely of traditional *ger* where recent immigrants from the countryside live who are too poor to afford western rooms. These neighborhoods are also crammed with simple shanties. In the winter months, Ulaanbaatar is one of the most polluted capitals in the world, the air hazy as if smudged, tens of thousands of people heating their homes, cooking their food with fires, the air filled with particulate. But in summer, the skies clear as the need for indoor fires lessens, the eternal blue sky once again blue and endless, perhaps the bluest in all the world.

Now we are just blocks from Sükhbaatar Square and the mammoth steel statue of Chinggis Khaan that looms over the plaza, everywhere his figure reflected in glass. Across the street is a three-story shopping mall. Although it is not yet eight o'clock, ours is a culture attuned to the hours animals keep. Already people pour out of the first-floor grocery store at the mall's entrance. I realize Mun's address must be highly coveted, a few feet of floor space in the heart of the new Mongolia.

It's not always like this, says Mun. At a wooden cart manned by a young boy he stops to buy some fried meat on a stick and a drink in a silver can. But it'll be like this all week.

Why, I ask.

He looks at me. Wow, he says, you really are living in the twelfth century. It's Naadam, he says. I feel a wave of stale rage crest in me. Mun acts as if he can't sense it.

Two blocks down we turn into a side street. A group of foreigners sits outside a shop with the words TUUL TOURS written on a big white sign mounted over the doorway. Each foreigner hefting a backpack, their whole world crammed in a single bag. A blond girl gets up and rushes over to Mun, throws her arms around his neck, kisses him on the cheek. Munny dearest, she says in English, you taking us to Terelj National Park?

I feel a heat begin to prickle in my chest at my twin's familiarity with women.

Not today, love, says my brother. The girl pretends to pout. Don't look so sad, says Mun, but already the girl turns her back on him and is running toward a tanned backpacker walking up the street.

As If Simply Stepping Over a Puddle

Inside the office, racks of brochures sprout haphazardly from the floor. Mun slips through the crowd and makes his way toward a desk. A woman sits in an office chair chewing gum, a map of Mongolia taped up on the wall behind her, yellow pushpins dotting areas of interest. A foreign couple sits in front of the woman's desk, a guidebook open on the man's lap. The woman picks up the phone and converses in Mongolian. From time to time she turns and speaks to the couple in some other language unknown to me though several foreigners in the room seem to speak it, each of them almost two meters tall, even the women.

Everywhere is chaos. People stand with backpacks, people in chairs, on sofas. Many stand fanning themselves with pamphlets detailing different attractions. Mun grabs a piece of candy from a dish on the woman's desk and unwraps it, pops it in his mouth. In the crush, I try to make myself as small as possible. There are so many languages being spoken I feel like the whole world is crammed in this one room.

The woman holds a hand over the mouthpiece and speaks to Mun You're late, she says, snapping her gum. From her tone and demeanor, I gather this must be Tuul.

I'm right on time, he says, never taking his earbuds out. I watch as he begins folding the candy wrapper into something origami-style, maybe a bird or a flower.

Tuul hands him a clipboard. Round up your group and get going, she says. The itinerary's there.

Mun looks it over. You expect me to hightail it all the way from the stadium out to Hui Doloon Khutag by three, he says.

You're supposed to be the best, says Tuul, grinning. She goes back to the phone.

The foreign man sitting before her begins to say something. It is obvious he is complaining. The woman holds up her hand. To me it sounds as if she is speaking sharply with him, but maybe this is just the way people in the capital talk, or perhaps this is how foreigners treat one another all the time. The man shakes his head, but he doesn't get up from his chair.

Oh, and don't forget I put a hold on the 66 for three weeks, Mun says.

For what? The way Tuul transitions between languages, as if simply stepping over a puddle.

Remember? Mun says. Private tour. He winks at me.

No way, says Tuul, swiveling in her chair toward a computer. I don't care about the car, she adds, it's you I can't lose.

Relax, says Mun, I'm not going. Ganzorig's driving. At the name, Tuul shakes her head. I wonder what's wrong with Ganzorig. I can sense that Mun also has reservations about him. You see my brother over there, Mun asks, pointing to me. I am standing by a bookshelf filled with notebooks in which past customers share written reviews. Says Martin K. of California, *Tuul is the best, but get out of UB into the countryside as soon as you can.* I see Tuul fix her eyes on me. I put my palms together and give a small bow.

Tuul gives me a quick bow in return. She looks startled to see a monk in her office. I notice a small prayer wheel sitting on her desk. Where's this private tour headed, she asks. Even though we are identical twins, I can tell she doesn't believe we are related. Mun with his scruffy beard, his hair in two shiny braids, the abomination tattooed on his arm, and me with my shaved head, my scarlet robe.

Top-secret Buddha mission, Mun says.

Some specifics would be nice, she says.

Mun ignores this. Three, he says.

One, she counters.

Mun keeps fiddling with the candy wrapper. Come on, he says. Two weeks.

I'll give you twelve days maximum.

Shit, my brother thinks in English, but he looks at her and grins. Great, two weeks with Ganzorig it is, he says. Tuul sighs but doesn't contradict him.

The western expletive echoes in my mind. Right thought, right speech, right deeds. *It is sufficient to rest in the unabsolute unceased,* I think, filling both my mind and my brother's with this calming mantra. My twin glares at me. A few western tourists stop what they are doing and look around with puzzled expressions. They are probably wondering what this sudden tingling is they sense in the air.

I feel my brother internally stiffen though he doesn't let it show. Fourteen days to drive across the country and back. For a moment I get a flash of his thoughts. Ganzorig is Tuul's nephew, which is why she keeps him on despite his proclivity to hit every sinkhole, get stuck in every river. In a land with few highways, two weeks means little to no sleep and no room for mistakes.

Mun lays the candy wrapper on Tuul's desk and grabs another handful of sweets. Already he is walking out the door with the clipboard. As I follow him out, I glance at the small offering he leaves on her desk, the candy wrapper expertly folded. I look again even though I see it forming in his mind as he brings it to life in his hands. Who is this being who resembles my brother but is not my brother? The thing winks at me as I hurry out the door. A tiny silver penis as delicate and beautiful as an origami crane.

Where I Walk, He Runs

Tonight at sundown my destiny awaits behind the gates of Gandan Tegchenling Monastery. At the thought, I pull my robe tighter around my body, elongating my spine so that it is not rigid but firm, my posture a reflection of my inner life. I must wait until this evening to find out why the world brings me here and who it is that I join in this journey.

From my seat in the middle of this crowded shuttle bus filled with tourists, I watch my brother grip the wheel. These tourists may be here to see Naadam, but I am here to mentally goad my brother into remembering his true self; it is imperative that he aid me in my quest. My brother and I are opposites in every way. Where I walk, he runs. When I look to the stars and see the emptiness at the heart of all things, the nothingness my twin sees is a kind of nihilism. We handle our connection in different ways. When I want to keep Mun from my mind, I imagine whiteness, the snowy steppes, winter as far as the eye can see, the ice on a mountain lake, the ice deep as the standing height of a man. In Mongolia, it is easy to fill one's thoughts with visions of snowy vistas. Winter here is like a visiting relative who refuses to leave.

To sever our connection Mun prefers fire. When he has a secret, I feel a heat building in him. I know not to probe, not to reach out and touch the burning stove, the red-hot iron, not to put my hand in the flame or risk the bubbling of skin, the instant blister, my mind seared like a piece of meat.

Ever since our days as children at Yatuu Gol, our connection grows both stronger yet more tenuous. Since learning to quiet our minds, to live the life of the spirit, we each establish methods of strengthening our defenses against the other, though Mun's strength is greater than mine, as he is the Redeemer Who Sounds the Conch in the Darkness, the heat of his inner eye unbearable. There is a place inside him, a spot the size of a grain of dust, but in this place deep within my brother radiates an infinite heat as well as an infinite anger. It is where he keeps his truest secrets from me, his twin, the one who shares the womb with him those long nights when we feed from one cord inside our mother. It is a place I am unable to access. A place that is completely off-limits. To touch this spot in Mun, to try to open it, would be worse than walking on the sun. He develops this spot as a child during our first months in the monastery. It is the place I can never go. It is more forbidden than even the Great Taboo where Chinggis Khaan is buried eight hundred years ago in the province of Khentii. I cannot imagine what it is to live with such a place inside me. I would cut this burning out of my twin, this spot like a cancer, but it is what fuels him, his eyes flaming at the mention of his spiritual name. When I think of the fiery space Mun hollows out within himself, this is what I imagine one would find there: memories of his previous lives, blocks of charcoal.

Even now as he drives these tourists through the city on this day of national sport, I can sense that he is already on to the next thing, already trying to work out what lies waiting for him beyond this day, and how he might benefit from whatever may come. And for me, I must spend this day being the small voice he hears above the flames, the voice that says: individually the self is nothing. But tonight the moon should look different here under this new sky. I must remember the Eight Reminders of the eleventh-century mystic Milarepa and not be tempted by the urban life surrounding me:

Castles and crowded cities are the places
Where now you love to stay,
But remember that they will fall in ruins
After you have departed from this earth.
Pride and vainglory are the lure

Which now you love to follow
But remember, when you are about to die,
They offer you no shelter.

May my twin remember the refuge of the Triple Gem. May the temptations of this floating world not engulf us both!

To Know the Self, One Has Only to Listen

There are eleven people on the shuttle bus. They're mostly young western couples, backpackers taking what in their language is called a gap year. The concept is mystifying to me. I cannot understand it, as the idea of searching for oneself through travel seems counterintuitive. As if self-knowledge can be attained through globetrotting. To know the self, one has only to listen, to slow the mind's inner dialogue and be content with the world as it truly is and not as one wants it to be.

Quickly I come to understand why Mun is so valuable to Tuul. He is both guide and driver, his English impeccable, his cheekiness an asset with the less formal westerners. This morning as we load ourselves onto the shuttle, I sit down next to a young woman traveling alone. Her toenails sparkle a brilliant cobalt blue. When I first sit down beside her, I apologize for my English. Even with Mun's fluency in the back of my mind, I cannot call on his knowledge quickly enough to mirror his proficiency. I can understand what is being said, but it takes me time to craft a response. The woman looks at me and coolly nods, then proceeds to seal a door closed between us. Outside the window I watch the city pass in silence. I try to make myself as small as possible. From time to time I glance at my watch only to discover that it is only a few minutes later.

As we file out of the shuttle bus, my brother tells his charges that Naadam is the country's biggest holiday, a day of national sport, a holiday bigger than even Tsagaan Sar, the Mongolian New Year. The largest Naadam competition is held right here in Ulaanbaatar, which means "Red Hero," he explains, but all over the country throughout the month of July, people compete in what are called the three manly sports of wrestling, archery, and horseback riding. He pantomimes each activity with an unlit cigarette clamped between his fingers.

The opening ceremony lasts an hour. I continue to sit next to the woman with the blue toenails. We watch as the procession of parade floats circles the National Sports Stadium, the people marching in wearing traditional dress, their furs gleaming in the July heat. Mun sits at the other end of the bleachers, a row of tourists between us, his earbuds firmly in place. Each time I reach out to him with my mind, there is nothing but silence. Eventually I stop and watch the performance.

By western standards there is nothing spectacular about the ceremony. No pyrotechnics explode in a brilliant shower, no performers magically suspended in the air. Though the heyday of the USSR is long over, the parade floats still call to mind Soviet-era contraptions with their thick lines and abstract geometrical shapes, their pastel colors sugary in aspect. Then the cavalcade of animals enters including the two-humped camels of the Gobi and the wild horses of the steppes, these creatures paraded in among beasts as mundane as sheep and goats while a battalion of singers and dancers fluidly morph into complex formations in the infield, singing traditional songs. A child marches into the stadium bearing a golden eagle on his arm, the bird as large as a small leopard. At the end of the ceremony, the nine white horse tails of Chinggis Khaan are paraded into the stadium on long poles, what Mongolians call a *sulde,* a spirit banner, each one like a head composed entirely of hair, this symbol of our nation's former glory.

After the opening ceremony, the wrestlers enter the stadium, each one almost naked. Men big as mountains, their bodies culled from a time of giants. Only their shoulders are covered in the traditional *zodog,* the garment that sheaves the arms but leaves one's chest bare. According to my grandfather, the *zodog* originates in the days of Chinggis Khaan after a particularly fierce competitor throws half the army to the frozen ground over the course of a single night. I remember Övöö relaying how, as the winner looms victorious in the circle of fiery torches, the victor triumphantly rips off his shirt, exposing two pale perfectly formed moons of what prove to be her breasts. I imagine the defeated men slinking off into the darkness, their skin flushing at the shame of losing to a woman. Now men wrestle bare-chested, leaving nothing in doubt. Similarly, the tight-fitting *shuudag* makes evident the sex of each competitor, the briefs red or blue and so short there is nothing for an opponent to grab on to.

As tradition dictates, each wrestler slaps his thighs and performs a dance as he enters and exits the match. Some competitors float their arms up and down in the style of the golden eagle. Other stalk about like lions or tigers. Now there is a rule that a match can go no longer than three hours. Some years ago two titans face each other for the title. For hours the men trade positions back and forth, first one man on the brink of throwing the other, then the second finds a reserve somewhere deep within and reclaims the dominant position. This goes on through the evening and into the night, the moon shining down on them as if cupping the opponents in her silvery palms. There are long spells where both combatants appear to be sleeping, the two men holding each other up like dancers. Finally, in the early hours of the morning, the loser places his foot in such a way that he simply slips to the earth, conversely the winning man as if gently laying a lover down to sleep. No one cheers.

If One Gets the Opportunity to Touch the Winning Horse

After an hour of watching men throw each other to the ground, our group departs to wander the grounds outside the National Sports Stadium. The archery competition is already underway. Everywhere arrows fly through the noonday air, their bright and colorful fletchings made from the tail feathers of the demoiselle crane. I can hear the arrows whistling in their flight like water boiling in a kettle. Though the sun is at its hottest, the contestants wear long belted robes and the traditional hat with the golden spike, the thing shaped like a cairn atop a hill. Here even women compete. I watch a young woman in blue walk up to the line and take aim. When the archer draws, she uses only her thumb to pull the string back. As a child I am never any good at it, my thumb seemingly bleeding before I even lift the bow. The woman lets go and the arrow hits just inside the bull's-eye.

A little after noon we reboard the shuttle bus for the long drive out of the city to watch the third manly art, though it is an art practiced by children, including girls. Much of the population of Ulaanbaatar is also headed to watch the horse race, the animals covering upward of thirty kilometers. If one gets an opportunity to touch the winning horse after it crosses the finish line, it is said that one is guaranteed good fortune for the rest of the year. In this, my brother and I do not hide our hopes from each other. We are both anxious to lay our hands on the sweaty flank of the winning animal. In the coming days we are hungry for all the good fortune this world sees fit to grant us.

At the wheel of the shuttle bus Mun makes a sharp turn. The woman with the blue toenails and I slide into each other, our shoulders touching, the bare skin of my arm surprised by the heat of her body. Then suddenly we are driving up on the sidewalk, the shuttle avoiding the occasional park bench, pedestrians moving off to the side, though undisturbed by our presence as we are not the only ones to seek a new path out of the city. This is how one drives in Mongolia. We are horsemen and the sons of horsemen, on and on back to the first generations born under the eternal blue sky. We make a way where there is no way. We drive our cars as if they are animals.

The shuttle slows down as even here on the sidewalk there is traffic. The woman with the steely blue nails closes her eyes. We are still pressed together. I feel the whisper of where her shoulder brushes mine as we continue to slide into each other like water lightly tumbling over stones. A light turns on in my chest. This is the first time I ever touch a woman in such a manner.

It is all I can do not to hold myself there, the skin of my shoulder pressed to hers, our shoulders briefly kissing. I breathe deeply. The sunlight flashing on and off on the side of my face closest to the window as the shuttle bus slips among the city's shadows. I recall the first time my brother fully touches a woman. It shames me to acknowledge that what I know of physical love I know only through the actions of my brother and our shared mind. The feel of the girl's palms on his shoulder blades. The unexpected smoothness of her body, the steeliness of it as well, the heat.

The morning after he first touches a woman, I encounter him in the hall when he sneaks back into the monastery, the light dawning like a new frontier, my look filled with reproach. My twin stares me full in the face, his eyes ablaze with Hayagrīva, the Horse-Necked One, the ferocious deity whose energy the senior monks are teaching him to channel. Mun's nostrils flare with defiance. Now you know, he sneers. Then he shuts me out of that part of his life forever. I am never again to experience the touch of a woman through him. In a way, I am grateful that he seals me off from such things. When it comes to my twin and what I can only assume are his innumerable conquests, I would rather be left in the dark.

Then just as easily the road curves, the shuttle bus veering, and with that, this blue-toed stranger and I slide apart. Maybe this is what happens when two people fall out of love. The path on which they are traveling together simply bends. This past year maybe this is what is happening between my brother and me. Perhaps our paths are about to reconnect.

Come with me, Brother, I think, sending my thoughts through the air. It is like shouting into a raging fire. In return, all I feel is silence and unquenchable heat.

The Leader of Ten Thousand

Listen without distraction: the worst day of my life occurs when I am seven years old. That is the age at which children are allowed to participate in Naadam, though sometimes a younger child who is bigger than his peers manages to slip among the contenders.

That year as Naadam approaches, it is all Mun can talk about. Summer nights before bed he shows me the space on the altar next to a picture of our mother in front of a backdrop of the Great Wall of China. After I win it, the medal goes here, he says. Each year, the winner is granted the title "Leader of Ten Thousand," though the most skilled rider does not always cross first. In thirty kilometers anything can happen; one year the winner crosses the finish line asleep in the saddle. Now that he is old enough, Mun wants to be the leader of ten thousand. Of the two of us, Mun is the better horseman, but he is too cunning, too impatient, too ready to kick the horse in the ribs to spur it onward, domination the only way he knows to communicate with the animal.

Two weeks before Naadam, Mun climbs up on Övöö's stallion, the one without a proper name. Our grandfather holds to the old ways that one never names an animal anything besides its color. About a kilometer from our homestead the beast throws my twin to the ground, breaking his wrist. Later, Mun claims a marmot startles the horse, but none of us believe him. Övöö says his horse is part wolf. This is the reason Mun and I are not allowed to ride him. Even our father prefers to walk long distances rather than try to saddle Övöö's stallion.

There is no one to ride for us, wails Mun as our grandfather sets the bone. I know the tears running down my brother's cheeks have nothing to do with the pain of the break.

My grandfather sucks in his cheeks. Of course there is, he says. Chuluun is also a horseman. And he can ride my horse. I feel a door open in my heart. I try to make myself as small as possible. Övöö cinches the bindings on Mun's splint. My brother stops crying. I feel a small stone harden in my twin's heart.

The night before the race I do fifty prostrations. Mun lies on the floor coldly watching me, his broken wrist bound to two wooden paddles.

Sometimes the universe clicks into place. Everything is as it should be. At first light, out by the animal pens I throw up my breakfast of rice porridge with milk. My grandfather pretends not to notice. He helps me climb up behind him on the unnamed stallion. A great being is fearless like a yak, he says as he pulls me up, but such a being also knows that fear can be instructive. I nod. We ride the eight kilometers to where the race begins. The whole way I can feel the animal's flanks rippling under my thighs, the animal so broad my legs stick straight out.

At the starting line someone pours vodka on the ground and asks the Eternal Blue Sky to watch over the few dozen of us. A whistle sounds and we're off. After the first thirty minutes across the plain, we are winnowed to a handful of riders, nobody truly in the lead, nobody lagging. I can hear someone among us singing to his horse. Another boy at my side, someone I do not recognize, rides with a face filled with an intensity that scares me. But on the way up a small ridge, his animal begins to flag, and though the boy uses his crop on it much the way my twin would, as an extension of his will, soon the boy and his horse drop out of view.

As time goes on, others begin to drop away, the animals tiring, the riders losing focus, until it is just me and the singing boy galloping together over the grasslands. Then it happens. I feel myself riding a wave of exhilaration, Övöö's horse beginning to edge out the boy's, his song trailing behind me. I imagine the whole region around Bor-

Urt waiting for me at the finish line, my grandfather lifting me off the hands of the cheering crowd and placing me back on earth, me, Chuluun, the new leader of ten thousand.

Unbidden, I hear a soft voice floating to me over the wind. The singing boy is just at your shoulder, the voice says. At the foot of the next hill, head east. Do not ride up the ridge. There is another, shorter way. I do as the voice of my distant brother suggests.

And so it begins. For the next twelve hours I wander through the grasslands utterly lost, slowly the earth growing dark under the horse's hooves, both me and the animal thirsting, the world an endless maze, the crescent moon little help, all the while bouts of panic and then moments beyond panic and then panic again. At one point I dismount to let the horse graze. Because he is not my horse, he does not come back to me when I beckon. He simply trots away.

There are wolves on this part of the steppe. I sit and huddle, rub my arms for warmth. A few hours before dawn I see a light moving over the grasslands. It is my grandfather riding his nameless stallion, the reins to a second horse in his hand. He comes and scoops me up in his arms.

For the next week, Övöö still refers to me as the leader of ten thousand. Each time he does, I feel Mun tighten. Even now in my nightmares, sometimes I still hear my twin's voice telling me there is another shorter way, don't ride up the ridge. Even all these years later there are days when I do not know if he is trying to be helpful or if he means to lead me astray.

We crest the first hill. The city long behind us. I can see the entirety of the dusty plain, the earth flat as an open palm. There are no structures, no *ger,* no wandering herds. Then we crest a second steeper hill, and the earth reveals that we are nothing but ants wandering in search of sweetness. Mun puts the shuttle bus into a higher gear. If there are just over three million citizens of Mongolia, and almost half of them live in the capital city, then it seems as if every man, woman, and child is here to witness who is to be crowned King of Horses. Later I hear reports that there are upward of fifty thousand people dotting this hillside.

Mun parks next to an operation selling neon-orange drinks in plastic bags. Be back in an hour, he says.

The tourists disappear down the hill, the woman with the blue toenails latching on to an Italian couple. The air smells of horses and meat being burned. Mun lights up a cigarette and locks the shuttle door. In all the madness I cannot even tell where the finish line is. It's over there, says Mun, pointing to a spot a kilometer away on a distant hillside. As we approach, I can already see throngs of people massing, each one jockeying for position. It is yet another twenty minutes before the first animal comes into view, but the crowd is already surging. I feel myself being jostled as if at sea.

When it happens, neither of us is surprised, though many of the westerners do not expect it. The rider is a girl. What I know now as an adult: we do not celebrate the rider but rather the horse. The noise is deafening. The horse crosses the finish line. The animal shines with sweat as if cast in glass. Sometimes the world can change in the span of a heartbeat. A moment on the verge of becoming a disaster. I try to make myself as small as possible. A hundred hands clawing the air, each one hungry for a touch of the winning beast.

We are on the verge of a stampede. The animal wheels about. A second horse comes crashing over the finish line and a hundred hundred hands turn and reach for it. The woman next to me falls to the ground, but I pull her up. Together the crowd surges forward, arms outstretched, pulsating, wanting just one stroke, one encounter with grace. My palm lands on something hot and damp. In the presence of so much good fortune, it is all I can do to stay on my feet.

My brother is standing on the edge of the mayhem, his earbuds plugged in his head. He thinks he is safe, that he is out of the roiling storm, but an errant rider is coming up behind him at breakneck speed, the young rider out of control as the horse panics at the size of the crowd. Move, I internally shout, filling my brother's mind with my warning. Mun leaps out of the way just as the horse goes barreling past.

Then at the same time we both spot her. The woman from our group with the blue nails. A horse is up on its hind legs, pawing the air with its hooves, its rider lost among the chaos. The woman stands frozen, gripping her camera. Slowly Mun and I approach the animal. I put my hand on its trembling flank, the muscle twitching like a live wire. I imagine a wave of tranquility emanating through my fingertips. Mun stands straight in the horse's path. He summons up Hayagrīva, his ferocious deity, this wrathful god whose tantric energy my twin learns to perfect while still living at Yatuu Gol. My brother's nostrils flare, the veins prominent in his neck. For an instant, the air around him goes stormy though only I can see it. Together through a mixture of compassion and fury we placate the animal. It stops rearing on its hind legs, lowers its head, and nuzzles Mun's hand.

Later, on the drive back to Ulaanbaatar, I can still smell the sweat of the horse on my palm. You guys make a good team, says the woman with the blue toenails. I feel my face flush. My hand smells like earth and grass and the summer air mixed with the mineral smell of blood. I know there is no such thing as fortune—there is only what is—though for the moment I let myself believe otherwise.

A Golden Deer Who Can Converse With Humans

An hour to sundown and Gandan Tegchenling, the Great Place of Complete Joy, is gleaming. Along the eastern wall the prayer wheels creak as Mun walks by, giving each a spin. The monastery is a maze of temples and courtyards and *stupa*. The buildings are mostly made of stucco and painted various colors. Several are topped by ornate green-and-gold Chinese-style roofs, their peaks adorned with tiles like the scales on a dragon, the roofs sweeping downward, then rising coyly at each corner the way a woman initially averts her eyes only to glance up at you as you turn from her. A group of tourists huddles in one of the courtyards. On passing I hear the guide mention that the roofs of the monastery complex, like a traditional *ger,* are not held together with nails but instead dovetailed like a jigsaw puzzle. She points to one roof in particular. Perched above the main entrance is a *dharmachakra* flanked by two deer. This is a reference to the Buddha's first teachings near the Indian city of Varanasi more than twenty-five hundred years ago, explains the guide. She goes on to say that in one of His many previous lives, the Buddha is a golden deer who can converse with humans.

Because today I have yet to sit as part of my formal practice, I convince Mun to arrive at the monastery early so that I might offer prayers with my fellow monks, together all of us chanting for the liberation of all beings. The courtyard outside the temple begins to fill with a sea of red. On the eastern tower two monks blow conch shells in the direction of the four winds, calling the monastery to the last *puja* of the day. In the fading light the two monks stand wearing the golden-crested lama hat, the yellow plume upright like the sheared mane of a horse. One of the monks holds a left-spiraling shell, the other blowing the rarer right-spiraling conch, the one symbolizing the motion of the stars and planets through the heavens. In Buddhism the right-spiraling conch is considered to be one of the auspicious symbols and has the power to awaken the believer from the sleep of the ignorant. Like a shepherd who milks his sheep, the animals feeling instant relief just at the sight of him, the call of the conch elicits a deep spirituality in the blood. Just hearing the music of the shells puts me in a state of peace.

When we are all in place at the entrance to the temple, the Abbot of Gandan Tegchenling Monastery stands before the doors. He intones the short-offering mantra.

For those who strive day and night to develop virtues,
The Universal Vehicle especially is a great tide of good,
So prepare to conceive its spirit and incomprehensible actuality,
Then, by dedication, fully retain them.

With that, he pushes the doors open and we enter. In his rock 'n' roll T-shirt, Mun stays behind in the courtyard, his fedora in his hands, earbuds sprouting from his head. He has yet to enter a temple since renouncing his vows. When living as the Redeemer Who Sounds the Conch in the Darkness, he might sit in prayer, wishing for the happiness of all sentient beings, for up to seven hours a day. Now he is too busy with the trappings of life to reflect on its very nature. For the first time since I arrive in Ulaanbaatar, I sense a small bubble of wistfulness rising in him, nostalgia for another world, another lifetime, for belonging, but then it bursts and is gone if it ever even exists.

According to the Great Liberation Through Hearing

Listen without distraction:

According to the Great Liberation Through Hearing, there are six types of hell where one may be reborn following one's time in the *bardo* between death and rebirth. One hell is a fiery world brimming with rivers of molten lava, the blood-red sky ablaze with sparks. Despite this hell's capaciousness, its ability to accommodate an infinite number of beings, everywhere within its lands there is a feeling of claustrophobia, of being wedged in tight places, the body slowly turning into charcoal.

When considering this first hell, says the Abbot of Gandan Tegchenling, one should meditate on the story of the beggar who finds the leg of a tender young lamb lying by the side of the road. When the beggar asks his teacher if it is all right for him to partake of it, his teacher advises him to mark the meat with an x and to return for it later. The beggar does as he is told, using his rusty knife to carve an x in the meat, thus marking it as belonging to him, before hurrying away to prepare a fire. Later, in the dank shelter of his cave, the shadow of the flames dancing on the cave walls, the beggar feels an uneasiness come over him, a low throb beginning to spread on his chest. Slowly he lifts his tattered shirt. On the papery skin above his heart, there is a bloody x etched in his own hand. This is the parable of the fiery hell, says the Abbot. It is a hell of self-directed anger. A hell in which we spend our energy raging against our enemies, but at the end of the day we are only raging against ourselves.

The Abbot glances at my brother. After the prayer offering in the temple ends, the Abbot tracks us down in the courtyard and motions for us to follow him to this room. Even though he is my twin, when his days on earth run their course, I believe Mun is doomed to this hell of which the Abbot speaks. I have no doubts. You can see it in his eyes. An orange aura burning around each pupil as if the iris itself is smoldering. Some days I think this is the journey he is destined to make. It is out of his control. Endlessly circling through *samsara,* doomed to be born in an infinite cycle from human to beast to hungry ghost until he lives every existence possible. Other days I think he is simply a fool.

Then the Abbot of Gandan Tegchenling turns to me. There is barely enough room for the three of us crammed here in his small study, the space obviously ancient and built for private meditations. I sit facing him, Mun behind me in the corner by the door. And what of the second wintry hell, the Abbot asks.

Like most monasteries in Mongolia, Gandan Tegchenling is a teaching monastery. The head monk serves as the Abbot. Most of the monks at Gandan Tegchenling are novices in their early to mid-twenties who, like me, have yet to take their final vows. I can hear them outside the window, a sea of robes clapping and stamping the earth as they debate the nature of the universe. For us, debate is at the heart of a monk's pedagogic training. Evenings filled with the sound of monks seemingly raging at one another.

I clear my throat, prepare my answer to what is essentially unanswerable.

Do Not Travel This Path

The second hell is a world of snow and ice, I say, coldness beyond anything imaginable.

Why are these two hells figured in terms of opposites, asks the Abbot. Why should even the world beyond this one present itself to us as a duality when the Buddha teaches us that duality is an illusion?

I can feel Mun's mind cloud over with boredom. My brother is no help. Theology is not the strong suit of the Redeemer Who Sounds the Conch in the Darkness. He slouches in the corner, his earbuds silently draped around his neck. At the very least I am grateful for this small gesture of respect.

The Abbot looks at me expectantly. A small bug the color of blood crawls along the ridge of his jaw. Hell is a projection, he says, eventually answering his own question. It is a creation of the human mind in the moment of death, he says, and as such it is subject to human error like the belief in binary systems. For a moment the small bug comes to rest on the tip of his chin. It flares its tiny wings but doesn't take to the air.

Like the erroneous belief that you and your brother are separate beings, the Abbot adds, when in reality there are no selves. I feel the half-finished letter tucked next to my heart begin to grow hot. Then the Abbot reaches out and places his hands on my head. Surprisingly they are the calloused hands of a herder. His nails black with work, the tip of his left index finger missing.

The Abbot keeps his hands on my head, slows his breathing. This second wintry hell is a hell of aggression focused inward, he says, a pride that doesn't reach out and communicate. Young brother, he admonishes. Do not travel this path. Accept your brother's aid.

This startles me. I look up at the Abbot. The Redeemer Who Sounds the Conch in the Darkness has yet to offer aid, I say.

I'm waiting to be properly asked, Mun shoots back. You know, in words.

Then the door opens and a light beyond anything on earth enters the room. My sons, says the light in a language I know mostly from reading. Please aid me in the quest to find the One for Whom the Sky Never Darkens.

Mun sits up a little straighter, but he doesn't bow his head. Sure, says my twin. What have we got to lose?

The Lotus of the Deep

We Rely on Nothing but What We Carry Inside Us

The ridge we are aiming for shoots up out of the plain, its profile like a camel kneeling on her two front legs. Already I can tell there is no way to drive the Machine up the butte. This means we must park at the base, and then Mun must scramble to the top if he wants to get his bearings. During our first day on the journey, from time to time my twin plugs a small box into the cigarette lighter, powering up a screen. After a while, a pale blue circle appears, the thing endlessly spinning. The second time Mun plugs in the box I hear a deep chuckle emanate from the back seat. Inwardly I laugh as well. We Mongols still reconnoiter in the old ways. We look for distinguishing characteristics in the landscape. We let the sun's position in the heavens tell us where we are. We rely on nothing but what we carry inside us, each of us a map and the world the journey. Eventually, Mun stows the box away, never looks to it again for guidance.

For the past few hours we find ourselves riding on virgin ground, lands where no cars venture. We are three hundred kilometers from paved roads, and only the ancestors know how many more from the deep tire tracks worn in the fibrous grass by countless vehicles over time, which in Mongolia are the equivalent of highways. There is a reason this land is empty this time of year when every herder is seeking to fatten his flocks for the interminable winter ahead. It means there is no water on this part of the steppe, the ground mostly pebbly dirt, almost lunar in its starkness. If we have to, we can sleep out here in the middle of nowhere, the temperature plunging at night to the point where summer frost is possible, but it is always dangerous traveling in uninhabited wastelands such as this. If something happens to the Machine, we could be stuck out here for the rest of the summer. In Mongolia, people die this way; more people die in the hot months than in the pangs of winter. They do not die of heat, but rather from being stranded in the grasslands. Sometimes it turns out they are only a few kilometers from help.

As we approach, the butte begins to take on the color of dried blood. It is a color I recognize as a type of igneous rock, its minerals fired deep in the earth. The same kind of rock is found a few hundred kilometers northwest of here near Khövsgöl Nuur where the first candidate lives among the Reindeer People in their tents sewn from hides. If all goes well, we should arrive there tomorrow.

I can feel the Machine make the slow turn toward the ridge. On the roof the jugs of water and gasoline slosh past level. Saran sits between Mun and me, her body a wall separating us from each other. She is the only woman in our group, which besides myself and Mun includes Venerable Uncle and Little Bat. Saran's head comes to rest on my shoulder, a dragonfly wafting out of the eternal blue to cease for a moment before traveling on. Once again she is awake before any of us, rising in the dark to start the fire and heat the milk tea, prepare the rice with raisins and sugar. Despite Little Bat's strong protests that he should serve as steward, the Abbot at Gandan Tegchenling insists Saran accompany us on our journey as we need someone to cook and look after us. Consequently, I do not begrudge her this small moment of fatigue. Her head is light and still smells of the wildflowers she laces in her hair at the start of our trip which is amazing after two full days in the Machine.

I cannot help but wonder why, of all the nuns and laypeople at Gandan Tegchenling Monastery, the Abbot picks her to accompany us on this mission. Her name, Sarangerel, moonlight, fits the dreaminess she exudes, her expression as if her heart is born aloft on a cloud. If I had to guess I would say that she is a few years younger than Mun and me, that maybe she is nineteen or twenty. Technically Saran is not a nun, though like us she speaks both Mongolian and Tibetan. Her Tibetan is more fluid than ours, which we learn through studying ancient texts. I wonder if, like us, she learns it in a monastery, or if there is a family connection. For the most part I am now used to sitting beside her, our legs brushing against each other intermittently. Still, there are moments when I feel an unwelcome heat spread through my body at her touch. Each time I must work to tamp it down. When Mun stares at Saran, he stares openly, the blood-heat apparent in his look. In my mind, I send him a sharp rebuke, a slap to the back of the head. I wonder if desire is something he picks up from westerners. As the first two of the Four Noble Truths state, in life there is suffering; the cause of suffering is desire. I add it to my twin's long list of shortcomings.

The Machine sails along through the early morning light, everywhere the colors crisp as if rinsed in milk, Saran's sleeping head on my shoulder. From the driver's seat Mun looks over at me and leers. Fire only knows fire. I see myself reflected in his sunglasses, one of me in each glossy lens, both of me looking vexed. It is only two days since leaving Ulaanbaatar. From what I am told by the Rinpoche at Yatuu Gol, it is urgent we find this reincarnation. Already a search is conducted in Tibet that lasts two years, the monks working secretly with the help of the local people, but something goes awry and now the monks are missing. If the child is not found soon, it could be difficult for him to acclimate to his new life. There is much hope surrounding this reincarnation. The child must learn to speak English. He must be well versed in western ways if he is to one day become the face of Tibetan Buddhism. There is a growing fear that the Chinese might anoint a reincarnation once the Dalai Lama passes, thus installing a puppet as the leader of the Tibetan people. Should His Holiness's reincarnation be politicized following His death, our faith requires a new leader, one the Chinese do not anticipate. This is why we are searching for a reincarnation from an undistinguished lineage, relatively speaking. In the past, this being serves His Holiness admirably throughout the ages, but in this current incarnation, this being is needed to serve at the highest level.

From the back seat Little Bat taps Saran on the shoulder. She wakes and turns, her thick black braid coming to rest on my arm as they converse. To my ears the sound of Tibetan is jagged yet watery, a language not all that different from Mongolian in that it too is filled with the music of the natural world—weather and hardship, long nights of dreams and the eternal blue sky.

Sometimes when he shifts, I can feel one of Little Bat's massive knees gouging my back. Really he should be sitting where I am in the passenger's seat which affords one the most space, but he prefers to sit next to Uncle, the two men mastering the discomfort of the body years ago.

Little Bat shifts again. I rearrange myself accordingly. I wonder if time and space mean anything at all to Uncle, the honored one with whom we travel, or if these material concepts slide off him like water off a lotus leaf. Then Mun jams on the brakes and the emptiness of the universe comes crashing in on us.

A Man's Got to Know His Limitations

Considering the seriousness of the situation we find ourselves in, Uncle seems light of heart, amused, like a young boy traveling into town to watch an evening of wrestling, his steps quick and eager despite his age. I walk at the back of our small procession, my hands folded at chest level. Little Bat walks in the lead, Uncle in between us, Little Bat's baby face as placid as Uncle's is jovial. In his hands Little Bat works an ancient set of ivory prayer beads carved from the teeth of a walrus. To my eye Little Bat looks even more tranquil now than he does an hour ago as we crawl one by one out of the Machine. His face remains serene though the world seemingly comes to an end, Little Bat a man who accepts whatever the universe parses out. A man who asks nothing of anything. His detachment attained after many lifetimes of practice. Though he shows no agitation, Little Bat believes we should not be going in search of help, that there is no help to be found, and that we ought to stay by the Machine and use what resources we have to help ourselves.

I focus on what Little Bat is saying, as I often have trouble understanding him. When he speaks, it is obvious that something terrible is in his past. His voice as if he once swallows a river of burning sand, his vocal cords damaged to the extreme, his voice the voice of a hundred-year-old man but somehow planted in the body of a forty-something baby-faced giant. The very first time I hear him speak at Gandan Tegchenling Monastery, I wince. It is painful to listen to him produce each word. At the sound of his voice, Mun remembers a man he sees in Ulaanbaatar, the man with a hole punched at the base of his throat and the sound gurgling up from the puckered skin. Besides his voice and his immensity, Little Bat appears unremarkable in every other aspect. I do not know what resources he is referring to, but when Little Bat suggests this course of action, Uncle vehemently shakes his head. No, Uncle insists, first we look.

When we hit the sinkhole, only Mun, who makes his living driving tourists across the vastness of Mongolia, is not wearing a seatbelt. Surprisingly, the Machine looks undamaged, its hood sunk up to the windshield in the ground like an animal burrowing into the earth. My eyes still sting from the smell of gas, the plastic jugs that are strapped to the roof having rocketed into the dirt, one of them cracking on impact, the leaked gasoline making the air go wavy. Standing there beside the Machine I notice a small bruise already marbling Mun's forehead, the thing pale blue like the spring egg of a bird.

I gotta go with you, Mun says, as we three monks set out to look for aid. My brother is sincere in his desire to help, but when he stands he wobbles drunkenly, a newborn foal finding its legs.

Uncle laughs. For the first time since we make his acquaintance at Gandan Tegchenling he speaks to us in English. A famous American cowboy says a man's got to know his limitations, Uncle explains. The twinkle deepens in his eyes. He taps his own forehead in the same spot where Mun's bruise lies shining. My young friend, he says, switching back to Tibetan, your third eye is opening nicely. Pray that it may continue to light your path.

Mun sinks back down in the shadow of the Machine, defeated, the bruise like pale blue dough rising on his forehead. Now would be a good time for him to practice the Buddhist reflection on death, the fact that we are of a nature to die, that as humans we do not evolve beyond dying, but already he is popping in his earbuds, he is tuning the world out. I know the reason why, despite his injury, he struggles to stand and come along with us to find help. It is because he resents that I am able to go in search of aid while he must stay behind. This is not the first time I step forward to make things right, our childhood filled with other instances, other places where I am the one to sweep up the broken glass, glue the world back together in the wake of his actions. The one time as children when I fire a gun at him, it is to save him from himself.

As I prepare to head out with Uncle and Little Bat, I feel the anger welling inside my twin as he once again finds himself dependent on me. Chuluun who is both doctor and medicine, Mun thinks, the sarcasm coloring his thoughts. Chuluun who nurses all the sick beings in the world until each is healed.

I am waiting, Brother, I silently respond. I am waiting for the day when things reverse, when you come and rescue me.

I consider reminding him that the *tögrög* wrapped in my robe is paying for this journey. Out here, I'm the boss. He is merely the driver hired to take our small party across the country on our journey in search of an ancient light. But for the time being, I let it go. Honestly, I am not sure if our relationship can ever be anything other than what it is. Me praying for the peace of all sentient beings. My twin looking out only for himself.

Still, I should be thankful he is with us. In two weeks' time when we return to Ulaanbaatar, most likely he no longer has a job. On our way out of the city in the old Soviet 66 owned by his boss, Mun calls Ganzorig, asks him to explain to Tuul that something's come up, that he is needed on this private tour. Though I do not know him, I suspect that Ganzorig is pleased not to have to drive to the ends of Mongolia and beyond. As for me, this is what life brings: two weeks on the road with my twin. It is more than a year since he disrobes.

Then Uncle claps his hands together four times, each clap offered in a different cardinal direction. When he finishes, he pulls a pair of stylish sunglasses out of the folds in his robe and puts them on. Sometimes I see young monks adorn themselves in the trappings of the modern world, mostly items such as headphones and sneakers, their demeanors changing as they robe themselves in such things. But Uncle? With or without sunglasses he is the same man who greets us just days before in the Abbot's study, instructing us to call him Uncle and leaving it at that though his full epithet is the Lotus of the Deep.

Like my brother, he is a *tulku,* a reincarnation of a spiritual teacher, a light who walks the earth many times before and on and on eternally.

Shall we, he says. Because I cannot see his eyes behind his sunglasses it takes me a moment to realize he is talking to me.

If it please you, I say, bowing, and then the three of us set off, Little Bat in the lead. Each time Uncle addresses me, I have to fight the urge not to touch the ground at his feet with my forehead.

Then a Door Opens

From the air I imagine we look like a trio of red ants. At the front Little Bat drifts contentedly along like a man without a future or past. Uncle seems to float over the ground, a leaf in the summer breeze. Everywhere the landscape is barren, the dirt possibly volcanic, the top layer oxidized and darker than what lies beneath. With each step we disturb the surface, leaving a trail of pale footprints in our wake.

We walk without speaking. For the moment there is nothing but the present moment—no past, no future, no desire. At times it feels as if you might drown in the vast blueness overhead, the way the clouds ripple like waves on the ocean. According to Övöö, in Mongolia the summer sky is so blue because the winters are so long and so dark. Övöö who lives through the destruction of the monasteries only to die just as we are coming through on the other side of history.

After twenty minutes there is only half a kilometer more to go until we reach the butte. The air is clean and does not smell of livestock. There are no dried patties lying coiled on the ground, no animal bones bleached white as snow. We are astronauts, explorers in an endless wasteland. How quickly the earth can change, and all because of a lack of water.

Suddenly Little Bat stops and turns. Perhaps the vast emptiness surrounding us is all the answer he needs about the prospect of finding help. He looks questioningly at Uncle. Uncle stops walking and the two men stand wordlessly facing each other in the desolateness. Something is being decided. Watching this, I have the feeling that they stand this way an innumerable number of times throughout the ages, a regent and his councillor. The first time I meet them I recognize what they are to each other. Little Bat is what we call Uncle's heart's disciple. The big monk appears to be decades younger than Uncle. From the short time I know him I can tell he is as resolute as a yak and beyond loyal. When the day comes and Uncle's essence leaves his body, it is already understood that Little Bat is the one who is to search for it.

The sun darts behind a cloud. The men's shadows waver on the stony ground. Then a door opens. Uncle relents. Go, he says, prepare yourself. The resignation in his voice like something giving way to nature. Little Bat bows his head and turns back to where the others wait. He wears the same look of stillness on his face that he sets out with, his face as though nothing changes. Uncle and I watch him go, his shadow twice the size of ours.

The path is steep, Uncle says, turning once again toward the ridge.

I feel the weight of the moment on my shoulders. If something happens to this man, a light in the tree of peace would be dimmed right when we need him most. After the search party goes missing in Tibet, the signs for discovery shift here to Mongolia. Now, based on what Little Bat tells us of his dreams, of whole worlds saturated in every shade of blue—blue ice, blue gems, the deep-blue sky over the ocean at night—there is the distinct possibility that we could be out here for weeks, heading as far south as the Gobi depending on what Little Bat can remember of his dreams and the ways of the nomads. Though this journey should only last fourteen days, already it feels like a lifetime. And it must not last longer than fourteen days. We must be back in Ulaanbaatar in two weeks as Uncle, who is among the Dalai Lama's most trusted advisers, is needed at the side of His Holiness, who is scheduled to deliver the rare Kalachakra teaching in Dharamshala at the end of the month, a teaching He offers only every few years. As He is getting on in age, this Kalachakra is rumored to be His last. We can only hope for the smoothest of travels across a land already proving that one must travel here anticipating absolutely anything to arise.

Yes, I agree, the path *is* steep. Truthfully I am not sure if by the path Uncle is referring to the stony outcrop that lies before us or if he is speaking metaphorically.

The rest of the way I concentrate on the beating of my heart, my pulse like a clock, like an icicle dripping from the branch of a tree. From time to time I scan the sky searching for scavengers circling on the winds. Scavengers are to the grasslands what the albatross is to the mariner lost at sea, namely, a harbinger of land; only in Mongolia the sight of vultures spiraling upward in the deep blue means that death lurks somewhere in the tall grass. Where there is death, there is life, a cycle at the very heart of Buddhism.

When we reach our goal it is not as hopeless as I expect. The ridge stands a few hundred meters above the plain. A few thin shrubs cling to its sides. About halfway around on the least-punishing slope we find a small path that clearly leads somewhere. Now that it is just the two of us, I am filled with an intense calm, a flower petal floating on the surface of a lake after the waters thaw. Uncle is younger than His Holiness by almost a decade, which would put him somewhere in his early seventies. From what I am told at Yatuu Gol, Uncle's lineage is one of the oldest. There are incarnations of the Lotus of the Deep serving at the side of the Lion Throne in one form or another since the line begins back in the mists of time. I know for him to be here now in Mongolia it must be a matter of the greatest importance.

I try not to let my heart race at the thought that I am in the presence of such an ancient humility, a grace that cycles through the world in the service of the Ocean of Wisdom since the fifteenth century, but every time Uncle looks at me I feel such unfettered happiness, a feeling a follower of the Triple Gem should not allow himself to enjoy for fear it clouds the mind.

I take a deep breath and fill my lungs with emptiness. The sunlight glittering all around us as if reflecting on water.

We Vow Not to Watch an Army Leave for Combat

Judging from the numerous spots where brush obscures the path, it is a long time since anyone walks this trail. Quickly Uncle moves forward. Somehow he intuits which rock can bear his weight, which rolls at the slightest touch. I pull my shawl up over my head. Considering I come from a line of nomads, I am now quite pale from hours spent poring over ancient prayer books in the monastery library, some of them so old they are handwritten on the smooth shoulder bones of sheep. It is difficult to believe that this very fall, when summer is over, I am to take my final vows, pledging myself to the Dharma forever. Among the additional vows monks pledge beyond the ones we initially take as novitiates, we vow not to watch an army leave for combat. We vow not to leave a mattress or a chair outside without arranging it suitably. Many of our vows are mundane promises that simply give order to everyday life. And after I am ordained, I intend to begin to study for my doctorate, a degree different from the one awarded in the west and which confers on the recipient the title of *geshe,* virtuous friend. In the Gelug tradition, the course of study to become a *geshe* can take anywhere from twelve to forty years.

Though a student like the rest of us at Yatuu Gol, at the age of eight, Mun goes through the ceremony formally naming him the Redeemer Who Sounds the Conch in the Darkness. Instantly he becomes an ordained monk. Because we believe Precious Ones are reincarnations, there is no need for them to live as novices.

Up ahead Uncle disappears around a bend. We are near the top. It is bare of all vegetation and smooth as a knee from the action of the wind through the eons. I blot my face with the edge of my robe, the sweat pearling down my back. I too reach the bend and walk out onto the crest. It is like walking into a small city.

A few rise tall as a man though most only reach mid-calf or to the waist, generally no more than six rocks or so balanced one on top of another. Everywhere the piles of stones like a series of stalagmites, their upright forms eerily human. I am panting slightly, but Uncle begins to move among the rocks, blessing everything with a touch of his hand. I stop to pull a stone from the heel of my sandal. Then I also begin to bless the *ovoo.*

Ovoo are a type of cairn and exist all over Mongolia at the top of hills and mountains, any spot deemed sufficiently high. In its simplest form an *ovoo* is a pile of stones that grows over time as travelers come and place a rock in the hopes of securing safe passage. Near the ancient capital of Karakorum people say there is an *ovoo* as tall as a five-story building. On Yatuu Gol itself there is an *ovoo* in the middle of the sleeping caldera. And in *ovoo* everywhere you can see where travelers leave personal offerings, items peeking out from underneath the stones as the *ovoo* grows around them—small bottles of vodka and paper currency, candy, and photographs, and always the flapping of *khadag,* the blue prayer cloth wedged under rocks or tied to sticks stuck upright in between cracks. Though we are both followers of the Gelug sect of Buddhism, in Tibet they call their prayer scarves *kata,* which are white like the snows of their mountains, but in Mongolia ours are blue, the color of the Eternal Blue Sky god, Tengri, our first deity. In many ways *ovoo* are a relic from Mongolia's shamanistic past. They are always built on an area's highest point, as such a place is the closest spot to Tengri. If you are traveling in a car or truck and do not have time to park and ascend and place a stone, you can honk your horn three times for luck as you drive by.

I cannot believe so many travelers find their way to this spot remote as the moon. Because there is no other evidence of them, no wrecks or boneyards littering the steppe, I can only assume they make it to wherever they intend safely. The thought makes me hopeful.

When we finish bestowing our blessings, Uncle and I walk around the largest *ovoo* three times in the same direction the sun takes through the heavens. The thing is the size of a car and sprinkled with blue *khadag,* some now just rags due to the elements. Then Uncle does a series of full prostrations. A cloud of dust rises in the air. He moves so lightly, like a man half his age, his forehead kissing the earth, arms outstretched on the ground. When he's done, he adjusts his robe and takes a seat. Within minutes he is in a deep place. Slowly I settle myself, clearing a spot of any sharp rocks. As we are a hundred meters above the plain, the sound of the wind sings in my ears, its voice mournful. I do not ask the question out loud, not wanting to reveal the existence of a shadow that is slowly entering my heart. Instead I think it to myself. How long do we wait?

Uncle sits with the half-lidded eyes of enlightenment. Already he is in the deepest river, a place the oldest ones can reach in a matter of minutes. The light as if bending around him.

I remember the half-finished letter tucked in my robe, the one addressed to the Rinpoche back at Yatuu Gol.

Most Honorable Rinpoche,

As it states in the Shantideva's Bodhisattva Vow:

May a rain of food and drink descend
To clear away the pain of thirst and hunger
And during the eon of famine
May I myself turn into food and drink.

May I become an inexhaustible treasure
For those who are poor and destitute;
May I turn into all things they could need
And may these be placed close beside them.

Esteemed Rinpoche, please know I have done everything in my power to serve you in a manner most befitting of one who wears the robe. But like a pond that is overgrown with moss, I find my heart growing turbid with doubt.

Late one night I write this on a scrap of paper after a wave of skepticism washes over me at the thought of all I am soon renouncing: what would it be like each night to unbraid a woman's hair, the smell of wildflowers suddenly filling the room? Three days after I begin writing this letter, the Rinpoche calls me into his chambers and tasks me with helping to find this reincarnation. Now I cannot help but wonder if it is the universe that arranges this series of strange events and slaps the rump of the wind horse that powers my life.

Here on this outcrop overlooking the endless grasslands, my watch beeps the hour.

Who sees the inexorable causality of things,
Of both cyclic life and liberation
And destroys any objective conviction
Thus finds the path . . .

I make myself as small as possible, then smaller still.

The Beautiful Arrives in Its Own Time

Days. Weeks. Years. Minutes. My backside tingling from sitting on the hard earth. I slow my breath and separate myself from the pain. What my grandfather would say at times like these: do not hasten toward doing what is beautiful; the beautiful arrives in its own time. I can hear the prayer flags woven among the *ovoo* snapping in the wind. The earth at its most elemental. Wind. Pain. Time. More pain. Then wisdom.

Each morning at Yatuu Gol I wake to practice *bodhicitta,* the wish to attain enlightenment for the benefit of all sentient creatures. I practice *bodhicitta* in a setting of like-minded beings, our brotherhood protected from the hungers of the everyday. Now there is no brotherhood to keep me centered, no smell of camphor, no call of the conch to help me focus. Instead, all morning Uncle and I sit among the landscape, our bodies like rocks. Overhead the sun moves through the sky like a hand making a sweeping gesture.

As a child, I learn about Buddhism from my grandfather. Where he learns it, he never says. When Mun and I are born, the only monastery in the country is Gandan Tegchenling in Ulaanbaatar, a place where even in the darkest of times the communist government allows a handful of monks to maintain some of the traditions. Unlike my twin, I naturally take to Övöö's lessons on emptiness and enlightenment. I enjoy pressing my body into the earth, prostrating myself in the name of compassion. It is with my grandfather that I first learn to consider a corpse, to stare long and hard at the desiccated body of a sheep or horse, to take comfort in the fact that my own body is made of the same materials, and that one day in the future my body also enters this state. It is my grandfather who tells me that to become a

Buddhist, one need only say the Triple Gem three times. *I take refuge in the Buddha, I take refuge in the Dharma, I take refuge in the sangha.* Even now I still say it to myself several times a day.

But now the quest for this reincarnation unleashes an uncertainty in me. I am like one who walks on shifting earth. Unbidden, my mind fills with such thoughts as are we destined to find the child, and, more important, is it the *right* child? This feeling of unease coupled with my own doubts regarding my upcoming ordination, and I find myself marveling at my brother's freedom. Though I do not approve of the way he sails through the floating world, a part of me wonders what it would be like to be my own master, to think of no one but myself. The longer Uncle and I sit without moving, the more I begin to feel my doubts infect me. In the coming days, should I finish penning the letter tucked in my robe? Am I to follow in my twin's footsteps and return to Yatuu Gol, renounce my vows? What would it mean to disrobe? And if I do, who am I then?

At the top of the butte there is no wind. A stone tumbles off an *ovoo.* Slowly I feel the action of time at work. The earth's plates coming together and moving apart. The seas rising and receding. Either my destiny is to pledge myself to the Dharma forever or I won't. Either I achieve some small measure of the diamond mind or I stay lost.

The Sun Shines on Both the Deserving and the Undeserving

And so it happens as it so often does in this life—when you come to fully accept where you are, a door opens. I remember the one thing I am sure of: suffering and the end of suffering. Everything else is bait. The way some creatures are born to die within hours, thousands of generations of life coming into being in the raindrop of a single day. If someone asks me how much time passes up here on the crest of the butte under the eternal blue sky, I would not be able to formulate a response. Days. Weeks. Years. Minutes. And yet it is as if only an instant passes, a dragonfly momentarily alighting on one's shoulder.

Uncle opens his eyes. May all beings have happiness and the tools of happiness, he says. He takes off his sunglasses and wipes them on his robe, the lenses flashing in the sun, a beacon to whatever is coming over the horizon. He puts them back on and stands up. The sky at the end of the sky trembles.

Before turning and heading back down the path, Uncle hands me a rock. The thing is dusty and fits comfortably in my palm. It is nondescript in every way. I wonder why he chooses this one. I know it is pointless to wonder. The Buddha says that in the moment of His enlightenment, He sees the very source from which life originates, but He does not address it in His teachings, as mankind often gets sidetracked by such fruitless questions as where we come from and why we exist. Not everything needs an answer. We must accept that some things just are. The sun shines on both the deserving and the undeserving equally.

I look at the options around me, the *ovoo* like a field of people. One of them catches my eye. The way it seems to stand in the shadow of another that is just off to its right, together the two *ovoo* like twin stars only one of them is taller and with more prayer flags woven among its stones, the other less robust. I place my rock on the smaller *ovoo*. Grow strong, little brother, I think. Your day is coming.

The walk down the butte is easier.

I Renounce My Vows, I Renounce My Vows

Mun is still lying in the wedge of shade the Machine casts on the ground. From the look of things it would seem he has yet to move. The bruise adorns his forehead like a small egg. It is lathered with a poultice Saran whips up from an old potato. By evening, the swelling should be gone, though the bruise itself remains for several days, his skin the pale blue color of a vein. When Uncle and I come back, he sits up quickly but winces. See anything, he asks.

Yes, says Uncle, one is always seeing if one simply opens the eyes. He winks at me. I am beginning to think that part of Uncle's journey, in addition to finding the One for Whom the Sky Never Darkens, is also to reopen my brother's heart, to bring him back to who he is, a Precious One. But then again I think this about every unexpected twist life brings our way ever since Mun says the words *I renounce my vows, I renounce my vows, I renounce my vows,* and in doing so, formally disrobes.

Little Bat is sitting in the lotus position off by himself on the scrubby earth. Not yet, my friend, says Uncle. Little Bat is too far off to hear, too deep in stillness, his form unmoving yet filled with light. Let us first give the universe a little more time to help, Uncle says.

Two years ago in early spring a herder on the edge of the Gobi discovers a young family of four in a remote area of the grasslands. Nobody knows exactly when they set out or where they are headed. In Mongolia people sometimes make long journeys by motorbike, bringing everything they need with them—extra inner-tube linings, a small compressor, a soldering iron, various tools and gadgets to fix anything that might go wrong, food and animal furs, photographs and keepsakes, a set of anklebones for the endless twilight evenings.

Of this family, all that is left is their rusted motorbike, the winter snows turning the metal to lace, the shriveled bodies of the young children huddling between the parents.

I arrange my robe around me and settle down on the ground, searching for the peace that exists even in uncertainty. I try to imagine the worst-case scenario, the five of us out here for weeks, the days growing shorter, the clouds graying with snow, our bodies moving less and less until all function ceases, the soft tissues of the face decaying first, maggots devouring the skin of our lips and nostrils so that our teeth appear elongated.

Noon approaches from the east, the sun at a standstill. The only shadows are those cast by clouds racing over the landscape. It is three hours since we hit the sinkhole. At one o'clock, Saran hands us each a bowl of milk tea and a block of *aaruul.* By two o'clock I notice a glittering when I close my eyes. Flecks of light dance in my vision even when my eyes are open. Three o'clock arrives. We have six more hours of summer light.

Little Bat rises and stands before Uncle, who remains seated but does not acknowledge the presence of his heart's disciple. After several minutes Little Bat prostrates himself before his teacher. He remains like that, face pressed to the dark earth. Time passes, the two men locked in silent strife. The sun lashing the world with its rays. Outwardly I also appear as one stilled, but inside me there is a great thundering. I envision a child's corpse hidden in the endless green. I imagine my own bones appearing through my skin.

Finally Uncle touches Little Bat's head with his palm. The way he touches him it is obviously a blessing. The big monk rises. He bows before Uncle. Then the giant with the baby face sets out to do what needs to be done. He displays the patience of one who knows that the yoke of this life brings what it brings.

Closing My Eyes Changes Nothing

Little Bat approaches the 66. In preparation, he ties a length of rope from one of our supply boxes to the roof rack at the back of the Machine. Methodically he trusses himself up like something about to be slaughtered. Now I understand Uncle's concern. The way Little Bat is tied I am worried his body could be squeezed to pieces, his insides compressed and bloody. The possibility is not that he is instantly killed. Instead what could come to pass are the kinds of injuries that occur in the dark. The body filling with its own fluids in all the wrong places, the death a slow and painful one, perhaps not even coming on for several weeks, the form internally leaking, a flood that cannot be stopped. I can tell my brother is thinking the same thing, but Uncle makes no move to stop his heart's disciple.

The distance between heaven and earth is no greater than one's intention. Little Bat lifts his face to the sky. I want to look away, but this is the world as it is. Closing my eyes changes nothing.

Impressive are horses and elephants which are well trained, but more impressive are individuals who tame themselves. It is not a miracle. Tomorrow as we bathe in an icy spring with the first candidate, the cost of this superhuman act of strength is evident. Little Bat's single-handedly pulling the Machine up out of the earth the way the yak pulls a plow, the rope merciless and digging into his flesh, the Machine slowly rising back up onto solid ground, a creature being raised from the underworld. As surely as our shadow never leaves us, so well-being follows when we act with a pure state of mind. Little Bat's entire body crisscrossed with welts and bruises, markings that are with him unto the end.

It's Not the Quality of Your Machine but the Quality of Your Mechanic

We drive another four hours. There is still time left before the sun sets that we can spend part of the day making for Khövsgöl Nuur. Thanks to Little Bat we are once again on the path toward the child. When all four wheels of the Machine are back up on firm land and Little Bat unties himself from the crushing rope, Uncle touches his forehead to Little Bat's. I expect him to say something, some words of blessing, but the touching of skin seems to be enough. I search Little Bat's form for signs of injuries, but it is too soon to tell. Should the worst come to pass, it could take time for the body to swell, for his insides to liquefy, his interior silently remapping itself.

After a few hours we come to a small outpost with a handful of buildings and an elderly couple manning the operation. We fill up with groceries, the gas jugs patched and back up on the roof. The woman gives us directions, detailing what to expect of the landscape. Despite his age the man crawls under the Machine and searches for any damage from our encounter with the sinkhole. He finds none. In Mongolia, we have a saying: it's not the quality of your Machine but the quality of your mechanic. Most cars in Mongolia are decades old cast-offs from the days of the Soviet Union. Most are completely rebuilt, the outer shell the only part that is original.

Mun hands me back my bag of *tögrög.* Carefully I wrap it up in my robe. We have yet to even meet the first candidate and already the bag is half depleted. Relax, Mun says, but he drives more gingerly than before. We do not travel as quickly. Now when he turns the car, he keeps both hands on the wheel. There is a small knot of concentration deep within him, his focus aimed completely on the landscape and the subtle markers that signify where we are. From time to time he fingers the bruise in the middle of his forehead, as if reminding himself of his responsibilities.

Far From It

Though we are told to expect it, what from a distance looks like a rip in the earth, the gorge still comes up unexpectedly. Beyond it we can see where the earth turns green again, the landscape shifting from the barrenness of Mars back to lushness. It's a dramatic moment. Let's take a look, says Uncle.

Carefully Mun inches the Machine up to the canyon's edge. The way the earth suddenly opens up in front of us, this the work of hundreds of millions of millennia, the world's smallest shovel patiently digging its way through stone. While the canyon is not wide, perhaps less than four hundred meters across, it is deeper than anything I ever encounter.

We get out to stretch our legs. At first I feel light-headed just looking at the gorge. But then I watch as Little Bat approaches with steady steps. He walks right up to the lip and sits down on the rim. A billion billion of him would not begin to fill it.

In our universe there are four previous incarnations of the Buddha. Each one is just a man and lives the life span of such. We believe that when the teachings of the Buddha are no longer remembered on earth, a new Buddha is born in the darkness and that each interval lasts for two thousand years. The teachings of this latest Buddha last five hundred years longer than expected. As I stare at this vast breach in the landscape, I think of the vows of the four great Bodhisattvas—Firm Practice, Pure Practice, Unlimited Practice, and Superior Practice:

However innumerable living beings are, I vow to save them all.
However innumerable hindrances are, I vow to overcome them all.

However innumerable the Buddha's teachings are, I vow to master them all.
However supreme the Buddha Way is, I vow to reach it.

I rub my eyes to clear my mind. We are standing in a place of wisdom, a place of unfathomable patience as practiced by the very earth itself.

Amazing, says Uncle. It reminds us of our place in the universe.

Yes, I say. We are nothing.

Uncle looks at me. Far from it, he says.

Saran doesn't seem to know how to enjoy a moment of leisure. She opens the back door of the Machine and begins repacking our supplies. It's okay, Mun calls. He waves her over to where he is standing. Just come see, he says. I watch as she stops, puts down a jar. She seems to be thinking it over. Finally she moves toward him. I remember the feel of a single strand of her hair in my mouth earlier in the day. I watch my brother pretend to push her over the edge, hear her delighted scream at being teased. I feel something darken inside me, a candle blowing out as a gust of wind rushes in through a window. The fact that I can feel such human pettiness in the face of absolute vastness is an indication of how much I still have to learn.

As we get back in the car, everywhere the shadows lengthening, Uncle spots an *ovoo* on the other side of the gorge. Because we cannot reach it to place a stone on top, Mun honks the horn three times as we head out on our way. It brings us luck. Each rock someone's inner light.

An Hour to Sundown

We stop to make camp. Tomorrow we should arrive at Khövsgöl Nuur and the summer settlement of the Reindeer People. Already we are in Khövsgöl *aimag,* Mongolia's northernmost province, a region famed for its beauty. After dinner, Saran piles the dishes in a plastic bucket and heads off toward the river. One of our water jugs is empty so I grab it and follow along. The spot where we choose to spend the night is idyllic. A lazy river winds its way through the landscape. The grass is filled with dung, the small black pellets that signify goats and sheep, and the large coiled droppings of yaks. A small herd of horses clusters on the far side of the river. The sun is still up though rapidly sinking.

I hold my free hand out at my side, dragging my palm through the tops of the grass, the long blades tickling my skin, the stems bowing down around me as if I am a boat cutting through water. Everywhere the loud mechanical stirring of insects in the grass, an impromptu symphony, the grasslands a metaphor for the mindlessness we attempt to achieve each day through meditation. In places, the grass is knee-high, its feathery tips gone to seed. With each step clouds of grasshoppers rise up in the air, my legs tickled by hundreds of tiny wings, the chirruping of insects like a sonic aura around me.

At the river's edge I dunk the jug. Instantly my knuckles start to ache. The water is cold. Siberia lies just on the other side of the Sayan Mountains. Despite the livestock, we drink freely of the rivers, usually boiling the water first but not always. The jug should be heavy when full, but we are not too far from camp and I should be able to manage it. Here by the river Saran and I have just enough distance for a conversation that can't be carried on the wind to other ears. Lightning flashes in my mind. This is another first for me.

Before this moment, I am never completely alone with a woman.

We Lower Ourselves into the Old Shafts

I remember places like this, says Saran. Once again there are wildflowers laced into her braid. I imagine what it would be like to pull them from her hair each night at day's end.

The water by the bank is shallow. Soon the jug is heavy enough that it doesn't float away. I let it go and take a plate from the bucket full of dishes, rub its face with my palm. Her statement puzzles me. Isn't all Mongolia like this, I say. I think of the places where Mun and I grow up in the shadow of Yatuu Gol, the beauty of the volcano something that is always there.

My family are herders, Saran says. I remember summers like this. Blue skies, endless herds, the rivers clear and cold. I'm four when the first *zud* hits, she says.

I nod. I also remember the *zud*. It is at the start of our first year in the monastery. We are eight years old. Our father moves the flocks south before it hits. The people who stay on the grasslands during the *zud* come to the gates looking for food. The Rinpoche gives what the monastery can, but when the *zud* drags on, turning the grasslands into a sheet of ice, there is no longer extra food to share. The older monks cut back, eating only one meal a day so that there might be something to give any supplicant that arrives at our gates.

There are two back-to-back *zud*, I say, one terrible winter following another.

Saran smiles but there is a sudden hardness in her usually dream-heavy eyes. She nods, tells me how in the first winter, two-thirds of their flocks die, while in the second, only a handful survives, though the next summer the grass is tall as her shoulders because there are no animals left to eat it. Without animals, she says, my family becomes ninja miners.

I take another plate from the tub. I am familiar with the term, which is used to describe people illegally scavenging in old Soviet mines that are abandoned after the USSR collapses, but I don't know where the phrase comes from. Why the word *ninja,* I ask.

She laughs, says the miners look like those cartoon characters—the Teenage Mutant Ninja Turtles, the way they carry green pans on their backs. We lower ourselves into the old shafts, she says, me, my siblings, my parents, my oldest brother staying on the surface to pull us back up. She tells me that clouds of coal dust can explode, how it gets in your lungs. We all have colds, she says, our noses constantly running a thick black sludge. Once a week a truck comes and we sell what we have. All over the landscape people crawling around under the earth. All of us trying to make enough money to buy new herds, to start over.

She tucks a loose strand of hair behind her ear. Three years later we have enough to buy new animals. Then when I'm twelve, she says, a convoy of trucks rumbles over the grasslands, and everything changes.

Who are they, I ask.

She sighs. The Chinese. She explains that after Mongolia becomes a democratic country, foreign companies begin to arrive, the old Russian mine where her family scavenges bigger than anyone knows. It also has copper, she says. The government claims it's the world's largest deposit of copper plus one of the largest deposits of coking coal, which you need to make steel.

Saran wipes her brow with the back of her hand. It's constant, she says. Trucks coming and going day and night. Construction expands the mine. The earth stripped open. There are no paved roads, so the trucks kick dust up in the air. It looks like darkest night even at noon. Our animals start to get sick. The babies don't thrive. The grass begins to die. Then our local well dries up. They say that in order to extract copper, the mine is using almost a thousand liters of water a second!

She places the last clean dish in the plastic tub. I remember this one time out with the animals, she says. We go to cross into one of our traditional pastures, but there's a barbed-wire fence where there is never a fence before. Several of the animals get caught in it. She nods to where the water jug is full and beginning to sink. I rush over and haul it up on land.

So we move to Ulaanbaatar. My oldest brother gets a job driving a cab, my mother sells clothes in the black market. She looks off toward the horizon. I can sense her slipping away, back to a world of clouds.

What's your family name, I ask.

Borjigin, she says.

I laugh. Yes, I say. Borjigin is my family name too.

Back when Mongolia is a communist country, surnames are unheard of. Then the Soviet Union collapses. We have no choice. We can go on being communists, a system that fails us at every turn, or we can change, open the door, and see where history might take us. With the coming of democracy, we are slowly brought into the modern age. For a while, everything is in chaos, though most of us don't know. Life on the grasslands goes on as it has for hundreds of years. On the steppes, the seasons continue, flocks fattening or not.

One day the government in Ulaanbaatar decides everyone needs a surname. It becomes a top priority. Previously, we never need to distinguish ourselves like that. It is enough to know your name and who your father is, your patronymic. I am Tsakhiagiin Chuluun, son of Tsakhia. There are three million of us scattered across the country. How would a last name change anything?

Still, we are excited by the prospect of reimagining ourselves, of becoming something new. People let their imaginations run wild. They consider various possibilities, like features of the landscape, dreams, horses. When it comes time to put name to paper, the most common surname adopted is Borjigin, the clan name of Chinggis

Khaan. According to *The Secret History of the Mongols,* the Borjigin lineage begins in the world's first dawn with Blue-Grey Wolf and his wife Fallow Doe. Today Borjigin is as common a name in Mongolia as I hear Smith is in English-speaking countries.

Nice to meet you, Borjigin Sarangerel, I say, *ta sain baina uu,* are you being well? Saran smiles. I feel my brother's presence somewhere in the growing dark, most likely smoking beside the Machine. What might he think to see me speaking so freely with a woman? Why do you speak Tibetan, I ask.

For the first time since we meet, I watch as she blushes. Something in her face tells me that she is one who holds the deepest of secrets within her, and that this secret is at the heart of her identity, that to be without it would efface everything she is. I don't pry. I know what it is to have a secret, the letter in my robe like an inner darkness waiting to find the light.

I just do, she says, the dreamy quality back in her eyes. She lifts the tub of dishes to her hip and turns to walk back to camp. The sun sets, the earth cooling. I struggle with the weight of the water jug but try not to let my effort show.

The One for Whom the Sky Never Darkens

Since the sixteenth century, it is said that the One for Whom the Sky Never Darkens always incarnates as a thoughtful prankster. Often he is born with thumbs that can be bent back at any angle, a trick he uses to fool others into thinking he is injured. His skin is said to take the sun at his will, darkening even when there is no sun in the sky if he so chooses. Unlike other holy men, what makes the One for Whom the Sky Never Darkens especially invaluable is that he is always birthed with all his memories intact, remembering the day when the first Ocean of Compassion is born in a cowshed in the snowcapped mountains of Tibet. It is said he can also recall his various lives in the animal kingdom—for example, the time his dark and juvenile feathers molt as he comes of age among the golden eagles, or the iciness of the water streaming past his gills during his existence as a trout.

If all goes well, tomorrow we should encounter the first candidate, a small boy living in the pine forests beside Khövsgöl Nuur. Details of the One for Whom the Sky Never Darkens must be kept secret lest some well-meaning grandmother inadvertently feed the signs to her grandson, telling the child of his life in Lhasa—the interminable hours spent at court, the sand mandalas constructed in the Potala's Great West Hall wide as the city's avenues, the sound of the beautiful sand being swept up and poured from a ceremonial urn into Lake Manasarovar.

And so, it is only now, as the five of us sit in the light of the fire, Saran carefully wrapping up the leftovers from dinner, that Uncle tells us these details of the one for whom we are searching, his voice tinged with the barest hint of wistfulness. Only Mun asks the obvious question, the one that plagues all our hearts, perhaps even Little

Bat's, though his stolid demeanor does not betray it, his baby face forbearing yet rosy.

Mun lights a cigarette. Already he is beginning to ration them. Today he wears a T-shirt with a red tongue sticking out of an overly large mouth. How you gonna know it's him, he says, gesturing to his own face as if to demonstrate what he means.

Saran hands Uncle an orange. He accepts it, head bowed, his left hand placed respectfully under the crook of his right elbow. He begins to peel it, the rind coming away in one long continuous strip. I'll know it's him, says Uncle with confidence. There is the usual gleam in Uncle's eyes when he talks of reuniting with his oldest friend in corporeal existence. He holds the peel in the air as if to demonstrate something about the nature of life. And he'll know me better than I know myself, he says, tossing the peel on the fire. For a moment, the air fills with the scent of orange. We'll know each other as we always know each other, he adds. In the way that true friends do. With our hearts. When Uncle smiles, I think of statues of the seated Buddha, His eyes heavy lidded with wisdom and nothingness. Anytime the smoke from Mun's cigarette drifts toward Uncle, Little Bat shoots a giant hand in the air to wave it away.

You Are Not Who You Believe Yourself to Be

Eventually the fire burns down and we prepare for bed. The others sleep in two separate tents. On occasion Little Bat drags his sleeping bag out in the open under the blanket of stars, his snores the night music of a big man with the yak's five-chambered heart. The first few nights of our journey Mun and I both sleep in the Machine, but mornings we rise more tired than when we lie down. The proximity to each other's mind at day's end is exhausting, the constant straining to discern which thoughts are mine, which his. Now Mun takes his sleeping bag and crawls under the car. In the morning he often smells of oil, but it is enough to keep our thoughts apart.

Tonight before Mun shuts the car door, he pauses. He is wearing a headlamp, what Uncle likes to call his third eye. All around us the world is dark and strange. Then something unexpected arises. I can feel my brother extinguish the fire in his mind. Tentatively, like a miner intuiting his way along a dark vein deep in the earth, I feel my way into my brother's thoughts.

We shouldn't be doing this, he thinks. We shouldn't be out here looking for some poor kid to pile all our problems on. For a moment I rummage around in his inner life. Among his doubts I feel something I do not expect. A glimmer of guilt.

Have courage, brother, I whisper out loud.

Forget it, he barks, shaking his head, and slams the door shut, angry at himself for allowing this moment of intimacy between us.

He's right, of course. I can never know the anguish of being told you are not who you believe yourself to be. To be handed a photograph of an old man and told this is you in your last incarnation. That everything about who you are is already established. That you are not original.

The sound of the car door slamming shut hangs in the air. I want to lift the icy sheet in the back of my mind and let all my doubts come rushing forth. To speak of my anguish with my twin who knows better than anyone what is lost when one renounces the body. I want to find out I am not alone in my loneliness, in my hunger to know the passions of the flesh. But the moment is gone. I do not know if it might ever come again.

Follow the Trail of Notes

Something is licking my face. The feeling soft and warm, amniotic, as if I am riding on a wave of good feeling that never crests. Though I do not want to, I open my eyes. Starlight, moonlight, blood-light, love. I am the sole being in the cosmos. The sound of my heart's drumming the only sound in existence.

In the sand, tiny hoofprints lead out into the indigo night, each print lined with silver. There is nothing else to do. I follow the prints through a world of tall grasses, rocky escarpments, trees festooned with prayer flags, small bottles of vodka strung on twine and draped in the boughs, the clear glass tinkling.

Someone is singing. Two notes simultaneously reverberating as is the ancient way that comes down to us from a time when people learn to sing two notes at once—one to tell the story and the other to flesh it out. I stand and listen. One like ice moving down a mountain, the other like a dragonfly alighting on a blossom. Then I realize the one singing is me, the sky filled with stars big as seashells, the night a reef alive with colors.

The hoofprints stop at the edge of a river. I kneel and wash my face and feet, the back of my head, my mouth and heart, the parts of me that err the most. All the while I hear it. What I am brought here to hear. Slow and rhythmic, building. The sound of the *morin khuur,* the horsehead fiddle, the most traditional of Mongolian instruments, the *morin khuur* with only two strings, a horse's head carved just above the pegbox, its sounds low and mournful, nocturnal, and in among the *morin khuur*'s music I hear a second music, one I somehow recognize as something new to the world. I follow the trail of notes as they hang in the air, each one primitive but stirring, my blood beginning to course faster through the rivers of my body.

I come to a tree. Moonlight slipping through its branches. Two figures lie in shadow. I walk right up to their coupling. The way a wild animal sometimes presents no fear and walks straight toward you to lick your palm. Both of them naked. The woman on top, her breasts swaying gently from side to side like ripeness itself, the man with his thumbs stroking the dark stars of her nipples.

This is what I can never have. I do not look away. I stand there all night and every night, watching these two dance each other toward ecstasy, the woman's face contorted with pleasure, a song the universe buries deep inside every one of us—man, woman, animal, and plant.

I am on the path to pledging my life to the enlightenment of every sentient being. And when I do, I must renounce the possibility of the sweetness of such music. Renounce the dark storms we carry inside us that break open from time to time. Renounce the hand-painted *thangka* depicting the gods with their female consorts straddling their manhoods, the union of wisdom and compassion.

Under this tree in this garden, woman and man rock each other toward a point of whitest light. They are two animals. They are pure. I can see from the looks on their faces that there is not a thought in their minds. They are attaining what I seek to attain with every breath. Sheer being.

May I never wake up!

The Tsaatan

From a ridge high up in the hills, Khövsgöl Nuur shimmers on the horizon like a blue mirror. Between the lake and the sky it's hard to tell where one ends and the other begins. Because he is a tour guide, Mun can't help himself as he launches into an explanation of the important facts about the area. Admittedly it is nice to learn about the landscape, to hear that at more than a hundred kilometers long, Khövsgöl Nuur is the largest freshwater lake in Mongolia and supplies most of the country's drinking water—travelers can even drink from it directly without boiling it first. Mun says on the other side of the mountains is the Republic of Tuva, part of the Russian Federation. Before World War II, people come and go across the border easily, but after the war, many of the Tsaatan, also known as the Reindeer People, settle in Mongolia because they don't want to lose their livestock to collectivization.

Khövsgöl *aimag* is different from Khentii where Yatuu Gol is located and Chinggis Khaan is born. Khövsgöl contains clear mountain lakes surrounded by the endless rolling taiga, the hills lush and green though the landscape is slowly changing as tourists come to spend time by the lake. As we drive farther up into the boreal forest, down below we can see tiny *ger* dotting the shore, camps created for tourists who come to ride horses or visit the Tsaatan, some of whom still speak Tuvan.

Consequently, we know exactly where we are going. Nestled among the lakeside camps is a Tsaatan family who comes down out of the forests during the tourist season with their animals to make money by charging tourists five thousand *tögrög* for the opportunity to take a picture. We stop and ask a teenaged boy dressed in traditional Tsaatan regalia where we might find the summer settlement of his clan. The boy explains that we must drive another hour up into the hills. He tells Mun what signs to look for in the landscape. A large reindeer lies at his feet, a handful of other reindeer scattered around on the ground in the shade. Some people believe that the Tsaatan should not summer by Khövsgöl Nuur with their reindeer, that the warmer temperatures here at the lower elevation are not healthy for the animals, and that there are too many tourists coming to this once-pristine place in order to see the Tsaatan, one of the last traditional cultures in the world.

By the lakeshore the bleached skull of a horse sits atop a pole. The thing is strangely compelling. The way its empty eye sockets seem to follow you wherever you go. Mun offers the boy a few bills, but he declines. We pull away, but the skull's eyes stay on us.

Look to the World for Signs

As we drive up into the hills, Uncle shares with us how the three candidates we are tasked with interviewing are discovered. The One for Whom the Sky Never Darkens dies almost eight years ago. As he lies on his deathbed in Dharamshala, the monks in all the Buddhist realms begin to look to the world for signs of where he might return. Anytime a *tulku* is dying, a monk is assigned to sit by Yamdrok Lake in Tibet, the lake said to be sacred and a place where visions often appear in its clear waters, the Himalayas visible in the distance.

Sometimes when a reincarnation lies dying, he takes up a quill before he breathes his last breath and draws something of significance. It can be anything. One dying lama draws a V, which his fellow monks interpret as a bird. Sometimes the soon-to-be-departed writes a word or a number, sometimes an entire letter telling his friends where to find him and telling his reincarnated self who he is.

Often those close to the dying lama begin to have significant dreams. They see themselves in strange landscapes where they move over the earth as an animal or as an element—water, fire, air, the ground itself. Sometimes after the *tulku* is cremated, clues are discovered among the ashes—pearls are most common. Following the ceremony, a general council is called and the evidence collected. Then one monk is charged with finding the reincarnation. This process can often take several years. Nothing is rushed. Most *tulku* are discovered between the ages of three to six. Mun is an unusual case. He is eight when someone arrives at our *ger* and changes our lives.

In the case of the one we are searching for, it is Little Bat who has the most dreams. Little Bat is not a *tulku,* but as a child, the One for Whom the Sky Never Darkens is his guardian, so it is only right that

Little Bat should be consulted along with Uncle, who many years ago as a young monk is the One for Whom the Sky Never Darkens's heart's disciple.

Mongolia is a land of contrasts. The jagged mountains in the west, the endless desert in the south, the grasslands and steppe centered in the middle, the taiga and the snow forests in the north. It is unusual that there is no specific clue to help pinpoint a more exact location of the child for whom we search. Just last night Little Bat dreams of a figure wrapped in the cloak of the eternal blue. This could literally be anywhere. A figure with a heart so big it could manifest wherever it pleases.

The Reindeer Is King

This is my first time so far north. The differences are evident, the flies thick and fat as berries, the earth almost spongy, the taiga often swampy in summer. As we are more than two thousand meters above sea level, the air is cool. In the rest of Mongolia, sheep and horses are the primary livestock; throughout the countryside there are four horses for every person, the grasslands littered with both their droppings and their bones. Here on the high steppe, the reindeer is king. Some are staked; some lie on their knees. Fur hangs in tatters from their summer antlers where they rub their horns against trees. In the winter, they grow new velvet as well as thicker coats for warmth in the harsh sub-Siberian cold.

Mun tells us that the Reindeer People are the smallest minority in Mongolia. He says some claim they are the descendants of the same people who cross the land bridge into North America thousands of years ago and give rise to the native peoples of those faraway continents. Much of their culture is similar. The shamanistic traditions. The ways they live off the land, taking only what they need. The houses made of animal skins stretched over wooden frames which the Reindeer People call *ortz* and which look like teepees. Their coloring, their cheekbones, their eyes, their beliefs. The way they weave feathers into their clothing. Their use of drums. Of fire.

It seems odd to me that a *tulku* would reincarnate among these people of a different faith, but nowadays, with Tibet under occupation, young reincarnations are found as far away as a city called Denver in America.

People are already standing outside as we roll down a ridge toward the settlement. The whole clan crowds in front of a large *ortz*. Mun whispers that there are less than forty families still living here in the traditional Tsaatan way. Many of the young people move to Ulaanbaatar, he says. I open my door and take a deep breath.

We've been waiting, says an elderly woman who remains seated on the ground. Her head is wrapped with a sky-blue headband, a spray of dark feathers sprouting from it, her fingers bejeweled with bright stones, colorful ropes hanging from her clothing. In her lap sits a small boy.

Mun tries to maintain our secrecy. We're a little lost, he says, stepping forward. Several people laugh. The region is remote. There is no way one would accidentally end up here.

Uncle steps in front of Mun. He speaks in a language I'm unfamiliar with. The sound of it like snow blowing in the trees.

The old woman nods her head and responds in the same language. Uncle bows deeply. You may take the waters, the woman says in Mongolian. The child, who we learn is named Belek, gets up out of her lap. He takes Uncle's hand and pulls him along.

Even After the Creature Bites Him

None of this is what I expect. I expect subtle encounters, a long evening of food and drink and storytelling, then Uncle pulling the child aside to ask a few questions, that we would never make directly known why we are here.

Instead, it seems Belek is waiting for us. There is a slowness, a deliberative quality, to the way he negotiates the world. The child moves as if he is already old.

How come they're expecting us, says Mun.

Uncle calls over his shoulder. They have their own traditions, he says. At his words, I imagine a shaman climbing a ladder of fire up into the night.

All of us but Saran follow Uncle and Belek down a narrow path through a stand of birch trees to an *ortz* pitched over a spring. Belek shakes his head when Mun tries to enter. Mun shrugs and slips his earbuds in, heads back to the Machine. Inside Belek changes into a pair of shorts. I follow Little Bat's lead as he removes his robes. Only Uncle remains clothed. There is a fire burning in a small brazier in the corner. Wooden planks are laid down so that the *ortz* is directly over the water.

I am too busy staring at Little Bat to notice much else, the sturdy brown walking shoes he always wears abandoned outside the teepee, his shoulders and back rife with young bruises. I cannot take my eyes off him. Not because his body is a map of injuries, the bruises like continents. No. It takes me some time to understand why I am staring, what is wrong with this picture. Then it hits me. Each of his feet is a simple oval, a lily pad. He has no toes.

Little Bat is the first in. When he slides off the plank, I am surprised that the water is up to his chest. Belek smiles. It's deeper than it looks, he says. He turns to the brazier and grabs a ladle, scoops a spoonful of water onto the rocks, sending up clouds of hissing steam.

Very good, says Uncle. All the best things are deeper than they look.

Belek considers this. A fly lands on his shoulder. I watch it scuttle about. It's triangular in shape, a biting fly, the kind that can draw blood and make a welt instantly appear. But the child doesn't shoo it away. Even after the creature bites him, leaving an angry mark. Instead, he catches it in the palm of his hand. Slowly and with great gentleness, he transfers the biting insect to his other shoulder, offering his flesh a second time. My own skin starts to itch. I fight the urge to reach over and flick the creature off. Instead I watch as the thing bites him again before flying away.

Do you recognize me, asks Uncle.

The little boy looks him up and down but says nothing.

Because I do not have the discipline of this child, I lower myself into the water as other flies begin to invade the tent. I am shocked by how cold the water is, but we are on the border with Siberia. The waters must be from the snowmelt only a few hundred kilometers away.

Little Bat rises out of the spring and begins to dress. I also get out of the water. We leave the boy and Uncle alone in the tent. They spend another hour inside. Hundreds of years between them.

Milk Is Like People

Life here feels familiar. Though we are on the border with Siberia, the landscape reminds me of the coniferous forests of Khentii. Both these woods and the ones in Khentii vie for the title of the oldest forests in Mongolia. Here, the Russian taiga stretches to the northwest. On some of the peaks I can see a glittering, what I can only assume is snow. The way the hills gently rise and dip in every direction, and the way broad swatches of land exist between the hilly forests is typical of both the taiga and Khentii. Tonight I should sleep well.

The Reindeer People spend their summers here at this higher elevation, letting their herds fatten for the long winter to come. More and more, their numbers are depleting as their young people head off to Ulaanbaatar. The natural beauty of the landscape is not enough to hold them.

I watch as a woman with a baby strapped to her back milks a reindeer. The animal stands eating grass as the woman deftly works her hands underneath the mare's belly. The rhythmic sound of the milk hitting the side of the pail is comforting. The woman sees me watching. When she's done, she motions me over and holds out the half-filled pail. There are no reindeer in Khentii. There are no camels there either, though I once taste the milk of such an animal, the taste like sand and unbearable heat. I lift the pail to my lips and take a deep swallow. It is richer than mare's milk. The taste somehow meatier. Somewhere in existence I know Övöö still likes to say that milk is like people—more similar than different.

Around the camp people ride their animals without saddles. I see a few wooden seats lying outside of various *ortz,* which the people must use for longer journeys. To them the reindeer is a sacred animal. Mornings they lead their animals up into the hills where they eat lichen and mushrooms; nights they bring them back down into the settlements and stake them to keep them safe.

A man is cutting the antlers of his animal. I imagine he uses the horn the same way the herders of the grasslands use the bones of horses to carve things like ceremonial knives or tiny flutes. The animal lies patiently on the ground, its front knees bent, its eyelashes long as a child's smallest finger. Everywhere flies mass like storm clouds. I brush them off my shoulders but am careful not to injure their delicate bodies.

Uncle and the candidate stay in the tent over the deep water until dinner. I wonder if it is a reunion of old friends. Perhaps our journey is over, I think. Mun looks at me and laughs. Get real, he says.

Why not, I say. The child is an ancient light. He could be the one to become the face of our religion.

I'm an old light too, Mun says. The world is full of old lights. He slaps a fly on his arm, then with his fingers he flicks its bloody body off his skin.

The First Man Comes From Fire

It is still light out when the fire is lit. Just before we sit down for dinner I watch a group of men pile wood up as if erecting an *ortz*. They pile so much wood, I wonder if, when lit, the fire might engulf us.

And it almost does. Up close it is as if the whole world is on fire. The people sit and gaze reverently at it, the sound of the flames so loud one cannot converse with one's neighbor without shouting.

Dinner consists of meat and soup. I watch as Little Bat intones a mantra before he eats, his lips moving but no sound coming out. Reindeer milk is also served, much of it fermented. Uncle accepts half a cup but pours it on the ground in an act of offering. Several times Mun holds his cup up for more. He does the same now as a bottle of vodka is passed around.

Fire and reindeer. The Tsaatan people believe that the first man comes from fire, that he jumps out of the flames when the world is still burning just after its birth. I sit next to Saran and watch the flames lick the sky. I am one of the mesmerized. I feel myself falling into a deep state of peacefulness. Quickly the heat becomes unbearable and I need to move away though I also feel the urge to remain where I am. Most of the Tsaatan stay seated as close to the fire as possible, just far enough away to avoid being kissed by an aberrant spark.

Through the flames I hear a heavy drumming. A man steps out from behind the fire holding a hide stretched over a round frame. The man hits the drum with his bare hand. Over and over, the sound of it like the beating of a heart. The man stands in front of the fire. His headdress of dark feathers resplendent as any crown, his body robed in blue, scarves and woven ropes, ribbons trailing his form, another secondary face painted on a headband wrapped around his forehead. He moves with such agility I wonder what animal possesses him. Lightly he jumps over the edge of the flames. Though the middle is too high to crest, somehow he weaves himself in and out of the fire. I can only see his silhouette, a black figure surrounded by light. The man's face is obscured by a fringe of ropes studded with beads that make a curtain in front of his face that swings back and forth as he dances. At one point, it appears as if he actually steps into the flames. I gasp. When he steps back out, smoke spires from his headdress. Two men approach and beat at the feathers with their bare fists as the man begins to convulse, his movements not in time with any rhythm on earth.

The child sits in his mother's lap on the edge of the flames. He closes his eyes. The shadows dance on his cheeks. I wonder if there are questions each person poses to the flames or if this is a demonstration of the power of their faith. The shaman stands up, lurches over the earth, the flames infinite, brushing the stars. When he removes his headdress, I see my mistake. It is the old woman who greets us earlier this afternoon. Her body smoking in the night.

I Could Walk It With My Eyes Closed

Sweat is dripping down my back. I look at Saran and see a bead run down the bridge of her nose. Mun sits fanning himself with the bottom of his shirt. A small dark stain is spreading on Uncle's chest. We are all subject to the elements.

Belek rises from his mother's lap. In the firelight, the child's eyes gleam. When he stands, a few people start to rise, but his mother makes a gesture with her hand and they sit back down. The child approaches Uncle. Yes, let's walk, Uncle says. Belek leaves the clearing and turns down a path past the night pasture where the reindeer stand hobbled to the ground. Saran and Mun stay by the fire. Little Bat and I follow Uncle and the boy.

Quickly I feel myself growing chilled. Away from the fire the summer air this far north loses heat within minutes of the setting sun. The light from the massive bonfire misleads me as to what time it is, the sun down for several hours. It is well after midnight.

We walk up into the hills. Soon the forest swallows us. A small dog joins our pack, its body misshapen and lumpy. Moonlight falls through the trees, the earth illuminated in patches. The path is well trod and smooth. There is no reason to be careful. I could walk it with my eyes closed.

I follow behind Little Bat. I wonder if this scene feels familiar to him. He is the one who dreams of the One for Whom the Sky Never Darkens. It is Little Bat who sees multiple visions in the polluted waters of Tso Pema in Dharamshala. I wonder if this night reminds him of anything, of a place he visits before, a spot where he feels safe for no reason he can fathom.

Then the trees stop and we are in a clearing. A few gray boulders rise up in an irregular circle. It is clear that they are not placed here by any human hand. Belek walks inside the rocks and sits on the ground. The child's face is serious, somehow both ancient and youthful.

Little Bat hands Uncle a small sack. Uncle lays down a white scarf and draws out several items. A singing bowl. A hand mirror. What must be the tiniest conch shell in existence. The child picks up the shell. My eyes are also drawn to it. It is perfectly formed but no bigger than the tip of a thumb, a mini-universe one can hold in the palm of the hand.

You want to know which of these things is my dearest possession, says Belek.

You can tell me anything you like, says Uncle.

Do you know a long time ago Mongolia is an ocean?

Really, says Uncle.

Belek nods. That's why Mongolian women cover themselves in coral. He runs a finger over the tiny conch. This shell forms during the life of the third Buddha, he says. Do you know who the third Buddha's disciples are?

I don't, says Uncle.

His is the Inanimate Buddhahood, says the child. He explains to Uncle how the Inanimate Buddha takes counsel with the wind and the rain, the stone and the stars. Now it is thousands of years later, Belek says, and each of His disciples still do only what they are meant to do. The child holds the shell up in the moonlight as proof.

In the Night of the Weeping Mare

No Matter How Much Butter I Lace in His Tea

Listen without distraction:

Each night that endless fall out on the grasslands of my childhood, I hear him tossing and turning, talking to someone in a loud voice as if that person is in the next room. I am eight years old.

Mun and our father sleep in the *ger* we use for animals. Our best mare is pregnant with twins though a local animal healer intuits that something further may complicate the event. Because of the difficulty of the impending birth, my father or Mun stays close to the mare at all times.

And so each night I sleep alone in the family *ger* with Övöö who cannot sleep. Övöö whose bones are beginning to stand out in his face. Just last month his beloved stallion breaks its leg when it steps in a marmot hole as Övöö is searching the grasslands for an errant lamb. There is nothing else to do. I watch the rifle shake as my grandfather takes aim. I believe he is shaking because he loves this horse above all others—it is the one he nurses by hand after its mother dies in labor. I do not think about the fact that the side of Övöö's head hits the ground when the horse falls, a fall which further injures my grandfather's already injured hip. Even before this accident, he walks with a slight limp, like a ship improperly ballasted. Now his right leg drags behind him, his tracks uneven in the grass, like something wolves would follow out on the steppe. Ever since the accident my grandfather spends the autumn days inside. Simply put, he is different, more inward. He is less like my brother, a spirit in need of open air. When I head out in the morning to drive the flocks to pasture, he is often sitting upright, a blanket pulled tight around his chest. I pour him another bowl of milk tea, dropping in a generous dollop of yak's butter to keep the bones from jutting farther out of his face. I can see them no matter how much butter I lace in his tea. Each day his cheekbones grow more pronounced like small scythes.

I tell no one that for the past several nights I hear my grandfather talking in his sleep, calling for *khüren,* the brown one, though there is nothing plaintive in his voice. He speaks as if beckoning someone who walks farther along a path to please slow down, wait. Around my twin I raise the icy white sheet in my mind. If Mun and my father find out that Övöö is calling for his dead horse, it would signal the obvious. That he is close to crossing over. I keep this news to myself because I don't want it to be true. Words have power. To speak something is to help ring it into being. Övöö is my world. In my eyes he can never die.

By the end of the week the mare has yet to give birth despite being in great distress. I am awakened by the sound of her whinnying, which seems to unspool forever, a brittle ribbon that cannot be cut. Mongolian horses don't cry like that. Even when they are in great pain, the horses of the eternal blue sky remain silent, only whinnying when spooked by the scent of a wolf on the wind.

I sit up in bed. My grandfather is standing under the hole in the roof of the *ger* where the stovepipe shoots up into the night. He pulls aside the small rug that is traditionally used to cover this opening, revealing the stars. Without turning to me, he asks if I'm packed.

Packed, I repeat.

He nods, still gazing at the sky. Someone is coming for you and your brother, he says. Slowly he closes the opening. Outside, the mare's cries continue, the sound not unlike a kind of music.

Every House Is a Hotel

The following afternoon I am the first to spot the dust from an unknown horse trampling over the grasslands. I feel my heart sink.

Why are you afraid, Mun asks. I wonder how much to tell my brother, but I don't raise the icy sheet in my mind fast enough and already he knows. Where does Övöö say we're going? he asks.

I don't know, I say. On the wind I hear scraps of song. Our father is inside with the mare, trying to coax the babies out by playing the music of the horsehead fiddle, an ancient method for bringing on a birth in any animal including humans. Mun and I are guarding the flock. We sit astride our horses and watch the cloud of dust draw nearer, hoping that this path might turn away from us.

Instead the path presents itself as one man on a horse. Because it is autumn, he wears a long *deel* and the traditional boot with the curled toe. As he approaches, he raises his hand and calls to us. How are your herds faring?

The goat meat is good when hot, Mun replies. I wince as he essentially tells this stranger to get to the point.

The man remains unperturbed by Mun's rudeness. And your horses? Are they yet to foal, the man asks. It is a strange question, not something a stranger normally broaches on first meeting.

I feel the suspicion grow in my brother. This year many of our mares are dropping strong foals, he says.

And are they done giving birth, the man repeats.

More or less, says my brother. At the word *less* the man nods, evidently contented by this.

Because ours is a culture of nomads, every house is a hotel. At any hour of the night a Mongolian may knock on your door and be allowed to claim a blanket and a bit of floor space, a bowl of whatever is cooking on the fire. Such hospitality can be traced back to the days of Chinggis Khaan. In that world, denying a man food and shelter is an offense punishable by death. Though I am only a child, to me, it is one of the best features of our country, a tradition born of the vastness of the grasslands. Often when a stranger knocks on the door, it is not unusual for the men to break open a bottle of spirits, to build a fire and sit around the flames for an evening of song as the bottle is passed from person to person. In a culture not centered around televisions, this is how we spend our nights on the grasslands. The few times strangers knock at our door seeking hospitality are always moments of great delight. But today, after what my grandfather tells me the night before, this stranger's arrival feels foreboding.

Though there is still plenty of time in the day for this man to put more kilometers behind him, he asks our father for shelter.

Aav is distracted. The four of us are standing in the *ger* we use for animals. The mare leans heavily against the wall. I can feel the tremendous heat emanating from her body. The smell in the room is strong. It stays on my clothes even after I leave. Father picks up his bow and places it on the strings. His own father lies in between two worlds, and the belly of his prized horse is unnaturally distended. As Övöö says: if anything is to be done, then do it and do it well. Wearily my father positions his fingers.

Perhaps I can be of some help, the man offers. When the only hope is a boat and there is no boat, I will be the boat, he says. Something beeps. The sound like two fingers gently tapping on your shoulder. The man smiles and presses a button on what looks like a brand-new digital watch. And so the world changes. My father begins to play. The music soft and sad, ice melting in the light of the chrysanthemum moon.

Buildings Torched, Relics Smashed

The guest says his name is Bazar. He is not a young man though there is a spryness about him. If I had to guess, I would say he is around the same age as my grandfather, perhaps a few years younger. He wears the clothes of a traditional herder. His horse is nondescript. From the looks of his animal, both man and horse have yet to travel far; perhaps they begin their journey in the nearby town of Bor-Urt. As it is not the Mongolian way to pry, we don't ask him where he comes from, though his final destination is fair game. Bazar says he is traveling over the grasslands to see an old friend who lives within sight of the volcano.

In our family I am the one who cooks. While my father tends to the mare and Mun works outside rounding up the animals for the afternoon milking, Bazar stays inside with me and Övöö, who lies sleeping. I can hear the air rattling in his throat. The stranger sits beside my grandfather, watching intently. He remains still, so still I wonder if he is meditating.

The year Mun and I are born, Mongolia becomes an independent and democratic nation. Since 1924, Mongolia is a socialist country like our neighbor Russia. Our premier at the time, Khorloogiin Choibalsan, styles himself after Stalin. Under his leadership, the monasteries are systematically destroyed. Buildings torched, relics smashed, nuns violated, the loose pages of prayer books shredded and tossed to the wind. I know these stories of the purges from Övöö. How one group of monks takes refuge in a cave. When the soldiers find them, they build a fire at the mouth of the cave and kill every one of them. Still, through the dark years, believers like my grandfather hold on to the faith in secret. Today Buddhism is on an uptick. There are rumors that a monastery is to be reestablished in the shadow of the volcano Yatuugiin Gol. This rumor is one of the reasons why we summer here instead of moving farther east to less inhabited grasslands. Övöö says that for once in his life he wants to live somewhere where there may soon be holy men. I am eight years old. I have yet to ever see a monk.

Bazar pulls a snuff bottle out of the folds of his *deel.* In Mongolia it is customary for old friends to offer each other snuff by way of greeting. Some bottles are quite elaborate, costing upward of half a million *tögrög,* but Bazar's appears to be a simple container made of plastic. He extends his right arm while touching under his elbow with his left hand in the ceremonial position one assumes when offering such things to another. Gently he waves the bottle under Övöö's nose. For a moment, the snuff works; my grandfather opens his eyes.

How are your herds fattening, my friend, Bazar asks.

The summer is good to us, says Övöö. He turns his head and looks Bazar full in the face. Something passes between them. In this instance it is obvious my grandfather recognizes this stranger kneeling beside him. He grabs the stranger's arm and grips it tightly.

If you walk the path, you arrive at the way that removes all suffering, says Bazar.

My grandfather sinks back on his pillow. For the first time since he kills his horse, he looks content. He never again opens his eyes on the visible world.

Generally the *Zud* Appears Once in a Generation

My entire life is shaped in the time it takes the moon to cross the night.

Bazar helps me make dinner. Surprisingly he demonstrates great skill in rolling out *buuz,* each dumpling stuffed with the meat of an old ewe who most likely wouldn't make it through the winter. My father's thoughts are elsewhere. Though today is the last week of September, already he is thinking about where we should spend the winter, if we should move to pastures farther south, or if we should head east toward the small city of Bor-Urt where we might spend our first winter off the grasslands. The *zud* can be fierce, the killing winds that come down out of Siberia, and can wipe out entire flocks within weeks. Generally the *zud* appears once in a generation, but as the climate changes, it is becoming more frequent, the Gobi starting to encroach northward as the grasslands die off. My father and his friends use the technical word for such change—*desertification.*

In winters past, Övöö is always against moving into Bor-Urt. He says he would rather die than be cooped up in a city with its smells and lack of space, like an animal in a pen. I know what it is to be contained, he says. Remember? My father hangs his head. The conversation always ends with Övöö proclaiming: if you go, leave me here, before saddling up and riding out to the herds.

During dinner, Bazar sits in the western position in the *ger,* the space meant for honored visitors. The rest of us take our places, though Övöö remains sleeping. If you'd like me to sit with him, I can, Bazar says. None of us ask what he means by this. It is plain to see—the quiet way he moves, his aura of calmness—that he is not a simple herder.

Please comfort him in any way you can, says my father.

Bazar nods. He crawls to where Övöö lies on the floor, tucked in among a pile of furs. Old friend, says Bazar. See your way through the *bardo*. Remember your essence.

Even after I clear the dishes and carry them outside to wash, the stranger stays by my grandfather's side. Even as the moon climbs in the sky, even as my father and Mun prepare to bed in the other *ger*. Even after I hear Mun's cries as the mare's time finally comes, kicking her legs and just barely missing my father's face, the two of them trying to calm her as the dark head appears under her tail. How my father catches her first baby as it falls out in a glistening sack, the creature a midnight blue. And minutes later as Bazar is kneeling beside my grandfather, another hoof appears, the second animal's legs splayed, lost somewhere in the darkness of the mother, our father sliding his hand up into the blood-heat and trying to steer the breached creature out, the mare eventually collapsing, the choice presenting itself of whether or not to slit the belly and save the foal or to cut the baby out piece by piece.

Within his nest of blankets, Övöö opens his eyes. There is something different in his look. Perhaps his sight is filling with what Bazar tells me is the clear light of mind. The indestructible drop at the center of his heart chakra splitting into the red drop of his father and the white drop from his mother, releasing his very subtle consciousness back into the universe. Bazar begins chanting in a language I do not know, by the sound of it the music older than the earth. I hold my grandfather's hand, rub his shoulder. He sits up and looks beyond the world.

The Spirit Is Fully Dissipated

Bazar stays for three days. He spends most of that time sitting in the lotus position beside the body of my grandfather. Occasionally he burns incense, chants, daubs the skin with yak's milk. Though Övöö is no longer breathing, Bazar says his death is not yet complete, that my grandfather is questing through the *bardo,* the intermediate state, and that we must not disturb him on this most important journey. At sundown on the third day, there is a flash of lightning in the sky but no thunder. Bazar places a finger between Övöö's eyes and holds it there. The spirit is fully dissipated, he finally says. I peer at my grandfather to see if I can notice a difference. Maybe the skin around his eyes looks looser, more relaxed. Maybe he appears less gray, less waxen, more like he is sleeping after returning from a long journey.

My father nods. There's a place about an hour's ride from here where no one ventures, Aav says.

Bazar looks off into the fire. Perhaps a full minute passes before he responds. You are aware of your father's final wish to be free, he says.

Now it is Aav's turn to fall silent. Our father simply peers at the same spot among the flames. Finally he sighs. Because of the hardship in his life, I know how my father wishes to leave the earth, he says.

And you consent to this, Bazar asks.

Aav bows his head. Do you know how it's done, he whispers. Bazar nods. A spark snaps in the fire.

That night Mun and I lie on our *leitur* wondering what is to come. We both know of a ceremony called *khödöölüüleh* in which the body is wrapped in felt, then transported by oxcart to a remote place and left in nature. Sometimes those accompanying the body howl to attract wolves, thus speeding the process along. Most times the body is simply buried. Whatever is to come, may our grandfather's journey back to this earth go smoothly.

Our father is sleeping out in the *ger* with the mare and her new foal, which for the time being needs to be fed milk by hand until the mare recovers. Ideally the foal should be born some icy spring morning, when the days are growing longer and the earth greening. Instead it arrives on the cusp of winter. If the *zud* blows down out of Siberia, the area herders could lose everything. We would be no exception.

The foal glistens redly in the light, his coat still slicked with afterbirth, which the weakened mare has yet to lick off. Father chooses to save the mare over her second baby, though the mare's survival is still in doubt. There isn't much time. The mare must regain her strength quickly before we move for the season. If she dies, the remaining foal is like my brother and me. Motherless.

Through Mun's eyes I relive the moment of my father's choice. How Aav takes a small blade and carefully slides it inside the mare, keeping the cutting edge toward his hand. Then slowly, piece by piece, he begins to cut the unborn baby apart, removing it from the mare's body before passing each part to Mun. It is the only thing to do. The foal is breached. There is no place on earth beyond the reach of death. Not in a mountain cave, in the ocean or sky. Mun taking the pieces and laying them on the floor, a bloody jigsaw puzzle, reassembling the animal instead of just tossing the pieces in a pile. When our father sees this, he shakes his head but remains silent, his arms and torso soaked in blood.

His Energy Giving Strength to Others

After declaring our grandfather released, Bazar now sleeps out in the third *ger* that we use for storage. Mun and I are left alone to sleep with the body. This is the first night Bazar does not sit with the corpse and burn candles and small herbs in a bowl, intoning words we cannot understand. Now that the consciousness is gone from the flesh, there is no need for such acts. Bazar asks our father for a felt blanket, and uses it to wrap Övöö up tight.

I cannot sleep. My mind is full of images of my grandfather. The idea that he is now nothing more than a pile of meat is discomfiting. There is no pain like the burden of attachment. I get up and walk over to where he lies. I lay my head on his chest. It is hard as stone. Eventually I fall asleep.

In the morning, Father and Bazar heft the body up onto the back of a horse. Our father eyes us as we mount our own horses, but Bazar nods and we are allowed to come.

I think of all the things our grandfather teaches us, about the cycles of nature and the way the spirit navigates the world, but most of all about Chinggis Khaan and the world the great Khaan inhabits, the world he creates in his own image.

After an hour on the grasslands, we ride down into a shallow valley. The grass here is short, stunted, not the tall lush grasses that grow closer to sources of water. The sky is gray, the wind icy. Aav and Bazar lay the body on the ground. Then Bazar pulls a plastic bag filled with raw meat left over from yesterday's dinner from his *deel*. He sprinkles the meat with herbs, and sets it directly on the ground beside the body of our grandfather. My father takes a seat behind him. We sit behind our father.

How long do we sit? Days? Weeks? Years? Minutes?

I see the first one circling on the thermals. The way it funnels down out of the sky, as if reeling us in. After it lands, I watch it study Bazar, the man and the bird as if silently communicating. Something in the way they face each other makes me think this is not their first meeting. Then Bazar speaks in the unknown language that sounds older than the world. The animal lumbers over to where the raw meat sits beside my grandfather. It scoops the meat up in its beak and throws back its head.

Bazar opens the strangely shaped fur bag he carries with him at all times. He pulls out a small hatchet and a hammer. The hatchet is silver and looks ancient, pieces of turquoise and coral embedded in the handle. He turns toward our father and presents it to him.

Aav takes a deep breath and accepts the hatchet. Somehow I know what is going to happen, but when it happens, I am still surprised. Perhaps this is the first time such a thing ever happens in the land of the eternal blue sky. Father approaches the body of his father and unwraps the blanket. Övöö lies stiff and gray and naked. Bazar points to a spot and motions for what needs to be done. Aav lifts Övöö's head. The blade winks in the sun as he works to remove the skin of Övöö's scalp. There is a ripping sound not dissimilar to when we flay the skin from a slaughtered sheep. Eventually it comes away in his hand. There is hardly any blood. Later, what blood there is is black and thick, unflowing.

It's done, he says.

He hands the hatchet to Bazar and sits back down. And so together we watch as this stranger proceeds to butcher the corpse of our grandfather, the skill evident in Bazar's cuts until our grandfather is just meat, his bones then pounded into a coarse powder that is sprinkled on the offering. Overhead the sky filling with vultures, the great ashy creatures massing, a vast storm. When he finishes preparing the body, Bazar begins to toss chunks of flesh up into the air at the feathered horde, the birds tornadoing in a frenzy.

I do not close my eyes. I watch the whole thing as does my brother.

Soon Övöö is gone. Later, Bazar tells us this is what Buddhists in Tibet call a sky burial. Though this act is not practiced in Mongolia, my twin and I are not shocked. We are accustomed to the many faces of nature, the cycles of birth and death. Rather there is only a fierce beauty as the dead are allowed swift passage back into the elements and the natural world from which we come. Years from now in Tibet, Chinese tourists begin to flock to watch such proceedings, to gawk at the sight of human flesh. But isn't human burial the more barbarous ritual? The act of preserving the flesh, dressing it up in its best clothes, embalming the organs, then burying the dead in the earth for hundreds, maybe thousands of years. Perhaps this way of leaving the world might catch on here in the land of the eternal blue sky. Maybe someday Mun might lift the knife and make the first ceremonial cut on our father's body. Maybe then it is my job to disassemble the corpse and feed it to the beasts of the air so that for a while at least our father may live on in them, his energy giving strength to others and then in turn these beings one day giving strength to countless others in a perfect circle that has no end.

Which of These Items Belongs to You?

Our father makes up his mind. We are to winter in the city. The government is predicting that a once-in-a-century *zud* is coming, the grasslands locked in ice. He tells us this the night Övöö is lifted into the sky, the flesh that is my grandfather set free to the four cardinal directions. At the news, my brother begins to cry, this child who does not shed a tear when the baby horse needs to be cut out of its mother's belly piece by bloody piece. My twin's tears are surprising as I am the one who takes after our gentle inward-facing grandfather, though it is true I do not feel Övöö's deep-seated love of the open grasslands like my brother does.

Bazar says he is leaving us in the morning. Out of respect, my father no longer looks him in the eye. After the skill he manifests as he dismembers Övöö, it is obvious who he is. With his knowledge of death and the *bardo,* he must be a monk, someone with a deep understanding of the old traditions, perhaps someone who spends time in Tibet. As my father is speaking, Bazar unties his strangely shaped bag for the second time and pulls out a series of small sacks. From one, he tips a set of anklebones on the floor. From another, he pulls out a silver pipe. From the last bag, he pulls out a small prayer book, the book wrapped in silk and no bigger than the palm of his hand.

Mun stops crying. Within my own chest I feel something dawning inside me.

These many decades there are so many unrecognized *tulku,* says Bazar. All this time there isn't anyone here to find them, he adds. I think of the way our grandfather would grow quiet anytime someone mentions the destruction of the monasteries by the communists. Centuries of tradition driven out into the killing snow. Our grandfather is born sometime in the decade after 1924, the year the Soviet Union helps bring the Mongolian People's Republic into being. How on the cusp of the great world war, the Stalinist marshal Choibalsan takes power and ushers in an era of purges, by the late 1930s killing upward of thirty-five thousand Mongolians and eradicating Buddhism from the nation. In the span of only a few years, more than five percent of the population is killed.

My brother and I are born almost seventy years later, in 1992, just as the country is putting communism to bed. Today everything is possible. Just one year before we are born, His Holiness the Dalai Lama announces the existence of His Eminence, the 9th Incarnation of the Jetsun Dampa, the spiritual leader of Tibetan Buddhism here in Mongolia. The Jetsun Dampa is born in 1932 but stays hidden, living secretly outside of Mongolia until the fall of the Soviet Union. Though almost seventy years of age, the Jetsun Dampa finally returns to our country in 1999, just as Buddhism is starting to flourish once again under the eternal blue sky.

Bazar smiles at us and beckons us closer. We approach the articles he lays out. My child, he says. Come find yourself. I realize he is not talking to me. The birthmark on the back of my twin's neck as if on fire.

Mun approaches the objects. There is an attentiveness in his eyes. I can feel every thought he is feeling, smell every smell. He picks up the anklebones and rattles them in his palm. He picks up the pipe and puts it between his lips as if he smokes a pipe every day of his life. He picks up the book and unties it. The writing on the parchment looks like the work of insects, delicate yet steely. Mun smiles and wraps the book back up.

Which of these items belongs to you, asks Bazar.

Mun looks at him. All of them, he says.

In the morning Bazar wraps his *deel* tight about his shoulders. Our father bows so deeply I think he may never stand back up. When a cloud obscures the sun, the light is diffused. The stranger touches his forehead to Mun's forehead and whispers something in his ear.

Later that night, I hear Bazar's words still rattling around in Mun's mind. It is written in the stars that I might find you in a house where one being is dying and another is being torn apart at birth.

Listen without distraction: we are eight years old the day we are found.

Our Eyes Have Vision to the Seventh Power

The Constant Arising of Uncertainty Is the Only Aspect of Life of Which We Can Be Certain

We are driving three days from Khövsgöl Nuur to the town of Olan Boyd in Bayan-Olgii *aimag* to meet the second candidate, a young eagle hunter. I am still unsure as to why the One for Whom the Sky Never Darkens would be reborn in a different faith. The hunters of the western Altai are mostly Kazakh, a people with more in common culturally with Kazakhstan just over the border and through Siberia than with Mongolia where most people are Buddhist. Though I am confused by this fact, I do not put my doubts into words.

My reservations do not stop my brother from voicing his own thoughts. He sits behind the wheel, eyes locked on the empty landscape. Even after meeting Belek and the night of fire, he remains conflicted. First the Reindeer People, now Muslims, he says. What gives?

Uncle smiles. If it is opaque to me, how can I explain it, he says, quoting Je Tsongkhapa, the fourteenth-century Buddhist saint. It is apparent that Uncle himself considers the same thing, but ultimately he is untroubled by not knowing. This is the very art of living in uncertainty. In some ways, the constant arising of uncertainty is the only aspect of life of which we can be certain. My twin, however, remains skeptical.

Our drive to the westernmost part of the country continues without incident. Mun credits our good luck to the old woman of the Reindeer People. How the morning of our departure, she circles the car three times sun-wise, her headdress of feathers casting colorful shadows on the windshield. With each circuit she turns and spits the ceremonial *aashkul* on the hood of the car, *aashkul* made from water or vodka in which one steeps an object of magic.

I watch the landscape roll past, time like sparks knocked off a piece of flint. We are leaving the places where the Siberian larch thrives, this tree that can grow for a thousand years. Soon the moon sits on the edge of the sky like the pit of some dark fruit. Then it is time to stop and rest. It is now one full week that we are on the road. Each day the mystery quickening as we search. Each night I find myself making camp as if in a dream. Tomorrow we should arrive in the mountains. Tonight I feel my eyes grow heavy, my milk tea long cold. Perhaps tonight I may find the words to finish my letter addressed to the Rinpoche back at Yatuu Gol. Maybe soon I am to know what the universe wants of me.

In the firelight Mun lies on his side, his head propped up on his elbow. The bruise on his face is gone, just a memory of what the body is capable of, a woundable thing. How come, he says, pointing at Little Bat's disfigured feet. This is how my twin operates. No segue, no run-up. He simply looks at Little Bat, this monk with his baby face, his ruined voice, his strength beyond anything quantifiable, of whom it is not too much to say that only the earth can stop him.

The big man starts to speak. His voice like blood-soaked sand. A star streaks across the sky. What I am always learning in my twenty-three years on earth: there is suffering. And sometimes at the end of it all a door opens. A hand appears on the surface of the water, reaches down to pull you up.

Go Inside the Door in the Mountain

This is what I know, rasps Little Bat. In the firelight his eyes gleam like precious stones. I am born in Amdo Province, he says. His Holiness is born in the same province in 1935. It is a land much like your Khentii, the birthplace of Chinggis Khaan. Hills and valleys, green everywhere. Do you know we are also the descendants of the Khaans? Many of the first settlers in Amdo are Mongols. Our lifestyles are similar—nomadic, summers in the mountains with our animals, the yak predominant, winters down in the valleys. But I have no memory of true nomadic life. All this is before. The Chinese invade Tibet in 1950. I myself am born in 1970. The Chinese force the nomads to settle, to become farmers. And so my grandfather builds a small house, the woodsmoke blackening the interior over time.

I don't know what is lost through the years. When my parents can afford the fees, we go to school. I am the fourth of five children. School is expensive. An uneducated population is easier to control. At the start of the day they raise and lower the Chinese flag. We are forced to learn Chinese. I go to school less and less. My brothers and sister, my neighbors, we go less and less. I don't know things should be different.

As kids, one of our favorite things to do is to climb a small nearby mountain up to the very top and play in an old cave where a holy man once lives. It is long abandoned. The cave has a wooden door wedged in the entrance, the thing rotten in places. A red bucket of dirt sits beside the door, a few weeds poking out of the soil. Inside the cave it is always dark, but as children we play there, pretending it is our house and that we are adults. Sometimes I pretend I am a holy man.

One night when I am seven years old, I see a light shining on the mountain. It's late fall. I get up to go to the bathroom in the place we use outside. The moon is up. I have no shoes on. I can see a glow coming from the mountainside as if a small fire is burning. There is nothing else to say. I go to it. It's like a dream. In a dream, there is never any question of whether or not you perform some act. You just do it. So I go. I am barefoot. The night air is cold but somehow I am not cold. When I get near the top, I see the wooden door. It looks new, the wood fresh and without rot. There are prayer flags flapping among the rocks. A small tree is growing in the red bucket by the entryway. One white blossom blooming in its branches.

The door is cracked open. There is a soft glow coming from inside. Light pours around the doorframe. I put my foot in the crack. I don't use my hands. I want it to seem as if the wind blows it open, like it is not an act performed by me. The door swings open and I wait for something to happen, for someone to yell at me to go away. There is only silence. I stick my head in. Then I go inside the door in the mountain.

Most times when I play there with my siblings, the cave is empty, but now there are a few chests, some blankets, cooking utensils, a bucket filled with water, the cave transformed as if all this time somebody is living there. And everywhere small candles burn solidly, their flames unwavering, even with the door open. They never seem to give off smoke. They never burn out.

I walk around and look at everything. I run my finger along a musical instrument which appears to be a human bone decorated with coral. In one corner there's a small altar, on it a silver bowl filled with fresh water. I dip my finger in. When I pull it out, my finger feels warm and tingly. I feel the warmth begin to travel up my arm. I know it is moving toward my heart. I'm not scared. I wait to let what may happen happen. When it reaches my heart, a contentment comes over me that never leaves even until this very day. I walk over to one of the chests and open a hidden drawer in the side of it. Somehow I know exactly where the drawer is and how to open it. Most people wouldn't notice there is a drawer. But I know.

Inside the drawer are a handful of drawings, sketches of landscapes, one of a very beautiful woman, her hair plaited like a horse's mane. And at the bottom of the drawer I find a second secret compartment. A kind of false bottom. I lift the cover and there it is.

I study the photograph a long time, says Little Bat. The image is faded and cracked, but it holds me. I look at it until it is burned in my heart, until I know every detail of it. If I put it back in the false bottom and close the drawer, my life would be different.

Little Bat stops talking. I look at Mun, but my twin is somewhere far away. I don't have any idea where this story is going. The fire hisses and pops. I feel my own toes begin to throb.

In the morning it seems like a dream, says Little Bat. As if the night before is an underwater world, a place where candles never waver and the moonlight hides you if you ask it to. Daylight I wake back in bed with my brothers. Our mother and sister already with the fire going, the three simple rooms we live in starting to warm. The only strange thing is that the bottoms of my feet are dirty, as if in the night I walk to the ends of the earth and back.

Over the next few days I hardly give that night any thought, though I know something is different. The warmth still echoing in my heart where the heat from the bowl of water touches it. I do all the things that are expected of me. I tease Pema, my baby sister, who is two years younger, chasing her around the yard as if I am a maddened yak. Only my mother notices a difference. She puts a hand on my forehead and asks if I feel all right. Yeah, I say. I walk outside and look up at the mountainside, scanning it for the faintest glow, but there is nothing. I know that if I walk to the cave that very instant it would be abandoned and empty as always. All the same I feel content. I touch my side where I am keeping the photo I find in the chest, tucked inside the waistband of my pants. It's still there.

One day there is a knock on the door. When I come home with my brothers and our animals from the high pastures, our father is gone, our mother inconsolable. A group of soldiers comes and searches our house before marching our father away. I am seven. I both understand and I don't understand. I know it is the Chinese. I know they hate us, are destroying us, that they disappear people, and now my father is gone.

Three days later he comes back. He looks the same on the surface, but there is something different underneath. That's how it starts. They don't tell us younger children anything so that we won't accidently tell someone and ruin it. One night a few hours after we go to bed my mother rouses us from sleep. She tells us what to do. I put on every article of clothing I own. I help my little sister do the same. Pema is five years old. It's hard to move. I feel hot and sweaty. Then a truck rolls up out front with its lights off. We take nothing with us. Absolutely nothing.

The truck drives us the many hours to Lhasa. We are my parents and my three older brothers and my little sister and me. We huddle among a herd of goats. After driving through the night we wake up in the city. There are so many buildings in one place! We walk down an alley and into the back of a restaurant. There is a man wearing a bandana so that we cannot see his face. He looks at my little sister and shakes his head. Lord Buddha, he says. Grant us safe passage. We stay in that restaurant all day, never venturing outside. I never see the Potala, the thousand-room palace of the Dalai Lama built on the side of Red Mountain.

The next day we take another truck up into the hills outside Lhasa. We walk for eleven days. Three days before we get to the pass, the landscape changes. We are at five thousand meters. The snow is up to my neck many times over. My sister and I are light. We can walk on top of it. My father and oldest brother and the guide kept falling in up to their waists. Then they have to struggle to get back out. The guide knows where we can stop to find food. There is food hidden along the way for travelers like us. We melt the snow for water. We also bring some *tsampa* with us, but it doesn't last. Most days we walk twelve, thirteen hours.

At first we walk only at night to avoid the Chinese patrols. Then we are high enough that there are no patrols. The pass we are headed to is located at sixty-seven hundred meters. Everest is eighty-eight hundred meters. My sister is carried by the guide. My father often carries me.

Somehow Little Bat's voice grows more scoured yet flat. It is like he is talking about something he hears, not something he lives through. Our party hits a crevasse, he says. All my brothers fall in it. The guide shines the light down into the endless hole. There is no sound. One minute they are there. The next they are gone. My mother sits down. She refuses to leave. I can hear her praying to the Green Tara, beseeching the Bodhisattva to intervene and keep us safe. The snow is rampaging around us. We have to press on, says the guide. The snow is coming down sideways. My mother won't get up. The air is thin. Taking a single step is like walking forever. My mother never stands back up. We keep going without her.

Little Bat stops talking. It is the most I ever hear him speak, his voice as if scorched. In the firelight it looks as if there is blood on his teeth. Uncle tells us the rest of the story, how Little Bat's father dies, then the guide, and then when there is no one left to carry them, how Little Bat tries to lead his sister down out of the mountains. Her hands big as apples, her fingers blackened and swollen until the skin splits. She never cries. She is beyond crying.

When Pema stops moving, Little Bat sits down in the snow and the darkness and digs out the photo tucked in his waistband, the one he finds on the mountainside in the secret drawer. He knows it is the reason the police come to his house and interrogate his father. He holds the image in his hands all through the night, and somehow he stays just warm enough. A Sherpa finds him in the morning, clutching a photo of the Dalai Lama. One month later when he reaches the Tibetan Children's Village in Dharamshala, India, he receives the medical care he requires. All his toes are amputated. His voice permanently altered, his vocal cords frost-bitten. He is the only survivor of his family.

I feel a wave of anger crest in my brother, the fires of anger and its corollary, helplessness. In Tibet, it is illegal to possess images of the Dalai Lama, says Uncle. One can be jailed for invoking His name.

I try to imagine living under such conditions, but I cannot. This is the reason why too many of the faithful arrive at a place where they lose hope. Who can be expected to live in a world without the freedom to believe in that which sustains you? There are one hundred fifty-seven self-immolations by Tibetans since 1998, says Uncle. Does the world know this? Twenty-six of those who set themselves on fire are under the age of eighteen.

In These Spaces, Spirits Are Always Appreciated

When we arrive in Oyan Boyd, the landscape is different. Bayan-Olgii is the westernmost *aimag* in Mongolia, a region more than a thousand meters above sea level. Little Bat speaks of a vision of mountains sharp as knives, so we know we must continue out on beyond the town. We pass square utilitarian buildings constructed in the boxy Soviet style. We pass the town's one disco. In front of the police station, there's a pool table, the green felt faded in a familiar way. As it is the height of summer, much of Oyan Boyd's population is up in the hills preparing for the endless winter to come.

Saran mentions that we should get more vegetables, that we don't know what we'll find once we drive up into the mountains. Roger that, says Mun in English. My brother has a nose for money. He can sniff out a black market within minutes of arriving in any town. Plus he is low on cigarettes.

The black market is on the edge of Oyan Boyd and housed in a series of rusty shipping containers. We park and walk around. There are vendors selling everything from western T-shirts to dried yak patties. What makes it a black market is simply the unregulated exchange of currencies. Otherwise, there is nothing untoward about it. I realize that most of the vendors must also call their containers home. I wonder what it would be like to sleep in one with the steel door closed, each box barely two by three meters.

Saran heads off to find vegetables. Mun goes in search of what he calls the "essentials." Though the population here in the Altai Mountains is predominantly Muslim, they are close relatives of the Russians just across the western border. What the people of both countries have in common: spirits are always appreciated wherever you go.

After making some inquiries, Uncle finds a man who says he knows a family where the young are learning the art of their grandfathers. He agrees to take us. I wonder if this man is Muslim. If so, he is the first I ever see. Nothing about the man's dress would make me think he is anything but Mongolian, his face lined in the same way as the Mongol herders of the grasslands, though his face has the ruddiness of one living at a higher elevation.

We follow the man on his motorbike to the end of town, then head out into the countryside. At times we lose him in the cloud of black exhaust trailing from the motorbike, but we never lose the cloud itself. On the horizon the Altai Mountains loom, foreboding. These are not the green-forested mountains of Khentii, the lush steppe and gently rolling hills. These mountains are serrated, each as if someone squeezes together layers of shale and balances the results on their edges, the peaks vertical black slashes that look razor thin.

Saran sits next to me. Somehow a strand of her hair once again blows into my mouth. I don't turn my head or fish it out with a finger. I leave it there, feel it tickling my tongue as I gaze at the nearest ridge. A handful of tiny specks scurry along the top. At first, I assume they must be goats as the height and sheerness of the rock face looks unnavigable. Then I realize they aren't. My stomach tightens.

Within the hour we make our introductions to the second candidate, the child a member of a clan of eagle hunters. When the family patriarch asks if we would like a demonstration, we are more than happy to accept whatever the world brings.

Stay and Witness What Is to Come

And so, hours after arriving at the homestead of the second candidate, we are on a mountainside in the western Altai. I am wrapped in borrowed clothes, my backside long numb from sitting on rock, the summer sun finally setting. It is more than thirty minutes since the bird is released. The little huntress remains hopeful, her arm still raised, a perch. Chala's younger brother Aibek is the candidate with whom we are here to speak. We are told the boy is only recently turned seven. Yet at the bird's disappearance, he berates his sister as if he is a grown-up. He chastises her for not training the eagle properly, for bringing shame upon their family in the presence of guests. After yelling at his sister, Aibek turns to his father, Makhmud, as if for approval.

Uncle clicks his teeth. Words are simply water bubbles, actions drops of gold, he says quietly to Little Bat in Tibetan. The patriarch Makhmud turns and begins to march back down the mountain with his two sons, one fully grown, the other a child, leaving Chala behind, her gloved arm still frozen in the air like a salute.

And Mun is turning too. My brother on the verge of following our host back to his homestead. I glare at my twin. Mentally I remind him that out here, I'm the boss. Then I take a seat on the stony ground. Let the men of her family leave, I think. We are to stay and witness what is to come.

Now the summer winds begin to pick up. Days, weeks, years, minutes pass. The moon peeks over a cliff. All around me the world is a dance of form and emptiness. And when the creature appears on the horizon against the setting sun an hour after it is released, I can see something dangling from its talons.

Listen to the way the bird comes soaring over the ridge back to the tiny huntress. The girl with her gloved arm stretched to the heavens, waiting to take the eagle back. This bird that can snap the double bones of her forearm with a single squeeze of its talons.

Chala buries her face in the eagle's feathers. At her feet lies the body of a wolf cub, the cub no bigger than a puppy, the animal's neck bent at a strange angle, a few bones visible at the top of the spine where the bird strikes it, veering down out of the sky at upward of a hundred and sixty kilometers an hour.

Little Bat intones a mantra, then carefully picks up the body. Together our small band winds its way back down the mountain. Thankfully the moon is out. In a few more days, it should be full, yet another light to aid us in our seeing.

Out!

When we arrive back at the family homestead, all lights are on inside the cinder-block house despite the hour, the household still awake. The bottle of Chinggis Khaan that Mun gifts the family earlier in the day is opened.

Little Bat places the dead cub in front of the father, Makhmud. Lubya is a wolf killer, Chala says. Indoors she wears the eagle on her arm, the bird a member of the largest species of eagle in existence.

Her brother Aibek, the one we are here to see, runs over and slaps his older sister across the face. Liar, he screams. Their mother, Karim, rushes over and folds the little boy back into her arms.

We do not hunt another animal's babies, says Makhmud sternly. He approaches the eagle carrying a tiny leather hood. As he moves to place it, the bird lashes at him with its tearing feet. Chala grabs the rope that binds the bird to her gloved arm to keep her father from being slashed. The eagle opens its wings, the sound of its agitation filling the room. Chala holds tight to the rope, the animal beating the air as if it would take flight. She grabs the hood from her father and places it on the animal's head. Once the hood is on, the eagle folds its wings and settles down.

Out! commands Makhmud. Chala bows her head and exits through the door.

In the corner on its wooden perch, her brother's eagle begins to flap its wings, the animal burning with some unseen force. Suddenly the eagle shoots off its stand and over to the body of the wolf cub lying on the carpet. Instantly it begins ravaging the near-perfect pelt with its feet. The bird doesn't even feed on the flesh. Nobody stops it.

I bow my head and step outside. Some feet away I can still hear the eagle savaging the pelt. The sound like heavy cloth being ripped.

After the Hunt, You Must Sing to Your Bird

Here at the foot of the mountain the summer night is warm. At first I don't see Chala, but I don't have far to look. Someone is singing. I follow the sound.

I find her nestled in a small nook behind a stone wall that separates the homestead from the mountain. From the look of things, she must come here routinely. The wall is old and crumbling; many of the stones jut straight out, like shelves. Chala uses these stones to store things like a hairbrush and a small wooden bowl. Out here there is also a perch for her bird to sit on, the perch simply a stick wedged in among the rocks so that it sticks out at a ninety-degree angle. Inside the house, the eagles rest on their upright perches, the top of each shaped like a Y. Here is no such formality. The eagle sits on its stick much the way it might out in the wild.

Chala rests against the stone wall and holds a small square-shaped piece of wood. A few strings, most likely hairs from a horse's tail, stretch the length of it. The notes it produces are dull and uniform, but Chala plucks away on the little makeshift contraption, her voice unadorned. Though I cannot make out a proper melody, her song describes a Kazakh girl who can never be with the Russian boy she loves. As she sings, I picture the river keeping the girl and boy apart, the long-standing enmity of their countries.

When she's finished, Chala takes a bowl from one of the ledges and fills it with water from a metal bucket. It should be vodka, she says. Skillfully she dips her ring finger in the water, then flicks her finger in each of the four cardinal directions before presenting the bowl to the eagle, who dips its beak in and throws its head back. After the hunt, you must sing to your bird, Chala explains.

Then you should feed it some of the meat from the kill, she says.

Despite her father's anger, she is tranquil. She is also seven years old, eleven months older than her brother Aibek, the candidate. Next month she turns eight. Both she and her brother are unusually large for their age. Their father towers over two meters.

There is such joy in this little being out here among the elements with just her eagle. After a long day in the Machine, I feel myself growing drowsy. The moon shines on us as if full.

Sometimes We Must Let Our Brothers the Animals Be Animals

Somehow the night passes. The eagle is still sitting on her perch when I open my eyes at the sound of feet walking by. After sleeping outside sitting up against a wall, I expect my bones to feel like iron in my body, but they don't. I stand, loose through my limbs, as if rising from a hot bath.

The older son, Kirill, comes around a bend carrying a small rug rolled up under his arm. There is at least a decade between him and his young siblings. Some years ago Kirill lives and studies in Kazakhstan. Now that he is back, he actively practices the faith.

Since the dissolution of the Soviet Union, more than fifty thousand Mongolian Kazakhs emigrate west to Kazakhstan, the world's largest landlocked country. Though Mongolia and Kazakhstan don't share a border, it is only a sixty-kilometer journey across Russia from country to country. The government there is one of the few nations in the world that pays to repatriate the diaspora. Many emigrate, as the Kazakhstan government offers free education and better business opportunities. Because most of Mongolia's Kazakhs are Muslim only in name, their traditions destroyed first by Stalin across the border and then by Mongolia's Stalinist puppet Choibalsan, there are fewer than a handful of mosques scattered across our country. Few Mongolian Kazakhs practice the five tenets of Islam; the Mongolian Kazakh who observes Ramadan is a rarity.

Inside the house, the mother Karim and the grandmother scurry about preparing our food for the day's adventure. Chala enters carrying a bucket filled with milk. On the floor her brother is lying on his back playing with a small plastic toy.

Uncle walks over and tries to engage him in conversation. Aibek barely looks at him. The child simply continues playing with his truck until it's time to leave.

Depending on who you ask, the eagle festival is either a new invention or as old as time itself. It is only an hour on horseback from the family's summer camp to the festival grounds. Each of us is given an animal. Saran rides as if she and the animal are one and the same creature. Little Bat is offered the largest animal in the herd, but he says he prefers to walk.

I accept an animal and do a quick intonation before climbing on its back.

For the sake of all mother beings,
I will become a Mentor Deity
So that beings in the supreme exaltation
May become Mentor Deities!

Beside me Mun looks somewhat rusty on his horse, but then again, how long is it since he's ridden? Uncle, on the other hand, trots lightly along, a great joy in his eyes. Sometimes we must let our brothers the animals be animals, he says, before racing off.

Now that he's mounted, Aibek seems more childlike. I watch him take off after Uncle. I can almost forget the scene of him slapping his sister last night. Instead, boy and monk play at chasing each other. Maybe they are indeed old friends, so old in fact that the one can periodically ignore the other, the casualness of their meeting as if to say, Ah, you again?

Both Aibek and his horse are wearing their finest clothes, the two of them ready to impress at today's event. As he gallops about, Aibek's eagle stays solidly perched on the *bajah* in which Aibek rests his arm, the *bajah* Y-shaped and attached to the saddle so that one can travel great distances with a six-kilo bird resting on one's forearm.

I search among our party, but Chala is not present. I wonder if she is to stay behind with the grandmother, the two of them left to look after the animals and do the milking, the animals with their animal demands rigid as any clock. But halfway to the festival site I spot a figure on a distant hill. From her horse she looks down on us, a huntress and her bird. Then Chala rides down out of the hills, and falls in place behind her brother.

A Hunger Turns On in Their Blood

We come around a bend and the landscape opens up. Down on the dusty plain hundreds of people are already gathered, a large rectangular area marked off and the spectators clustered around the edges. People coming from all over Bayan-Olgii Province, from as far north as the Siberian border, from places a two-day drive away or even a week on foot. This is their chance to show off their birds and to gather tips and pointers, to see friends old and new. On Chala's arm her eagle unfolds its wings and gives a shriek as if to announce its arrival.

We ride into the thick of things. I can feel the eaglers eyeing each other. Despite the fact that almost two hundred square kilometers are represented, most of the challengers know one another. Chala's older brother Kirill rides beside Uncle, filling him in on the details of each competitor. He points out a man resplendent in regalia lined with the silver fur of a wolf, the man sparkling in the sunlight. Kirill mentions that the man wins last year's competition and is favored to win this year as well. I can see that the hood his bird wears contains coral and silver embedded in the black leather. It makes the bird look like a warrior, like something out of the age of warlords and Khaans.

Kirill says there is grumbling among the eaglers about the way the man in the silver fur treats his bird. Though no one can say for sure, allegedly the bird the man flies is with him for more than ten years, some saying as many as fifteen. Tradition dictates that when a man partners with a bird for ten years, he must kill a sheep and lay the carcass on a mountainside as an offering of thanks. Then he must untie the strings attached to the eagle's feet, unhood the creature one last time, and let her go. Each eagle must be given the chance to live her own life, start her own family. Because the birds are often taken as fledglings, at ten years of age the females, which are the ones trained due to their larger size, begin to grow restless. A hunger turns on in their blood. Despite this call of nature, Kirill says there are stories of eagles returning to their handlers after being released. One famous story says that during one winter's killing *zud,* which left half the area's livestock dead, as one family teeters on the brink of starvation, from time to time they wake to find a dead rabbit or fox outside their door, each body with the telltale talon marks at the back of the neck.

The fact that this man in the silver fur hunts with the same eagle for so many years gives him an unfair advantage, says Kirill. Raising a new bird is time consuming. As we ride by, Aibek shoots the man a look of such disdain, as if the man is his inferior, that for a moment I imagine Aibek riding in a palanquin through the streets of Lhasa, a regent on his way to see his king.

Karim runs her fingers through the fur of her son's coat, smoothing the hair. It's hot, and standing in the sun in a landscape with few trees, I don't envy him. He holds still and lets his mother fawn over him. At one point she licks a finger and wipes his face, though I cannot see any dirt. Chala doesn't wear any of the traditional clothes of the eagle hunter. All she wears is the special leather glove. Despite its thickness, the bird can still crush her wrist, exerting almost three thousand kilopascals with its talons.

This is a one-day competition. The Golden Eagle Festival for which the area is famed is actually held in October before the start of the hunting season. Now that we are in the peak of summer, this festival is much smaller and only started up in the last few years for the benefit of foreign tourists, many of whom are in the country to see Naadam. Often younger trainers participate in this festival as well as the more seasoned eaglers, men with years of experience who are looking to put their birds through their paces, birds that perhaps are young or out of shape, some lethargic and fat, as there is no true hunting in the summer, only training in the long pale summer nights.

Though the people here are Kazakhs, several come over to shake Uncle's hand. Already word is spreading that a Buddhist lama is traveling in the area. Despite the fact that most of the people in this province are Muslim, there is no animosity between us the way there is in some countries in other parts of Asia, countries where Muslims and Buddhists are at war with each other, which Uncle says distresses His Holiness to no end.

Someone gives a sharp whistle. The contestants begin massing on horseback. Together they make for a nearby hill and momentarily disappear behind it. A man begins to play the Mongolian national anthem through the speakers of his car. As the music plays, the eaglers reappear from the shadow of the hill and stream into the clearing behind someone carrying the flag of Mongolia. Among the riders Aibek adjusts his hat. I look at Chala. She is smiling, her cheeks pink and dewy with sweat. She turns her horse toward where the others are now lining up and rides off, the bird a good head taller than she is. She is the only girl among the riders, but I only know because I know. If you don't look for it, you would never see a difference between her and the others. If there is any difference, it is that she carries herself like a true horse lord.

Happiness Is Infectious

The first event is essentially a beauty contest. One by one the contestants trot by the judges' table. The contestants show off not only their riding skills but also the magnificence of their birds. Despite the high heat of summer, last year's winner glitters like mica in his silvery wolf fur. His horse is also robed in white, ribbons plaited through its mane, its tail braided and shining. The man in the wolfskin looks as if he rides straight out of the days of Chinggis Khaan, his bearing regal, his bird equally haughty.

There is no order. Older trainers mix with the younger ones, who appear to be teenagers. Aibek and Chala are the youngest.

When his turn comes, Aibek rides out, his clothes made from the skins of multiple animals—rabbits and foxes, a wolf as well. Aibek doesn't smile. He rides as if he owns the world. One judge gives him a nine, perhaps because of the family he hails from, but most others give him fives or sixes. Technically there is nothing he does wrong. Perhaps there is something about the way he carries himself that makes one want to remind him he is only a child.

When Chala's moment comes, she takes a deep breath and spurs her horse on. In many ways, she rides too quickly, which doesn't give the judges time to admire the bird, but in her case, it's not important. The rapport she has with her eagle is apparent. Her happiness is infectious. She gathers a few nines, but mostly eights. The audience claps as she rides out, the women clapping the hardest, though several of the older men do not hide their disapproval.

In between events, the spectators play games for fun. As we wait for the contestants to prepare themselves for the next portion of the competition, we watch as an animal skin is tossed among a group of riders. Two men at a time vie to wrestle the skin out of each other's hands while staying on horseback. It is comical to watch. The men sit astride their horses, each man with a hand on the pelt. The two ride around among the others, who cluster about until one of the two men is vanquished, then the others simultaneously try to land a hand on the fur in order to have their shot at it.

Because the eaglers are not yet in place, a different game breaks out when the first one ends. In this, men gallop around on horseback trying to throw the headless body of a goat into a basket. The men ride hard against one another. At one point, two horses collide and go down, but no one is hurt. The game lasts only a few minutes. In that time, no one scores.

Later, toward the end of the day, several of the women get a chance to mount and show their skills. In this game, a man rides out after his wife who has a head start, and tries to capture the scarf wrapped around her neck. The two ride around a cone. On their way back to the starting line, they reverse positions. Instead, the woman tries to land a few blows with a small whip as she chases her husband.

When Chala's parents take their turn, I can see where Chala gets her riding skills from. Karim outrides Makhmud the whole way; he never comes within an arm's length of her. After racing around the cone, she whips him several times, her blows so hard I can hear each one. Something in her face tells me this feels good, that she savors this moment all year long until the next competition.

I wonder what would happen if I play this game with my twin, who would whip whom, how satisfying it would feel to make physical the struggle between us. I look over and see Mun staring at me. When he nods at me, I realize the thought I am thinking is his.

Disaster!

Everyone is in position. For this event, a helper looses the bird from the top of a nearby outcrop. Each animal is timed to see how long it takes the creature to land on the arm of its trainer far below on the dusty plain. The first bird is let go; the stopwatch starts. The bird comes swooping down from the rocks, its wingspan almost three meters, its shadow gliding along the earth like a cloud, and in one perfect move it lands on its trainer's arm. The crowd claps. The judge calls out a time. Nine point three seconds. Excellent. Anything under ten seconds is good.

The next bird is released. I hold my breath. Disaster! The bird goes sailing over its trainer's head and keeps going, banking back toward where it comes from and away over the ridge. The man hangs his head. People clap all the same though there is also laughter.

For the next hour it is like this. Some birds making straight for their trainers, other taking side trips, others going where they will. Aibek takes his position on the plain. From the outcrop Kirill lets the eagle go. Quickly the bird flutters into a craggy nook nestled in the shade. Aibek calls out in rage, but the bird does not budge. One of the judges comes forward with a dead animal tied on a string and hands it to Aibek. Aibek takes the lure and walks back and forth on horseback, running the carcass along the ground. Eventually the bird takes off and flies down, swooping onto the desiccated corpse. Aibek scoops up his bird and rides off the field.

Chala's bird also has a mind of its own. It doesn't come immediately to her arm, but flies overhead circling on the wind. For a moment it seems to stall, hanging in the air before diving like a hammer and harrowing one of the smaller horses tethered by the side of the field, the animal's coloring gray and silvery, much like a wolf's. The eagle persists until someone drives it off with a stick. The spectators remain silent. After it menaces the horse, the eagle flies to Chala and perches on the *bajah.* The little girl rubs her face in its feathers. Coolly the eagle rearranges its wings.

Perfection!

The last event is a simulated hunt. We watch as once again each eagler climbs the ridge on horseback, then releases his bird into the air. Down below, someone scurries along the ground dragging the body of a fox tied on a rope. Kirill explains that this is how young birds are trained. Some eaglers tie their birds to poles so that each time they attempt to fly away, they get thwarted after just a few meters, the rope tethering them to the earth. Then, when the birds learn not to flee, the men untie them from the pole, though their feet are always kept bound, and when they are ready, they lengthen the rope little by little and release the bird, letting it land on the carcass that the handler drags along the ground.

When his turn comes, Aibek's eagle performs well. Within seconds, she comes thundering out of the sky, her powerful talons squeezing the lure. People clap. She won't let go. Nobody can get her off the corpse. It is only after Aibek rides down the ridge and takes her up on his arm that she loosens her grip.

Only Chala remains standing on the outcrop with the bird on her arm. She cuts a forlorn figure, silhouetted against the sky. One of the judges resignedly raises his arm to give the signal. The lure is positioned. A few mothers with small children pull their children closer.

The eagle comes screaming out of the air. Perfection! She lands on the lure, tearing it with her feet. Quickly Chala rides down from the butte. Nobody approaches the bird to remove the lure from its talons until this young girl does it herself as if taking a toy from a naughty child.

As This Is the Century of Women

The man in the silver wolfskin places second. Perhaps the rumors about the age of his bird are just too much. The bird's performance is perfect, as if it spends whole lifetimes wafting on the currents back to the arm of its trainer. Maybe in another life, the two are king and commoner, master and servant. Instead, first place goes to a seventeen-year-old boy whose eagle performs well.

There is no reason for anyone in our contingent to hang their head over Aibek's or Chala's performance. Makhmud is in good spirits. Even Chala's eagle's terrorizing the small horse doesn't seem to foul his thoughts. For the first time all day I see him smile as other eaglers congratulate him.

Because there are things he would like to discuss, Makhmud and his family remain chatting with the other eaglers. There are questions about the government in Kazakhstan's latest offer, the government there eager to bring the Kazakh diaspora home to the motherland. This time they are offering land and business prospects. After the collapse of the Soviet Union, fifty thousand Mongolian Kazakhs head west to Kazakhstan, but ten years later when Kazakhstan doesn't prove to be the land where flowers rain from the sky, twenty thousand of them come back.

Many of the other eaglers travel from far enough away that they intend to camp out on the dusty plain for the night. In celebration there is to be music and singing and food and drink. Toward the end of the night there may also be fighting. Chala offers to take us back while her family discusses politics. We ride slowly as Little Bat is on foot, carefully picking our way over the butte from which the eaglers launch their birds. There are other buttes beyond this, each one tall and thin, a piece of flint set on edge. It should take us an hour to reach home.

Too bad Aibek's not with us, says Mun. Now would be the perfect time to question him.

Would it, murmurs Uncle. The sack he is carrying rattles lightly. I feel a breeze caress my shoulder. A ripple radiates through the muscles of the horse I am riding. And just like that, I realize the mistake clouding our thinking. The way my twin and I make certain assumptions when the facts point elsewhere. This is the power of what the Buddha calls "misknowledge," how it blinds us to truth.

Little Aibek is not the candidate. Last year His Holiness the Dalai Lama says that as this is the century of women, maybe He Himself might choose to reincarnate as such. Chala is just up the path. Yesterday when we arrive here in the westernmost region of Mongolia, I believe it is to evaluate her brother, as that is what seems most logical. But now I realize that consciousness knows no boundaries as it migrates from vessel to vessel.

Uncle rides toward Chala. When the chance arises, he leads her off the path and dismounts in an auspicious place. In time he pulls out the three items he carries with him. He lays them on the ground and listens to what she has to say.

This Is Not for Show

The cat comes out of nowhere. A mountain lynx. It jumps up on a rock. My horse whinnies and bucks, but I manage to stay on. Mun is not so lucky. We are at the rear of our group. The cat is right in front of him. His horse goes up on two legs. In a flash Mun tumbles off. I feel an immense pain in my wrist. Instantly I know it is broken. That is the least of our worries. Two small tawny heads appear in a crevice on the other side of the path. Her cubs. She is ready to kill anything in her way, and right now, Mun is in her way.

The lynx shifts her weight to her back haunches, prepares to pounce. This is not for show, a demonstration meant to make the other creature turn back. This is an attack to protect her offspring. Mun cradles his arm. I can feel his heart pounding. I stir my horse into action, putting it in between the cat and Mun, the whole time my wrist also throbbing, my mind seeing everything at once.

Then the hammer falls. The lynx is startled. She twists and swats, clawing. The eagle is on her back, the bird riding the lynx the way a man rides a maddened yak. Uncle is thundering straight for Mun. He scoops him up onto his mount smooth as any horseman. I turn my horse and ride to be far away on the other side of the lynx and her babies.

Farther up the path we regroup. Chala stands on a ridge and gives a sharp whistle. The eagle releases the lynx and rises up into the air, a small cloud dark and furious. The cat is not seriously hurt, though there are scars to come from the attack. Blood is lost, but life is not taken. The lynx flattens herself to the earth and slinks across the path toward her cubs.

Right Time, Right Thought, Right Speech

All the way back to camp I can feel my brother's pain. I can also feel his humiliation, the fact that I am able to stay on my horse while he cannot, that this is yet one more instance of Mun being in need of rescue. I want to say something to comfort him, but nothing comes to mind. Right time, right thought, right speech.

Do not speak—unless it improves upon silence!

As we bump and jounce over every rock, every ridge, I can feel the nerves in his wrist on fire.

We ride the rest of the way in silence—Saran on one side of Mun, Little Bat on the other to keep him from falling. Chala rides beside me. There is an air of determination about her, a quality of fixed resolve, as if childhood burns away, a decision reached. Something about the encounter with the lynx precipitates this. Sometimes there are moments in a life where a path is presented, where one must decide which road to take. Chala is not the same girl as earlier this morning. She looks at me and smiles.

When we get to camp, Uncle helps Mun dismount. Inside the house we find the grandmother, who then takes my brother's wrist in her hands and turns it this way and that for the better part of an hour. Words are spoken, water steeped with herbs and the pink rhodiola that grows on the mountain. And so it is healed. She is a bonesetter. She is the first I am to ever encounter. They are a kind of shaman. Generally the skill runs in a family and is never revealed to outsiders. Somehow, the bonesetter can simply touch a person, turning the injury in their hands, and in time all is healed, the spot perhaps bruised and swollen, but healed absolutely. Mun's wrist is good as new before the rest of the family even returns.

All during my childhood my father would say that an injury is not a break if it can be healed so easily, but I know what I feel in my brother's body, the pain like a million suns throbbing under the skin. Afterward, Mun heads to our car to find a bottle of vodka to gift this old woman. It is the least he can do.

Chala's mind is on other things. When we ride into camp, she dismounts and walks straight into the house, leaving her bird outside on its perch. When she comes back, she is carrying a knife, the kind small but deadly sharp and used in the killing of animals. Please help me, she says. I nod though I have no idea what she intends.

Together we walk up the path toward where the sheep and goats are kept in a small enclosure. Chala walks among them, eyeing each. I think of the little girl near Yatuu Gol with her ash-blackened face, how she knows which animal to select.

Chala picks one and steers it out of the group. It is an older female though something about the animal is still plump, still worthy. Quickly she ties the animal up and together we throw it over the back of her horse. There is nothing for me to do but follow, which I am doing all my life.

There Are a Myriad of Ways to Exist in This World

We ride for more than an hour. We are headed to what seems to be the highest point in the area. I can feel the temperature drop. It is well after seven o'clock. Though it is summer, we are high up, the ridgeline thin like walking along the edge of a blade. I wish for a second jacket, but such is life as it is.

Chala pulls up and I stop beside her. I help her lay the sheep on the ground. The thing bleats weakly, a thin stream of urine wetting the dirt. Chala flips the animal on its back and unties its front legs. The animal kicks and kicks, but she straddles it. I move forward and help to pin back its limbs. How many years is it since I usher a being out of this life? From its perch on the horse the eagle sits watching us, its yellow eyes all-seeing.

Chala takes the knife and begins to thin the hair on the sheep's chest. When she finishes clearing a spot, she makes an incision, the cut just big enough for her to slip her hand inside. She reaches in as if putting on a glove. I know what she is doing. She is searching for the vein, the artery that one must pinch in order to give the animal a painless death. She finds it and eventually the animal stops kicking though its eyes stay open.

May you find refuge in the Dharma, I intone.

There is blood all the way up to Chala's elbow as if she dips her arm in a river of blood. I wonder if this is the first animal she kills, as it is usually a job delegated to men. The efficiency with which she makes the incision and how quickly she finds the artery make me think she aids her father countless times. The sheep gives one last shudder. A final tension drains from its body. Together we carry the carcass over to a spot on the ridge. The wind whips around us, the smell of blood on everything.

We ride back down the ridge, only stopping a half hour away from camp. The temperature changes. The mountain where the body of the sheep lies is long behind us. I cannot see it anymore. I am not sure what is going on until Chala stops and lifts the great bird. Slowly she begins to untie the tethers from its feet.

Why now, I ask.

Chala doesn't look at me. Lubya saves the life of your brother. Now she deserves her freedom, she says. I consider this. Chala holds the tethers in her left hand, the bird on her right. She buries her face one last time in its feathers. There are a myriad of ways to exist in this world. I rub my wrist. It no longer aches. Later, as we are driving back toward the center of Mongolia to see the third and final candidate, I ask Uncle if this visit proves fruitful, if he sees what he needs to see.

One sees, he says. One is always seeing.

But here on this rock face, Chala throws her arm up into the air.

Who are you, I think. She has to throw her arm up three times before the bird takes flight.

In the Shadow of the Volcano

Oracles Are Consulted

The first week of March and my brother is still crying intermittently. It is six months since the Rinpoche sits him down in the brisk October air of Yatuu Gol's courtyard and takes a straight razor to his head. Although half a year passes since our arrival in the monastery, tears still cloud my twin's eyes for no earthly reason the *sangha* can discern. His ordination as the 5th Incarnation of the Paljor Jamgon, the Redeemer Who Sounds the Conch in the Darkness, is to be held in April, the dignitaries traveling from as far away as India.

And so when Mun through tears asks his personal cook Namrut to make him *boodog,* this labor-intense Mongolian dish, Namrut does not say no right away. Instead, Namrut asks the Rinpoche. In turn, the Rinpoche asks me.

I am eight years old.

It is a new millennium. The world is still intact. Two months ago we celebrate Tsagaan Sar, the lunar New Year. In the Chinese zodiac it is the year of the Golden Dragon, a year of power, prosperity, good fortune. In October when we enter the monastery, I too feel the burn of the Rinpoche's razor on my scalp. But at Yatuu Gol, my brother and I are entering into a slow reversal. With each hair that falls to the ground, I feel myself paring down to my essence, like a tree readying itself for winter. For Mun, the shaving of his head is the beginning of losing his identity, his inner fire slowly cooling. As he cannot hold still and submit to the blade, his scalp gets nicked in a hundred places, the skin beading with blood. For the first few weeks this patchwork of scabs is the only thing distinguishing him from the rest of the *sangha.*

Oracles are consulted. The surfaces of lakes read for signs. The Rinpoche says spring is the auspicious time for Mun to take his official title. These past six months the elder monks teaching him the rudiments of what he needs to perform at his ordination. Everywhere people clamoring for his blessing, prostrating themselves on the ground. He must not allow himself to be spooked like a startled horse by the commotion, the people thronging just to touch him, just to brush the sleeve of the Redeemer Who Sounds the Conch in the Darkness after all these years deprived of the faith. He must remain stoic, impassive yet loving, and perform his duty, taking each of the thousand or more sky-blue *khadag* he is offered from well-wishers in both hands before lifting the scarf to his face and touching it with his forehead, then wrapping the *khadag* around the person's neck as they bow before him.

I feel an uneasiness for my brother. Mornings he sits on a golden pillow at the head of the assembly. He is learning when to take the bell and the *dorje* in his fists, how to ring the bell in a manner that is both sonorous yet grave, twisting his wrists hypnotically like a dancer as he recites the words only he can say, leading us, his fellow monks, as we pray for the salvation of all sentient creatures in this and all universes.

After two hours of chants there is always a break. The novices on kitchen duty scamper about filling each monk's bowl with milk. As it is March, we still eat the traditional New Year cakes, each *ul boov* filled with cream and sugar and shaped like the sole of a shoe. Some mornings we drink from juice boxes. I can sense how my brother likes to unwrap the tiny straw and stab it through the hole. How he likes to keep sucking on this straw even after the box is empty so that he can watch the sides of the box move in and out like a set of bellows. Ever since I can remember, mornings my brother and I would ride out with the herds. On the steppe there are no walls, the grasslands stretching before us all the way to Hungary and the Volga River. On our horses we are as fast as the wind. We are Mongolian. Nothing can contain us. In our life before Yatuu Gol, the eternal blue sky like a mantle protecting us.

Tell Me: Is *Boodog* a Good Idea?

The Rinpoche comes to find me in calligraphy class where we are learning to write Old Mongolian, the traditional Mongolian script from hundreds of years ago during the time of Chinggis Khaan. Our people's oldest surviving history, *The Secret History of the Mongols,* is originally spoken in Old Mongolian, then transcribed phonetically into the Uighur script before being transcribed a second time into Chinese. The only remaining copies of the ancient originals still exist in Chinese characters.

Old Mongol is one of only a handful of languages written vertically from left to right. I love learning the twenty-nine characters that comprise the alphabet. On the page the letters like the tracks of some fantastic bird. My favorite letters are the sound for *du,* which looks like a woman's earring, and the sound for *ja,* which looks like a man walking with one overly long leg. Old Mongol is still used in places like Inner Mongolia. During the Stalinist purges, Old Mongol is all but abandoned here in Mongolia in favor of Cyrillic, but in places like Gandan Tegchenling Monastery in Ulaanbaatar, there are always monks who can read it even during the dark times.

The Rinpoche stands by my bench and takes off his glasses. Because I am the brother of the Redeemer Who Sounds the Conch in the Darkness, the Rinpoche often consults with me. As this is the case, I am always trying to humble myself and to give whatever aid is needed; I don't abuse the distinction granted me. I can sense that the others don't mind the special treatment I receive. I suspect that many of them feel sorry for me, that I must live in the shadow of my brother. Some use an old idiom to describe Mun, saying he is a bad dog who can't stomach ghee butter, meaning he is unworthy of the privileges heaped upon him—the separate living quarters, the private cook, the tutors, the gifts, the golden pillow elevated above all others in the temple.

Little Brother, says the Rinpoche. All these months after he rides up to our homestead and sometimes I still do not think of him as a Precious One. When Mun and I are alone, my brother still calls him Bazar. Bazar, like Mun, is a *tulku.* I remember the way he butchers my grandfather, the focus with which he handles the blade. Your brother asks that Namrut prepare *boodog* for him, he says. I know the others in class are listening intently though they keep their eyes on their work. The Rinpoche pauses and studies the script I write. I wonder if it is legible, if this passage from the *Jangar* still holds meaning hundreds of years later. The Rinpoche doesn't comment on my efforts. Instead he asks: what do you think might be the result of this?

As he and I often converse like this ever since Mun and I ride out of the grasslands, I know what he is truly asking. Do I think the meal may make Mun more homesick and recalcitrant, or do I think it can help?

Though I try not to show it, I am growing weary of answering for my brother. When he is named the Redeemer Who Sounds the Conch in the Darkness, I am to be given the honorary title of the Servant to the Redeemer Who Sounds the Conch in the Darkness. It is decided that because we are twins, we are not to be separated. It never occurs to me that I might stay behind with my father out on the grasslands and carry on with the life of a herder, that I would not come to Yatuu Gol and do what I can to help my brother while also working on achieving Buddhahood for myself.

One month after Bazar discovers Mun, our father brings us to the monastery gate. Though he is invited in for tea, Aav comes no further, saying the driver he hires to drive the herds south should arrive shortly. Our father doesn't smile or cry as we walk away with the Rinpoche. I try to ask him one last question about the red colt born earlier that fall, but there isn't time. Aav is heading south with his brother. At night I hear talk of a woman, a widow with small children. The next time I see Aav I expect him to be remarried. A baby might be on the way. Our father never lives in a world with religion. In his eyes life at Yatuu Gol is like life on a faraway planet. I can sense his bewilderment, that the idea of losing two sons to the monastery is unimaginable to him, but he knows it is what the spirit of Övöö counsels. In places like Tibet or Nepal or Bhutan, there is an unbroken history of Precious Ones, of children being taken from their families and the tremendous honor such a parting bestows. But here in Mongolia that tradition is long dead. My father suffers in this new world filled with ancient ways. Consequently, he requests that Mun not be sent all the way to India, as most *tulku* are trained in one of the three great monasteries in that country. Instead, we are to remain right here in the shadow of the volcano.

Little Brother, repeats the Rinpoche. Tell me: is *boodog* a good idea?

Since arriving in Yatuu Gol six months ago I learn that the best way to help Mun is to win the other novices to his side. I try to do this in whatever way I can. Like having Mun ask for a soccer ball, or establishing one night a week for foreign movies so that together we can improve our English.

My brother likes eating *boodog,* I say. I don't lie to the Rinpoche. He is a Precious One. I never lie to him. But sometimes the truth can be stretched, and sometimes it is best to do so. He likes it even more when shared with others, I say, the way we eat it with our neighbors and friends out on the steppe.

The Rinpoche nods. Hope sparkles in his eyes. Once in the late hours of the night when I step outside to wash a sheet which one of the younger novices wets, the novice too embarrassed to do it himself, I hear the Disciplinarian speaking frankly with the Rinpoche. At most monasteries, the Disciplinarian is an older monk who is second in charge after the Principal. That night, the Disciplinarian, an aged monk from China via India, says that perhaps a mistake is made, that maybe I am the Redeemer Who Sounds the Conch in the Darkness and that Mun is my servant. Quickly I scurry away to wash the sheet outside at the well. Outdoors in the moonlight I do not hear the Rinpoche's response. I cannot let such thoughts enter into my heart as they make my path more difficult.

The Volcano Always Stays in Sight

And so, because of my small conversation with the Rinpoche, in two days' time my brother and I go out on horseback along with a handful of other novices chosen by the Disciplinarian as being in need of "open space." Mun is told not to ride too fast or too recklessly, which only makes him ride like the wind created by a maddened horse. Together our small band thunders forth from the monastery. We ride so far away that we can no longer see its walls despite the flatness of the landscape, though the volcano always stays in sight as a reminder of who we are and what we strive to be. When one in our group finds a string of holes that look inhabited, my brother dismounts and dons the hat that has the ears of an actual fox, the marmot's natural enemy, and by making a series of calls through his cupped fists, he lures the marmot into poking its head aboveground to find out where the danger lurks. Then together we flush it, and Namrut shoots it with the monastery's one gun, an old relic from Soviet times, as only he is allowed to kill the meat we eat.

In this way we pass an afternoon out on the grasslands, a group of Mongolian youths, Namrut the oldest at twenty-two. We take the three marmots we are blessed with back to Yatuu Gol where Namrut guts them and pulls out their innards for cleaning, after which he carefully stuffs everything back inside the animals' stomachs. Then he crams several hot rocks, which heat for hours in an open fire, inside the bodies before sewing them closed with wire. We watch the final step in the process as he takes a blowtorch and burns off the animals' fur. The corpses are then allowed to sit. When the meat is ready, we come together, the *sangha* of Yatuu Gol, the young and the old, Mongolian and foreign. The Rinpoche says an offering, and Namrut takes a knife he sharpens on a rock and makes the first cut. Steam comes shooting out as one by one the carcasses deflate. He takes out the viscera and cuts up the meat, and we eat of our fellow sentient creatures. And that night and into the next day there are no tears, no stamping of the feet of the Redeemer Who Sounds the Conch in the Darkness. True, there is also not the same carefree happiness among us as there is when we go hunting for these marmots out on the grasslands, all of us riding hard like the Mongol horde of yore, an ancient brotherhood sworn in blood and capable of taking over the world.

The Snows in Lhasa

April and the most sumptuous day of my life arrives.

Just last year the 9th Jetsun Dampa, the head of Tibetan Buddhism in Mongolia, is enthroned in Ulaanbaatar after a lifetime of living in hiding. But because there is no ordination of a *tulku* in this part of the country in almost eighty years, the celebration starts a full week before the ceremony. People travel from all over the region to the nearby outpost of Bor-Urt. A small *ger* city begins to sprout. All week the faithful trek up the rocky slopes of Yatuu Gol to make an offering to the *ovoo*. All week, Mun is fitted and poked, measured, rehearsed, quizzed, bribed when necessary, reminded that he is an ancient light in our new country in a new millennium of hope. Each day I feel him grow more resigned, more listless, the fire in his heart slowly dying until all that is left is an orange glow in his eyes, the rage of Hayagrīva, the horse-necked deity whose energy he is learning to generate within himself, a deep burning, a resentment that is never extinguished.

It is in the days before he is saddled with his title that I first feel the new intensity of the fire in my brother. As herders we roam over the grasslands, our thoughts moving freely between us until sometimes I cannot distinguish which thoughts are Mun's and which are mine. Perhaps this is only logical. On the grasslands we share a life. There is little difference in our experiences. Now all that is changed. I can only experience secondhand what it is to have old men pull me onto their lap and talk about the snows in Lhasa, or to suddenly be expected to be the paragon of goodness and compassion every day when one is anything but. Most *tulku* are discovered at a much younger age, often before they are five years old and sometimes as young as toddlers, when the personality is still malleable. Perhaps as we are eight, almost nine, it is too much to expect my brother to conform to his new life.

Instinctively, I think the Rinpoche knows this. After discovering Mun, he flies to Dharamshala to consult with the Dalai Lama's council. He is warned that in a culture long deprived of a tradition of *tulku,* it might be difficult to get the seed to take in one so old. The Rinpoche listens respectfully, but the wheel of Dharma is already set in motion. April arrives, and my twin and I both receive our new names.

There Is to Be Chanting and Incense and Candles

The night before the ceremony I feel my brother calling me to his quarters. Unlike the rest of us, who sleep eight to a room, Mun occupies a series of rooms by himself that include a separate chamber for his private meditation as well as a side room with an altar that stretches from floor to ceiling. Even the Rinpoche sleeps in a small nook cluttered with books, his room more of a storage space for the things he reclaims along his journey toward reopening the monastery. Despite all the work the Rinpoche does to rekindle the flame of Buddhism in this area, at eight years old, Mun is the senior monk at Yatuu Gol. While they are both Precious Ones, Mun's lineage is older.

I leave my bed and walk along the empty halls. A few of the old masters who travel from abroad are sitting in the main hall. They meditate all night and into the morning, the butter lamps burning, making the air smell sweet, the altar piled high with offerings of store-bought biscuits, cookies, liters of soft drinks and fruit juices, *tögrög* crammed in the offering bowls.

I enter my brother's chambers and find him sitting in his altar room among his booty. I'm not allowed to keep it, he says. All week gifts pour in. Stuffed animals, sports equipment, electronics, candy. It is all to be whisked away tomorrow and donated to the local school, places where children are allowed to be children.

And so my brother and I spend the night playing with objects we don't even know exist until now. One is a remote-control truck that has a siren on top that flashes red and blue lights, washing the walls with color. Tomorrow my brother is to don the gold brocade lama hat like a horse's mane. He is to be carried on an open-air litter through the crowds, the *sangha* of the whole country and beyond gathered so that the community here at Yatuu Gol looks robust and plentiful, the monks rocking back and forth, lifting the great horns to their lips, beating the drums, sending a wall of sound up into the eternal blue.

I am to sit off to the side on a platform in a place of honor with my father and his new wife and her three children, two girls and a little boy who wriggles in the woman's arms like a fat slug. It is October since I last see my father. He looks both thinner and more worried. I wonder if, besides my shaved head, I look different to him. The people come and bow down to Aav and lay items at his feet, my father a simple herder. I can tell that the people think this woman at his side is our mother. Each time they bow to her it makes me want to scream.

There is to be chanting and incense and candles. Walking around the altar in the same direction the sun moves through the heavens, a stick of incense clasped between the palms. Heads bowed, food eaten. Old women crying at the return of the faith of their childhoods.

Tomorrow our father may bow to us, his sons, and touch his forehead to ours. As always, we do not hug. But tonight we are two little boys playing among a pile of treasure the world mysteriously brings into our lives.

My brother and I are different people. This is evident to me during our life on the steppe. The way I sit on my horse, body square and balanced, and the way he rides as if about to fall off. Still, I understand why he is about to do what he is planning. Perhaps if our roles ever reverse, I might do the same.

Don't go, I say out loud. I can tell what my twin is thinking. That at first light he is planning to wrap himself in a simple robe and head out to the stables where he finds a good strong horse and rides it to the ends of the earth and beyond, out into the larger world he dreams of seeing. Don't, I repeat, but the toy truck with the colorful siren drowns me out.

Some months ago when we are still living with my father out on the grasslands, the Rinpoche visits to finalize plans for our entering the monastery. After everything is decided and the adults go to bed,

I intuit Mun's childish thoughts. How he is planning to make the incision in Bazar's chest and slip his arm inside to pinch the artery that gives life, as if killing a grown man is as easy as killing a sheep. Perhaps the fire first burns uncontrollably inside my twin that night when I go out after him with Övöö's old hunting rifle. Maybe Mun foresees the life that awaits us here in Yatuu Gol—him burdened with the happiness of all living beings, and me burdened by him. Maybe I should allow him to slip into the *ger.* Maybe I should trust that this is only for show, a way for my twin to express his feelings of powerlessness. Somewhere deep inside I know that my brother is not capable of such darkness. All the same, I raise the rifle. Mun glares at me, the knife glinting in his hand. Go away, he commands. I close my eyes. The sound of the blast scares the clouds off the face of the moon. When the smoke clears, my twin is still standing. Our father and Bazar come running.

There's a wolf about, I lie. The two men eye us suspiciously.

This is what I am capable of. Of rising in the night and taking a gun, of aiming it at my twin. Of ruining his deepest plans. Of betraying him.

Since arriving at Yatuu Gol my brother trains with a Precious One from India. He is receiving advanced tantric instruction I do not have access to. Tantric practice is an important part of Tibetan Buddhism. There are endless levels of tantric study. One must spend thousands of hours with a teacher in order to ascend to the highest levels of practice in which one learns to manipulate energy itself by entering the state of what we call foundational clear light mind that most beings can only access at death. Through mastering such states, one can, when needed, learn to generate within oneself the energy of wrathful deities, enlightened beings who incarnate in ferocious forms in order to lead others to enlightenment. In tantric practice, one's teacher often decides on a wrathful deity that is already in alignment with one's personality, and that deity becomes one's protector. Mun's wrathful deity is Hayagrīva, the Horse-Necked One. Sometimes Hayagrīva is depicted with three faces, each of his mouths filled with fangs, his sword raised to cut through the fog of delusion and ego. Though still a novice, when Mun tries to summon the energy of Hayagrīva, his eyes burn.

Each day my twin is learning to focus, to shut out the world entirely. I am of the world. Tomorrow after his ordination, a spot gradually opens inside my brother, a hole like the vastness of outer space but filled with fire. If I try to enter it with my mind, instantly a searing pain rages between my eyes as if looking directly at the sun.

Tomorrow everything is to be different. But tonight in his chambers piled with gifts he has yet to perfect this inner burning.

Don't go, I say a third time. Don't, but it is the beginning of something new between us. If he is ever to escape this life, he must keep secrets, even from me. As the toy truck rampages around the room, siren wailing, I can feel my brother testing the limits of his ability to shut me out.

When Mun gets up at dawn to put his plan into action, he finds the stables locked, one of the old monks sleeping in front of the doors as the Rinpoche orders. I have no defense, no hidden spaces inside me. The icy white sheet is not enough. My brother knows the actions I take. How after leaving him with his toys to return to my room, I stop in the Rinpoche's quarters. All the while my eyes locked on the ground as I speak with the Rinpoche of my twin's plans.

As the sun rises on the day of my twin's ordination, I wake to a sudden pang, a conflagration in the front of my skull, a feeling as if the whole world is burning. I sit up in bed. I am not able to catch my breath until late into the morning. By the time I do, it is done. We both have new names.

In My Hands, It Is Both Heavier and Lighter Than I Expect

A week after Mun's ordination I am allowed into the small closet where the instruments are kept. Right from the start Mun is taught to ring a large brass bell in his left hand while wielding the *dorje,* a small scepter, in his right. The left hand represents wisdom, the realization that all is nothing, while things held in the right represent compassion, or skillful practice. The bell and *dorje* are often used together during ceremonies. The *dorje* is the physical representation of the thunderbolt of enlightenment. On his golden cushion, my now-fully-ordained brother sits at the head of our assembly and marries these two elements together in his eight-year-old body. Now it is my turn to choose an instrument, to decide how I want to be heard.

I am well versed in the appeal of each. Most of the younger novices play the *tsingsha,* two small cymbals attached by a leather cord, the sweetness of the *tsingsha*'s one note calling hungry ghosts to the altar to accept the offerings. Other younger novices gently shake their wrists as they play the two-sided drum called the *damaru,* causing a pair of wooden clappers to bounce off the drum's opposing heads. Some of the senior monks play the double-reeded *gyaling,* a wind instrument resonant like the western oboe, though the *gyaling* is usually decorated with silver and coral. In order to play the *gyaling,* one must master breathing in a circular fashion, inhaling through the nose while exhaling the air held in the mouth. Finally the *dungchen* can always be heard during *puja,* this long horn often up to six meters in length, the end of the horn placed on a cushion, though if need be, the instrument can be dismantled into three sections for ease of transport. While I am told some say the sound of the *dungchen* is like the singing of elephants, to my ears, it sounds like cold water on a moonless night, the peace that arises from stillness. There are a handful of various other drums and cymbals, flutes including one the Rinpoche plays made from a human femur, the instrument gilded in silver and with a sound like the winter wind.

Well, says the Disciplinarian as I look over the possibilities. What is your choice?

I gave him a shy look as my eye lands on the instrument I long to master. I hear an especially beautiful one can cost upward of millions of *tögrög*, but the expense aside, something in the shape of the instrument, the smoothness of its folds, calls me to it. I run a finger along its perfect spiral.

The Disciplinarian nods and takes it off the shelf. In my hands, it is both heavier and lighter than I expect. This one is fitted with a silver mouthpiece on one end, though some monks learn to play it without. Try it, says the Disciplinarian not unkindly. I lift it to my lips and imagine every sentient being to ever exist.

Than this, what could be more wondrous?
Than this, what miracle could possess more awe?

I blow.

The conch makes the most beautiful sound ever. The sound of all four elements—earth, sky, water, fire, death as well as life. When I lower it from my lips, the sound seems to hang in the air.

The Rinpoche pokes his head in the room. He looks at me, then the two men look at each other.

His first note, says the Disciplinarian. Auspicious.

For once I truly feel I am the Servant to the Redeemer Who Sounds the Conch in the Darkness. I lift the mighty shell again, its surface intricately carved with small swastikas, one of our many symbols for peace and auspiciousness, the word *swastika* from the Sanskrit, meaning "conducive to well-being." The swastika is almost three thousand years old. Here in the East, this holy symbol still retains its original meaning despite its vile corruption in the west. Its true meaning continues to shine in the hearts of those who walk in love. May all sentient beings find a path over the water!

In the Auspicious Month

May arrives. The *puja* begins at five in the morning. The youngest novices prepare the temple, lighting the butter lamps and filling the silver offering bowls with water, in some cases with soda. Flowers adorn the statues of the Buddha and the deities, fruits meant to remind us of impermanence. All week we make small figures sculpted from *tsampa,* a dough made from flour and water and then left to harden in the sun before being painted with bright colors. Later today a rich man is driving out from the capital with his wife and daughter, who plans to attend business school in London. As we are in the auspicious month, the month when the Buddha achieves enlightenment, it is the most propitious time to schedule a *puja*. Monasteries all over the Buddhist world make the majority of their money in the month of May.

In May, many Buddhists give up eating meat and refrain from intimate knowledge of the body during daylight hours. They visit as many temples as they can and make offerings to the Buddha. They try to argue less with their loved ones, to be more compassionate to strangers. If they die in this month, it is said they can achieve much merit for their next incarnation.

This is Mun's first *puja* on behalf of a patron since becoming the Redeemer Who Sounds the Conch in the Darkness. It is his job to lead us in our chants, which begin at sun-up and last until late afternoon. There are occasional breaks, for milk tea, for juice, for lunch, for studies and napping, the monks coming and going all day as needed though only Mun and the Rinpoche are expected to be seated each time we are in session.

The Disciplinarian wanders up and down the rows. As he originally hails from China, he is filled with tales of Confucius, stories of the power of surrendering to the Way. Throughout the temple we sit on scarlet cushions placed on low wooden benches. The higher one sits, the higher one's station. When people come in from the countryside to chant with us, they sit directly on the floor. A few western tourists wander in and sit in chairs. So much time spent sitting with crossed legs is difficult for them.

Because we are reestablishing an abandoned monastery, in Yatuu Gol there are fewer than fifteen of us from Mongolia. The Rinpoche supplements our numbers by bringing in novices and ordained monks from other countries. Many are from Tibet via India. My favorites are from the tiny mountain kingdom of Bhutan, which some say is the happiest place in the world. The Bhutanese do indeed seem to be filled with an inner bliss. They often walk around with betel leaves stuffed in their cheeks, which eventually turn their teeth black.

Most monasteries are teaching monasteries like Yatuu Gol. Our youngest novice is only six, the oldest twenty-seven. In the days before the Soviets, families send their sons to the monasteries for an education. Back then it is one of the few places where a child can learn to read.

Eight months in and I love everything there is about monastic life. I love the learning, the sitting for hours among my brothers and developing a strong sense of calm. I like helping out where I'm needed. I like the nights when we are allowed to watch movies on the monastery's only TV with an attached VCR. I like thinking about my consciousness and how it is connected to the consciousness of every other sentient being on the planet.

Conversely my twin is growing pale. This time of year we would normally be outside for most of the day. There would be games played on horseback, nights filled with singing. My brother is living proof man's happiness lies out on the vacant steppe. Here, the only singing we do is chanting, though one monk likes to wander the monastery grounds in his free time with headphones on, belting out the song from *Titanic*.

The rich man and his family arrive an hour before lunch. I can tell it is them because, when they enter, the wife is holding two shopping bags filled with *tögrög*. It is mostly in small denominations so that it can be easily distributed among us. This is how the *sangha* makes our spending money. We are each paid to participate in this *puja* meant to increase the good fortune for this girl who is to study abroad. Already we are eager for day's end when we are to receive ₮2,000 each. Over time, we can save up and buy things. Because we are only a few hours from Ulaanbaatar, we can get our hands on almost anything.

Mun watches as the man and his family enter the temple. They are dressed in traditional clothing, but the fabrics have a sheen to them, a richness, brocade like the kind Mun wears at his ordination. The man's boots are also of the best quality. The girl herself wears a pair of western cowboy boots with her *deel*. She is quite beautiful. Some of the older novices openly stare.

We get up and march around the altar once more, each of us holding a joss stick in our hands. Then it is time for lunch.

My brother is required to eat lunch with these people who are paying the monastery a huge sum of money. I also sit with him and the Rinpoche and eat a simple meal of *khuushuur*, dumplings fried in mutton fat. My brother quizzes the girl about her upcoming trip. He doesn't hide his interest in her travels. He wants to know how much it costs, how one obtains a passport, the necessary visas issued, her budget. Silently I remind my twin of what Övöö would say in this situation: the rich can eat carrots or candles, it's not our concern. Finally the Rinpoche intervenes and moves the conversation along. But my brother sits back, content. I feel the fire within him building like a bomb that's about to go off and destroy everything.

Do Not Let My Brother Die

Summer passes, then autumn and on into year's end. We are in the dead of our second winter. Late afternoon and it's already dark. The day moon like a vestigial bone in the sky. Namrut goes outside in only his robe and fills a small zinc basin with snow using his bare hands. Namrut whom the novices declare to be part yak, impervious to temperature. All week out in the sun the air never warms above -20°C. Most days it is faster to melt snow over an open flame than break the ice on the surface of the well. For morning ablutions the *sangha* washing themselves with icicles. Taking the icy points and rubbing them along the crowns of our heads. From the kitchen I watch as Namrut hefts the tub onto his bare shoulder. He carries it inside the same way he carries the skinned body of a goat in summer, the animal leaving a bloody print on the side of his face where he holds it firmly against his neck to keep it from slipping.

Nights I can hear the snow accumulating in the courtyard, the sound of flakes compounding, universes being born and falling dead, the monks floating wordlessly through Yatuu Gol, each of us deep in prayer. Mun has a fever, the birthmark on the back of his neck hot as any flame. The Disciplinarian's thumb and index finger swaddled in bandages where the old monk's skin instantly blisters after touching it.

Everywhere there is talk of death, though during that interminable week we are asked to speak only when necessary. In the hours of silence, everywhere I hear the language of death. The altar is kept lit at all hours, the offerings refreshed daily. As novices, we are told to lose ourselves, to go as deeply as we can in praying for the salvation of all sentient beings and for our brother the Redeemer.

I follow Namrut as he carries the tub of snow into my brother's chambers. The room is dark, unbearably hot, though two of the windows are open. At my brother's bedside I hold a silver bowl in my hands and watch as Namrut dishes some of the snow into it, then lays a wet towel over the top. With the Rinpoche's help he takes the bowl from me and positions it under Mun so that the back of Mun's neck rests on the snow. Instantly steam curls up around the sides of my brother's head. The sound as if someone throws water on hot coals. Within seconds the bowl is full of lukewarm water. Namrut fills it again.

When we enter Yatuu Gol in the previous year, the fire in my brother's pupils brings to mind the color you see in the eyes of some animals, mostly raptors, birds that need vision to the seventh power in order to spot their prey. A golden yet fiery hue. A smoldering, embers that lie quietly among the ashes. Now one year later the few times he opens his eyes there is less and less molten gold. His eyes turning into dark pools of stagnant water, like mine.

Colds and infections are not unusual at Yatuu Gol. We are a community of all different ages living in close quarters. Viruses race through our ranks with nothing to stop them—no vaccines, no antibiotics, our diets scarce in vegetables and fruits. Occasionally when a cough is rampant among us, one of the older monks takes on the work of compounding herbs into tiny brown pellets that taste like dirt. Depending on your symptoms, sometimes you have to chew them, though just as often the monk boils them in water, then soaks cotton balls in the scalding liquid so that he might press the soggy cotton to the corresponding energy vectors on your body, the compresses so hot they leave marks.

On the third night of his sickness, Mun's breathing begins to grow ragged. The Rinpoche decides it is time. Because Yatuu Gol is too remote to house a telephone, in the morning I set out on foot with Namrut for the fifteen-kilometer trek into Bor-Urt to phone the monastery in Ulaanbaatar. I am chosen because I am born in the region and know how to navigate in winter, the snow erasing the few landmarks that would normally orient a traveler.

We leave at sun-up and arrive back well past midnight. Namrut breaks through the snow with each footfall, always struggling onward. There are times when the whole world is an icy sheet, a whiteout, like being trapped inside a snow globe.

The whole way there and back I am praying to the Green Tara. Do not let my brother die, I intone. In the weeks to come, I discover that my twin resents the fact that it is me sent to phone for help. That the world once again calls on his twin to save him.

When the Red Horse Stops Running

During his sickness I sleep in his chambers. Nights I am tangled up in his dreams. Each time I slip into our shared world, without fail he is dreaming of horses, the earth itself turning thanks to the power of a red horse that forever runs along the horizon, like a treadmill, the horse's feet powering the revolutions of the planet. I know this horse is my brother's *hema,* his wind horse, the animal that energizes his being, what in the old shamanistic tradition is believed to be a person's essence. I know that when the red horse stops running, my twin could die.

Four days after the call is made from Bor-Urt an old Soviet jeep pulls up at the monastery gates, its headlights sliding over the 108 snow-covered *stupa* surrounding Yatuu Gol, the ring of *stupa* like a mountain range hemming us in. Two figures climb out.

There is a rumor circulating that a traditional medicine man arrives. This doesn't require medicine, says the Rinpoche. Nights in Mun's dreams I witness the red horse's coat building a lather, foam issuing at its mouth. And so I agree with the Rinpoche's assessment. Something is blocking Mun's *hema,* his wind horse struggling to stay ahead of the turning earth.

One of the monks who exits the jeep is an old man. The other is a young monk, his frame slight as if he is still a boy though I am told he is fully ordained. I assume the old man is the one the Rinpoche summons, but once the ceremony starts, I realize my mistake.

Every member of the *sangha* is called on to participate. We chant for more than two hours. Incense fills the temple. The chants are different. We read them from the folded books the pair brings with them, the pages yellowed and delicate. It becomes evident fairly quickly that we are trying to invoke something, that we are seeking to bring something that doesn't exist into existence. The old monk from the jeep walks among us, pouring mentholated waters into our cupped palms. We sip it, then dribble the few remaining drops on our heads. We feel ourselves cool. The energy in the room building. A sea of red rocking itself into frenzy. The long horns blaring, the *tingsha* ringing, the drums booming until our blood courses through us to their rhythm. Even when I am not playing it, I can feel the conch in my lap emitting a deep humming sound.

Mun is lying on a golden cushion at the head of the assembly. The young monk who travels to be here sits by his side staring at him the way one sometimes stares into the flame of a candle without blinking. Finally the muscles in the monk's back begin to ripple. He begins to shake his head from side to side. Something about his movements reminds me of a panther. Some animal of immense power that keeps said power contained until the one percent of its life when it needs it.

The monk is a medium, one who channels an oracle, an ancient spirit that protects and guides. We in the Gelug sect of Buddhism have a long tradition of consulting oracles in times of need. In 1950, it is the Nechung Oracle, the official state oracle of Tibet, who on several occasions counsels the young Dalai Lama to flee His country after the Chinese invasion, but the young leader doesn't obey immediately. Only after the last consultation, the medium flinging himself around the chamber as the oracle fills his body, does His Holiness finally acquiesce, dressing as a soldier and letting Himself be led out of His beloved country and over the Himalayas along trails used by herders. The local people bowing to Him along the route though His counselors try to keep His leaving a secret.

Here at Yatuu Gol, hour after hour the energy grows exponentially. The music intensifying. The incense thickening until I can hardly see. Then the young monk leaps up off his cushion and throws himself into the air. Others rush forward to grab his arms. He snarls like an animal and fights them. Eventually they work him into his costume: a series of brocade robes adorned with gold and precious stones, on his shoulders a wooden harness that supports four banners that stream behind him as he runs to and fro. Last, an enormous headdress is tied on his head, the thing more than a meter tall and weighted with jewels. Anchored in the center of the headdress is a circular mirror big as a man's face. It flashes light around the room. It is said that the headdress weighs more than fifteen kilos, the many splendid robes an additional ten, and that if the oracle is not in a true state of trance, the headdress could break his neck. Only a being in a state of possession can bear the weight of such a helm.

In the case of the Nechung Oracle, the medium channels the spirit of Dorje Drakden, a warrior who back in the mists of time is charged with protecting the line of the Dalai Lama. Here I don't know what spirit this monk channels, but the way he bandies himself about with no concern for his physical being, the power of the possession is evident.

The monk runs around the room. He spits. He claws. His voice deep as thunder. Though I know better, I would say he is possessed by a demon. One of the younger novices begins to cry. The oracle hisses out a series of unintelligible sounds. Eventually he collapses. Monks rush forward to relieve him of the neck-breaking headdress. He is carried to a room where it takes him two full days to recover. His body convulsing until it eventually quiets. The old man who travels with the oracle translates. The oracle speaks in an ancient tongue of Tibet. It is a language few people know.

The old man turns and speaks with the Rinpoche. The Redeemer Who Sounds the Conch in the Darkness does not know where he comes from, the old man says. He does not know the true history of his family. Knowing it may give his wind horse strength.

The Rinpoche nods and bows deeply. And so it is my brother and I come to learn the secret history of our grandfather.

The World Is a Mystifying Place

The Rinpoche takes a deep breath. This is what I know, he says. We are in my brother's chambers. The walls painted with scenes from the life of the Buddha as well as images of deities, many of them wrathful in appearance, their mouths filled with teeth, their skins all sorts of fantastic colors. Outside, the snow is falling fast, each flake a light in the billion-billion-armed cosmos. When we are younger, our grandfather would tell us stories of blue wolves and deer, a mountain with the power of the world steeped in its sides. The room takes on the same hue as those nights, a fire burning in the stove.

My brother is lying on the floor on a *leitur*. He is covered with blankets. His forehead draped with a wet cloth. Today he does not open his eyes. Namrut carefully pouring broth into his mouth, most of which runs down his chin. Namrut claims that at the exact moment when the oracle falls into his trance, steam rises off the skin of my brother.

Your grandfather is born in Khentii, just a few hundred kilometers from God Mountain, some years after the birth of the communist Mongolian People's Republic, says the Rinpoche. The old monk's eyes gleam. For the first few years it is easy to forget that we are a new country, he says. We are like the mouse that hangs itself for the state. What happens in Ulaanbaatar is so far away from the lives most of us live out in the grasslands, out on the steppes. The politics of the capital are inconsequential to us, and vice versa.

Then the Rinpoche's eyes harden in the firelight. I am the last *tulku* discovered before the purges, he says. I am found when I am three years old. I remember my ordination day. There are monks from Tibet, from all over. I remember the smell of the butter lamps, the butter rendered from the summer milk of yaks who feed on wildflowers. The purges start when I am seven. I am living with my brothers in Gandan Tegchenling in the capital. One day, soldiers come and tell us we have to leave. The soldiers are Mongolian. Many of them are only teenagers. The *zud* is hard that year. Many animals die. There is famine. War massing in various regions of the faraway world. I remember seeing a snowy field covered in blood. The look of the blood on the ice in the winter sun. Monks being shot, clubbed. The sound of the Heart Sutra filling the air. I remember walking unfathomable distances in the snow. I remember someone carrying me.

I am the youngest Precious One. I am a child. I am saved, he says. An old herder and his wife take me in and raise me among their eight children. Your grandfather is the youngest of those eight. He becomes my brother. Though he is a few years younger than I am, nights I teach him to read, I teach him the chants as we lie together under the blankets. I am a herder like the rest of the family, but I teach your grandfather what I know of Buddhism. His own grandmother remembers much of the Religion of the Yellow and would periodically sit us down and light a candle, and together the three of us would make our prostrations, praying that our enemies and every living being attain peace.

Your grandfather excels at learning. When he is a teenager, he is sent to the capital to study. He works hard, gets a job working for the government. For many years, he prospers until eventually he becomes a government minister. One summer your grandfather is sent to China on government business. When he comes back, he tells me he's seen it. There are always rumors circulating of its existence. A text written for the noble Mongolian family during the days of Chinggis Khaan. A secret history of the Mongols. But the Soviets are afraid of it, afraid lest it stir up nationalist sentiment, and so for years and years it is only a rumor, something scholars talk of, an ancient text in Old Mongolian originally written phonetically in Uighur script, one of the languages of Central Asia, and then transcribed into Chinese. Under the Soviets it remains banned in Mongolia.

Your grandfather does the unthinkable. The next time he travels abroad, he brings a handwritten copy of it back from China. It is the only copy in Mongolia. He doesn't read Chinese. Underground he begins to amass a group of scholars to work on the text, pairing those who can read the script with others who still understand the ancient tongue. When Stalin dies, there is a period of cultural thawing. It looks safe to bring the research out into the light. But within a few years, another round of purges begin. Scholars are kicked out of the university. A man is hacked to death with an ax just for suggesting that the warrior banner of Chinggis Khaan be placed on a commemorative stamp.

One day soldiers come for your grandfather. Someone, under the pain of torture, denounces his work on *The Secret History of the Mongols*. Your grandfather is sent to a gulag in Siberia for ten years. His family assumes he is dead.

A decade after his arrest, he comes back from Russia an old man with a deep limp and a mouthful of broken teeth. He goes back to living a life on the grasslands. He starts over with nothing. In this life he is a herder, a government minister, a prisoner, then a herder again. He is forty years old when your father is born. Because of the work of your grandfather, today there are copies of *The Secret History of the Mongols* all over the world. It is the history of our people. The Mongol people come from a line of warriors. Your grandfather pays a heavy price. If I know anything, I know he would pay it again.

The Rinpoche's watch begins to beep. The world is a mystifying place, he says. I don't see your grandfather again until I find you at his deathbed. His watch falls silent.

For the first time all week my twin takes a deep breath in his sleep, a breath that fills his belly and seems to run all the way down to his toes. He sighs and rolls onto his side like one contented in a pleasant dream.

We Walk Among the Bones of the Ancients

A Pile of Bones Lies in the Corner

The Altai Mountains loom a day and a half behind us, a line of black teeth still visible on the edge of the world. We are headed into the southern reaches of the country, into the endless ocean of sand and bones, to see the final candidate. But rather than drive directly from the Altai into the Gobi, we make a slight detour. The tire ruts we now follow in the grass are well trod. This means many travelers follow this route. True, such a detour could add hundreds of kilometers to our journey, but here, everything is relative. A hundred kilometers on previously traveled land can go smoother than ten kilometers on virgin earth. The more direct route would take us through uninhabited regions where any unforeseen troubles can be disastrous. Even though we travel out of our way, it is a safer option. I am glad Mun chooses the more conservative path. Perhaps my twin is maturing.

An hour before nightfall we arrive at a ghostly spot. There are no paved streets, the dirt black, volcanic. The whole outpost covers a single city block, the buildings gray and blocky and built in the old Soviet style of right angles and squares. It is as if the heart of some industrialized city is picked up and dropped in the middle of nowhere. A pair of black boots hangs from a fence. A child's wagon lies on its side. A statue of two workers in headscarves stretch their arms up to the sky, but there is no plaque, no writing.

In the middle of the square is a tree. A chair hangs in its branches, the kind you might find in a school. The chair looks inviting, as if you can climb on up and take a seat.

It's just a mining town or old military post, says Mun.

There are abandoned outposts like this all over Mongolia, old towns built by the Russians and then junked, the landscape dotted with their ghostliness. Because it is an hour to sundown, we make camp in an empty building with no doors or windows. Inside, the floor is covered in soil, a carpet of weeds blanketing the space. A pile of bones lies in a corner; on a wall, things written in what looks like gibberish. It's uncanny to see letters I can read but words that are foreign. Both Russia and Mongolia use the same Cyrillic alphabet, but our languages are different.

The building shades our fire from the endless winds that meet no resistance out on the long plains. Half the roof is gone so that the smoke travels up into the night. I feel like the world is turned inside out, my viscera slung on the outside of my body. Everything is inside that should be outside, a whole ecosystem blanketing the walls.

Little Bat tears apart an old desk with his bare hands and feeds the wood to the flames. Mun sits across from Uncle. In the silence, I feel a sudden fissuring inside my brother, a sinkhole opening in him that he must scramble to fill.

Isn't it weird how only Tibetan Buddhists believe in the reincarnation of their lamas, he says. He speaks as if this thought just occurs to him. I feel myself growing angry. Between the two of us his skepticism is one thing, but to talk this way in front of the Lotus of the Deep is another matter. Stop, I think. I think it so hard Mun shudders, his head filling with my rage. But he continues. No other Buddhist sect hunts down their reincarnations, he says, just you guys.

I know where this is headed. Once at Yatuu Gol, Mun encounters an old monk from Nepal. The monk tells Mun ancient stories of great estates that prominent monks amass through their teachings. Gradually their followers gift them with treasures. In the beginning, these rich monks bequeath their estates to a nephew or a family member. But over time, the monasteries begin to institute a process by which to discover the reincarnations of these wealthy holy men. Essentially it begins as a way for a monastery to keep an estate under its control.

As if to say, look—here is the same man born again in the flesh of this child. His wealth belongs to this child, who is one of us.

In the firelight, Uncle's face is a map of shadows. Yes, existence is quite a racket, he says merrily. In among the grime something goes scurrying from darkness to darkness.

Do I Really Fly on a Magic Saddle Across the Himalayas?

Don't you ever doubt, Mun whispers.

I am off by myself leafing through an old magazine I pull out of the debris. I keep another magazine folded over it, the outer one a nature magazine in Russian. Pictures of mountains and crystalline lakes, people in traditional dress. The magazine I am really looking at contains things I am never to see in this world. In one photo, two women lie inverted on top of each other, each woman straining with her tongue to lick the other's darkness. I feel myself stir. Nobody looks my way. There is a lesson here, in the fact that the earth doesn't open up and swallow me whole, but I am not sure I am reading it correctly.

Do I ever doubt, says Uncle. He smooths the folds in his robe. Of course, he says. My lineage goes back hundreds of years. Am I really the man who defeats the Chinese in 1572? Do I really fly on a magic saddle across the Himalayas at the side of Guru Padmasambhava, the two of us leaving our impressions on the side of a mountain where we sit one afternoon to drink milk tea? Imagine, he chuckles, bum prints hundreds of years old!

Mun doesn't smile.

It's different for me, says Uncle. I'm found quite young. I'm barely three years old. I don't remember another way. My whole life people prostrating themselves before me, touching my forehead to theirs.

Don't you ever think of leaving, asks Mun.

Uncle takes a deep breath. The tradition is different in Bhutan where I'm born and raised, he says. Buddhism in Bhutan and the Dalai Lama's Buddhism in Tibet aren't exactly the same. One is the Drukpa Kagyu tradition, the other Gelug. They are similar enough that we move back and forth through each other's worlds. Thanks to my parents' wishes, I'm not taken away and raised in Tibet as most *tulku* are back then. I stay in the Land of the Thunder Dragon near my people. I come of age in a little mountaintop monastery a day's walk up into the hills outside Punakha. I live with other monks, many of them my own age. The Principal is a kind man who understands that Bhutan cannot remain isolated forever.

In his right hand, Uncle works a set of prayer beads. The way he nimbly slides them along, I wonder if they help him think. One day we receive word that one of the royal wives is coming to visit, he says. At our monastery there's a holy relic that is said to cure any sickness imaginable if one only holds it in one's palm. No one knows if the royal consort is sick, or if she's simply out on holiday. One month later she arrives with a small retinue. She is robust and in unbelievable health after walking all the way from the capital, Thimphu, a journey of ten days.

But that isn't what you want to know, says Uncle. You want to know if I ever consider leaving. He stares into the fire as if for clarity.

Pen, Butterfly, Milk

The prayer beads click in Uncle's hands as if time itself is being marked. The queen consort stays one week in our monastery, he says. It's only a week, but as we are taught, time is an illusion. There's a young western woman with the queen. Uncle winks. She's from Canada on the other side of the world. She speaks both Dzongkha and Tshangla, has a wide-open smile, freckles vast as the stars. It feels odd to say it now, but until her, I never see a westerner, the color of her skin the same pale pink like a sheep if you remove its hair. All week I follow her around, this westerner in her early twenties. She teaches me my first English words. Pen, butterfly, milk. She says she's from a small town on a great and icy plain.

One afternoon she and I are walking through a nearby hamlet. The farmers are out working their paddies, at four thousand meters the main crop rice. It's a staple of the Bhutanese diet. We eat it with cheese, with small green chilies. In the sound of Uncle's voice, I can hear his happiness at the memory. Something about the farmlands of Bhutan always makes my heart settle, he says. Seeing the women with their short-cropped hair, a baby often strapped to their backs, and the men in the traditional *gho* belted at the waist. Yes, it's true, back then it's the national costume—it's mandatory that everyone wears it. It's the same with the houses—in Bhutan, all buildings must be built in the traditional style with the painted scrollwork, the white walls. Everything in harmony. It's what makes the country so happy—everyone like everyone else.

That afternoon the Abbot is with us, the senior monk who discovers me when I'm a child, Uncle explains. We're walking toward an ancient *stupa* Carol wants to see. It's the temple of the Divine

Madman. In Bhutan but especially around Punakha people paint giant phalluses on the outer walls of their houses. Sometimes they nail wooden penises on their roofs. Uncle pauses a moment to let this fact sink in. The temple of the Divine Madman houses an unusual relic, he says. Carol wants to be blessed by it.

I look up from my magazine. I know something of the Divine Madman. The Divine Madman brings Buddhism to Bhutan from Tibet. He uses unorthodox ways to enlighten the people, mostly women. He has sex with them, saying why shouldn't sexual activity be a tool of enlightenment? His penis is referred to as the Thunderbolt of Flaming Wisdom.

In the temple we're headed to, says Uncle, there's a small *stupa* built on the spot where it is said the Divine Madman once overpowers a demon with his penis and traps it in stone. There are a million stories of the Divine Madman's sexual prowess taming the powers of darkness.

We walk through the neighboring paddies and up the long hill to the monastery. Prayer flags adorn the way, a giant Bodhi tree at the top. The Abbot finds a young monk wandering the grounds memorizing his chants and sends him to bring the Principal of the monastery to us. We three are already in the altar room admiring the beautiful *thangka* when the Principal arrives. He looks startled at Carol's presence, a white woman wearing the traditional *kira,* but when she greets him in perfect Dzongkha, he nods and walks toward the altar where the relic is kept. Carefully he takes it off its stand. The bow is said to be the bow the Divine Madman carries with him when he travels from Tibet. Tied to it is a ten-inch wooden phallus decorated with silver and bone. The Abbot instructs Carol to kneel. The Principal pours camphor water in her cupped palm. She sips it, pours the remaining drops on her hair. Then the Principal touches the top of her head with the phallus.

But she giggles. Uncle smiles at the memory. She is being touched on the head by one of the most sacred objects in Bhutan and she giggles. With that laugh, I fall in love. I want to be with her always, says Uncle. She's twenty-two. I'm fifteen. I remember as if it happens yesterday.

There are others, says Uncle. A nun who lets me kiss her behind the altar. A laywoman who appears at my door one night with a bag filled with money, asking me to make her a mother. But Carol is the first to make my heart sing.

Uncle folds up his prayer beads and slips them somewhere in his robe. You and I, he says, we don't choose this life. But the ones among us who thrive, like His Holiness, at some point, we do choose it. We choose it with every breath.

He looks through the fire and directly at my twin. But to answer your question, yes, I know what it is to doubt, he says. Imagine, I am a young monk from a country with no paved roads—today there are still no traffic lights in Bhutan. If you want to go anywhere, you have to walk. It can take a week to get where you're headed, but there's never any rush. The mountains, the forests, the rivers, the clouds that hover beside you as you walk, the land so high up, everywhere the beings of the sky like neighbors.

My brother is waiting to hear more about Uncle's crisis of faith, but Uncle rises, stretching his arms overhead as he moves off to find his sleeping bag. I struggle, I suffer, I move beyond suffering, from time to time I slip back into suffering, he says, yawning. This is the path.

In my dark and far-off corner I am no longer looking at the rich images of naked women that I hold in my hands. My stomach hurts, as if I eat too much food too quickly. I pull the unfinished letter addressed to the Rinpoche out of the folds in my robe. I reread what is written:

Esteemed Rinpoche, please know I have done everything in my power to serve you in a manner most befitting of one who wears the robe. But like a pond that is overgrown with moss, I find my heart growing turbid with doubt.

I take a pen from my pocket and add a single line, then fold the letter back up and once again hide it on my body. I finally stumble onto the heart of the matter. All night as I sleep the words burning into my skin.

I do not trust myself.

Here in the Dreamscape

Midnight and I am back in the garden. The silver hoofprints yet again leading onward to a river. The sound of music, of laughter, the smell of wildflowers garlanding the night air.

Two figures coupling by the riverbank. Many nights my dream self stands here watching the act unfold. But instead of the slow and steady movements of love, this time the man is driving himself into her, a hammer pounding a nail into stone, the woman doubled over in front of him like a four-legged animal, the man like an overseer, his hand pulling her long black hair as if riding a horse, yet when the woman cries out at the apex of the moment, her cry is one of pleasure and not of pain.

The two come apart. Together they lie in the grass. I walk right up to them. I want to know. It is only when the woman turns to face me that my heart stops. His arm lying across her naked breasts. The grasslands chirring around them. Even in the moonlight I cannot see his face in the tall grass, just his arm, a long dark scratch running up the skin. The woman grins at me, her teeth dark as if covered with blood. The four streams of the world shatter. I recognize them both, woman and lover, even in this moment of animalism, the woman with a dreamy quality in her eyes, like one who walks through puddles but remains dry, and the man and his forearm inked with words.

Then Saran is gone and the landscape is changed. My twin is walking toward me with a knife in his hand, the tattoo gleaming on his inner arm. I know that he intends to walk past me and out into the night. I cannot see into his mind, his inner eye a blazing field. All the same I know I must stop him. That to do what he is seeking to do can set his being on a dark path for eons.

Bazar is sleeping in the *ger* where we store food. My brother doesn't want to go to the monastery. He doesn't want to be the Redeemer Who Sounds the Conch in the Darkness. Here in the dreamscape he is eight years old, yet he looks as he does now, a grown man, his hair in braids. He doesn't want to be told that he exists on this earth before, that his life is not his own. I pick up my grandfather's old gun from the corner and race out into the night to stop him.

In the moonlight Mun is standing out in the open grasslands. He does not walk toward the *ger* where our guest lies sleeping. I know this is only a dream as all those years ago he does indeed turn toward that *ger* and I do indeed stop him. Here in the dreamscape, I train the gun on him anyway. We are standing in an endless field of grass, the whole world rippling. I feel him lift the burning sheet in his mind only to reveal a second burning sheet. I steady the gun.

I open my eyes just in time to see Saran pick something up off the floor. A bird wafts overhead. Sunlight pours though the ravaged ceiling. Though I am awake, it is as if I am back in the dream. I cannot tell her quickly enough. My mouth won't work. I watch her curiously handle the thing, which is rusty and cylindrical, wondering where to put it now that she holds it.

On the edge of my vision I see Little Bat rush forward, his shadow like a tree on the floor. Mun is sitting on his sleeping bag, eyes closed, his legs folded in the lotus position. His right hand moves hypnotically through the air as if ringing a bell. At first I don't realize what I am seeing. My brother is meditating.

The thing in Saran's hand is old, parts of it jammed in dangerous positions. Her turning it this way and that is enough to loosen the rust, to awaken the object to its true purpose. Then the inevitable happens. The sound somehow both sharp and dull, quick and echoing. In the enclosed space the noise crashes off the walls before floating up into the air. Saran begins to cry.

Mun is still sitting upright on his sleeping bag. Behind him a large hole is blasted in the wall, the hole right where his head would be if he is sleeping. The hole big enough for an animal to climb through.

Debris hangs in the air. My twin opens his eyes, wipes loose grit off himself. He remains eerily composed. For the second time in his life a gun is fired at him, and he is once again left unscathed. Today he is not meant to leave this world.

Uncle is sitting in his corner also in the lotus position. He isn't roused by the blast. Inside each of us there is another world we can access through one-pointed concentration. In that space we are untouchable. Everything is forever all right. Despite the blast, Uncle continues his meditation for another fifteen minutes before he opens his eyes, fully refreshed.

Grow Up!

The first hour in the Machine and the air as if burned. My twin and I do not speak. Saran sits between us with that mysterious smile sketched on her face. I think of my dream of the night before, his arm lying across her naked breasts, skin inked, and Saran with her normally shy smile frozen in a grotesque rictus.

Is it possible, or am I just imagining it?

My twin sits behind the wheel, the white earbuds sticking out of his ears like plugs. I imagine them holding in his brains, that if I pull one out, the contents of his head would follow. Mentally I hurl question after question at him—*nights do you sneak off to lie with her?*—but his thoughts remain ensconced behind a wall of fire stretching up beyond the clouds. The air in the car thick with our mental electricity. All I can sense behind the flames is an air of bemusement, an occasional phrase. *Grow up!*

I try to calm myself.

O Thou of Diamond Body
Whose wheel of speech benefits all beings,
If thou wish me to remain in life
Pray arise right now happiness.

How dare he? And us on this mission of faith. I remember my twin's first physical encounter, the woman's hands on his shoulder blades. How I can only imagine the numerous women that follow that first one. True, I have no proof except my dream, but dreams are often more real than reality.

And so we ride toward wherever the path is taking us. The Redeemer Who Sounds the Conch in the Darkness and his servant. All around us the silence as if ablaze.

Many of Us Are on Facebook

After a few hours, we hit a paved road, our first in almost two weeks. Large signs hang over the highway. It feels strange to be moving so smoothly over the earth, to not be jostled about. We drive into Kharkorin a few hours before noon. The modern town of Kharkorin has a main street with a few shops and cafés catering to tourists. We turn into a parking spot to stretch our legs and eat before heading out to the monastery. Mun pulls an inexpensive cell phone out of the glove compartment. He plugs it into the cigarette lighter and checks to see if he can get a signal.

Little Bat grabs his day bag out of the back of the Machine. From one of the bag's pockets Uncle produces an iPad. I see my brother eye it, can sense the sheepishness he feels at the inadequacy of his own device. Most monks have such things. I also have a phone, but it's back at Yatuu Gol. Many of us are on Facebook, some of us with hundreds, thousands, of friends. Mostly we talk with other monks at other monasteries, some in other countries. We chat about monastic life, food, the European Football League. I have friends in Bhutan, a monastery located in the mountains of Punakha not far from where Uncle is born. The monks there like to watch western movies. They love the American wrestler known as The Rock. One monk, named Sangha, posts more than fifty images of The Rock on his wall.

Uncle points toward a café that says it has internet service. Saran looks happy not to have to cook. The five of us saunter over and sit down at a table by the window. There are a handful of customers scattered around the room, most of them western tourists bathed in the light of their devices. Uncle takes my wrist in his hand and looks at my watch. Good timing, he says, then powers up his iPad. It takes some minutes for the miracle to occur. Everything about the way it transpires is utterly mundane—the tablet turning on, joining the network, then Uncle opening FaceTime and searching among his contacts. But when the miracle does occur, all the same I do not believe it. I wonder what would happen if these western tourists would just look up from their screens for one moment and glance our way. What would they see? An elderly monk speaking in Tibetan, chatty as any teenager. But in this case, the monk is talking with one of the lights of the world, His Holiness, the 14th Dalai Lama.

Would you like to say hello, Uncle asks. The image of His Holiness fills the screen. *Tashi delek,* He booms cheerfully. *May only auspicious things come into your environment.* Uncle holds the tablet out so that we are all in the picture. Little Bat smiles and waves. Among the three of us who have never met Him, only Saran maintains her composure. Of my brother and I, together our hearts beating fast as any schoolgirl's, the sound filling the world.

Where Marco Polo Once Walks Among the Nations

Even after the two men say their goodbyes and hang up, my heart still thunders through the rest of our meal. For the moment my anger at my twin's lasciviousness is washed away. May I always remember this moment when the 14th Living Incarnation of Avalokiteshvara, the Buddha of Compassion, wishes me *tashi delek!* I can feel a difference in my twin, a looseness spreading through his being.

After lunch we drive out to what is once the center of the world. All around us the plain is flat and expansive, large and utterly empty. Erdene Zuu Monastery is the oldest in Mongolia. It is built in the 1500s and then abandoned during the Soviet era. The white wall mounted with 108 *stupa* rings the monastery, each like a snowcapped mountain. And just north of the wall lies all that remains of the ancient capital, Karakorum, the place where Marco Polo once walks among the nations of the world. When the wind blows, dust spires up in whirlwinds. The emptiness feels planetary.

We don't tell anyone we're coming. Stealthily we pull up in the visitors' lot like a pack of sheep wranglers in the night. Even if we want to tell someone that a high-ranking counselor of His Holiness is making an unannounced visit, who would we tell? Somehow I would have to notify the Rinpoche at Yatuu Gol, who would have to inform someone, perhaps in Ulaanbaatar, who would maybe call someone in Dharamshala, who would then try to raise someone here.

Instead we walk around the perimeter of the monastery. A small sign points to an exit, saying this way to the turtles. We follow the path a hundred meters beyond the monastery walls. Already Saran is standing beside one of them. This is all that remains of Karakorum, the thirteenth-century center of civilization. Two stone turtles that once decorate one of the courtyards. There is a lesson here for anyone who chooses to listen. Pride. Impermanence. Desire. The thirst for legacy.

Mun is here countless times with tours and yet this is his first time as a tourist. The connection to this place surges within my brother. I don't understand his preoccupation with a man who bloodies the steppes more than eight hundred years ago. This pride seems like the very act of clinging. Övöö also spends a part of his adulthood obsessing over the great Khaan, and it costs our grandfather everything.

Then my brother opens his mind to me. Educate yourself, Mun thinks, and suddenly I am awash in his knowledge:

This Is His Millennium

They say he is born with a blood clot in his fist. Like my brother and me, the stars predict his birth. As a child, he kills a half brother to claim his place at the head of his first small band of warriors. He eventually goes on to conquer the world. His empire is as large as the continent of Africa. In modern terms his realm covers an area of more than thirty countries with more than three billion inhabitants. His offspring found dynasties around the globe including the Yuan in China, the shahs in Iran, the Mughals in India. It is said that one out of every twenty males on earth carries his DNA. Karakorum is his legacy though he never lives to see it in all its splendor.

In 1253 William of Rubruck, a Franciscan monk traveling from western Europe, makes his way across the steppes that stretch from Hungary to Manchuria. Today in Hungary you can still find horsemen who gallop upright on wooden saddles as they shoot arrows while racing along at fifty kilometers an hour. From his letters home, we can ascertain that William of Rubruck is not overly impressed with Karakorum. Unlike western Europe, the Mongol Empire is not interested in amassing treasure. Chinggis Khaan is not a leader who collects loot and builds monuments. Rather he is a man interested in ideas, which last longer than booty.

He launches the first international postal system. He strengthens the trade route along the Silk Road and establishes the largest free-trade zone the world has ever seen. He creates the concept of diplomatic immunity that allows ambassadors of nations, even those he is at war with, to visit his capital without fear of retribution. He dismantles the old aristocratic system and institutes a process of promotion based on merit and loyalty rather than birth. He allows religious freedom through his empire, each nation free to worship as it pleases, though the Eternal Blue Sky rules over all. In Karakorum, William of Rubruck can walk past Buddhist temples, mosques, Nestorian churches, shamans and animalists, Zoroastrian fire worshippers, and countless other forms of worship.

Legend has it there is a golden tree crafted by a Parisian prisoner of war named Guillaume Bouchier. It is one of the wonders of the city. The tree is reported to serve different libations—*airag,* mead, wine—which one can pour by pulling on various branches. Like the tree, Chinggis Khaan brings together distant and diverse cultures. Before the Mongol Empire, China doesn't know Europe exists and vice versa. He helps spread scientific data and art, combining Chinese gunpowder with western iron to create the world's first fusible arms.

The Khaan's army revolutionizes siege warfare. No wall can keep him out. When he reaches western Europe, he finds the region poorer than he expects. He turns around and returns home.

Our grandfather Övöö is imprisoned for his research into the great Khaan. During the Soviet era, the government tries to suppress the memory and achievements of Chinggis Khaan, claiming he is a monstrous overlord. The Soviets are afraid that the memory of the Khaan might lead to the destruction of their union. If Mongolian national pride is allowed to be fed by the accomplishments of Chinggis Khaan, the people of Mongolia might rise up and throw the Soviets out, sending a signal to Russia's other satellites that it's open season on Moscow. And so men like Övöö, who simply want to search for historical artifacts about the Khaan, are fired from university positions, jailed, sent to Siberia. As a nation we are taught that the Khaan is a stain on the Mongolian people. The western view of him as a bloodthirsty barbarian wins out.

Centuries after Chinggis Khaan's death my brother wears his hair braided in a traditional style. The Khaan and all that he accomplishes lives on. Though I am one who knows little of the world, I do know that this is his millennium. Global networks spreading ideas from country to country at the speed of light. There is nothing barbarian about this.

Everything Works Itself Out in Its Own Way

The sky is just beginning to darken. After driving all day, we are back on unpaved roads. Technically we are in the Gobi, but it doesn't look the way I imagine.

It's the biggest desert in Asia, says Mun. Most of it's exposed rock, but where we're headed, there'll be sand dunes just like in the Sahara.

Yes, says Uncle. It is what we call a rain-shadow desert. He sits looking out the window at the darkening plain. The Himalayas drive moisture up to a great height, he says, and the Gobi sits in the shadow of the Himalayas. The rain doesn't come down here but farther away over Southeast Asia. In a way, it's a metaphor. I feel my twin's confusion compound with my own. Displacement, says Uncle. Everything works itself out in its own way in its own time. Perhaps not where you would expect, but eventually.

Silently I ponder this. Everywhere great outcroppings of rock like heralds guarding the earth.

Who wants to take a shower, Mun says. None of us respond. It is almost two weeks since we properly bathe, which is not unusual when one lives out on the steppe. My guess is it is my twin who is accustomed to regularly bathing, Mun now saddled with the habits of city living. Well, we're going, he says.

Thirty minutes after we stop and make camp, the five of us walk a kilometer in the last dregs of daylight to a spot in the middle of the desert. The landscape looks utterly empty, like walking on a red moon, then we crest a dune, and the world changes. A sprawling complex appears nestled in the sands. And the luxury! Everything made of stone and blond wood, glass and chrome. It's as if we are stepping straight out of Mongolia. People walk the grounds in bathrobes, westerners with small white buds in their ears, many of them carrying bottles of water, zazen pillows tucked under their arms. Little Bat stumbles around, amazed. I can tell that he doesn't know what to think. We pass a cafeteria, groups seated at round tables of ten, everyone eating, their plates piled with more greens than I eat in the past year.

Everywhere the sound of bare feet padding across hardwood, the sound of air being recirculated, the temperature like floating in a warm broth. It's a meditation center, Mun whispers. People from all over the world come here to cleanse themselves on the edge of the Gobi. For a fee, they let travelers like us come use the facilities, then it's back out to the desert for us.

I notice a group of people with deep tans, sunburned lips, sitting around a table. Mun sees someone he knows, another guide, and goes bounding over. See you later, he says.

Our camp is a little more than a kilometer away among the rock and sand. The sun is down, the night dark, the showers heavenly. When I come out, Saran is standing by the gift shop.

Mun is off with his friend, she says, and the others are already heading back.

Inwardly I smile at the fact that she waits for me. Shall we, I say. And so we set out across the desert.

Two Notes Spiraling Up into the Dark

This area of the Gobi looks like what I imagine a desert should look like, the dunes vast as an ocean of sand. The wind is chilly. I pull my robe tighter around myself. After twenty minutes, I realize I have no idea where we're going. Behind us the meditation center looks like an oasis. In the other direction, distant lights shine in the desert, but which one is ours? Saran walks serenely by my side. We walk and walk, the night deepening all around us. I realize she would follow me to the ends of the earth without question.

Finally I concede it. I think we're lost, I say.

We stop and look around. The lights don't seem to be getting any closer. I know this feeling from growing up out in the grasslands. In a place with no man-made landmarks, it is difficult to orient oneself. I imagine the two of us wandering all night over the desert plain, then with the morning sun realizing we are within feet of our camp.

What should we do, I ask. I try to imagine what Mun would do. Would he stop and wait to be found? No, never. An image of him lying with his arm across Saran's naked breasts comes to mind. No, he would wander all night, like a lost sheep. Wander and never admit it. All the while claiming he is just where he wants to be.

Then I hear a note rising over a nearby dune. Someone is throat singing. The two notes spiraling up into the dark, weaving themselves together. We continue on. In the distance I see a fire burning, animals shackled in the darkness. Figures appear.

Uncle is sitting beside Little Bat. Both are holding a bowl in their hands. Little Bat sits on a blanket. He is the one singing. I listen to him accompany himself. One melody like thunder on a distant plain. The other a small yellow bird flitting through a sunbeam. Miraculously when he throat sings, producing two notes at the same time, his voice sounds whole, smooth as water on ice.

But this isn't our camp, I say.

It's a good sign, says Uncle.

A child, a boy, something about his skin not right, wanders out of a nearby tent and offers me a bowl of milk tea. The boy has no color, is all light. In the morning it all makes sense.

The World's Largest Dinosaur Graveyard

In the desert night Mun never finds us, though truthfully he never looks. Early this morning Uncle texts him—incredibly there is cell service out here in the middle of nowhere. One of the westerners explains that the desert is good for signals, that they can travel hundreds of kilometers unimpeded. When Mun stumbles into this camp, it is obvious he is still feeling the effects of his night. I feel my head pound, then quickly I imagine a snowstorm raging between us in order to keep my twin's night of drinking at bay. Still, all day I feel a slight throbbing like a rainstorm off in the distance.

My brother is surprised he doesn't know this place. Who are these people, he asks.

Dinosaur hunters, says Little Bat in English. He grins from ear to ear, then wanders off to help carry a silver cargo trunk.

Uncle thinks it's a sign, I say.

What is?

That he is so easy to find.

Who?

The candidate, I say.

At the mention of him, the candidate floats by, a small figure dressed in white, a hat on his head with netting carefully draped to cover every inch of his face and neck. The child also wears long gloves all the way up to his shoulders. Last night the one time I see his eyes full on in the light of the fire I am not sure what I am seeing. His eyes red as if filled with blood.

Sain bainuu, says the child to Mun, and hands him a bowl of milk tea. Mun nods, speechless. He doesn't offer a hello back.

Last night decisions are made, generosity extended. Today we ride out to the dig site two to a camel. Uncle rides behind Tömör, the candidate we come to see. Because of their positions on the camel, Uncle seems like the child, Tömör the adult, which, if he is who we think he is, seems right.

Each day in the summer season the teams work until eleven o'clock, then rest for two to three hours when the sun is at its worst before picking back up. To get to the actual site, many in the expedition ride camels, though the heavier equipment is hauled over by truck.

Tömör is staying in the camp by himself, his family a hundred kilometers south tending their herds. Though he is only seven and his family lives year-round in the Gobi with their livestock, for the last two years Tömör spends his summers here with the paleontologists—he even learns English. Three summers ago his family makes their summer camp in the shadow of what turns out to be the world's largest dinosaur graveyard. Each day, rather than help with chores, the pale precocious child sprints off on his camel to see what the scientists are up to. His parents cannot keep him away. He shows such an aptitude for finding bones, for spotting where the researchers should dig, that Stevie and Jess make him an unofficial member of the team. When he points to a spot on the side of a hill that produces a dinosaur nest complete with a dozen unhatched eggs, the scientists decide to make it official. Now when Stevie and Jess and their team return each summer, Tömör joins them in camp. As his family entrusts his well-being to them for the season, the two scientists treat him like their own son. Eagerly he helps out with all aspects of the expedition. Although a congenital albino, he is the only member of the team never to complain of the heat.

Zeal for Bones

I ride over the landscape seated behind Billy, a graduate student from California, who tells me about the expedition and the history of the area. In 1922, American paleontologist Roy Chapman Andrews, whom Billy calls the real-life Indiana Jones, makes a perilous overland journey from China in his quest to find dinosaur bones. As I watch the landscape roll by, I try to imagine what it must be like to transport thousands of kilos of supplies over such terrain. Andrews uses a motorcade, driving the most technologically advanced cars of his time, but he quickly learns that animals are better. He has to carry everything his expedition needs with him. Between 1922 and 1925 he makes four journeys deep into the Gobi, discovering several new species of dinosaurs as well as the first-ever intact dinosaur eggs. Then the Soviets come into power through a series of puppet regimes and close the borders. The paleontology world loses access to the richest trove of dinosaur artifacts on earth. Andrews goes on to direct the American Museum of Natural History. Even today stories still circulate of the abuses he heaps on the local people in his zeal for bones.

Billy has long sun-bleached hair and is working on getting his doctorate. We chat a bit about our studies. Both our educations must culminate with a defense of our ideas, though in Billy's case the rules call for a defense in front of a committee of mentors about a theory he is proposing involving the evolution of hollow bones. I am to spend an evening debating several peers on deep cosmological tenets, like at what moment does consciousness enter the body and where does it come from?

After twenty minutes, I begin to feel sick, the motion of the camel like riding in a small boat. I tighten my grip on one of the camel's soft humps, each like a burlap bag filled with fat. My nausea is coupled with my twin's distant headache thundering on the horizon, his hangover a cloud hovering over us both. I reinforce the wintry scene in my mind more resolutely than before. I am one who never over-indulges with drink. To have the after-effects of drinking without the experience of drunkenness is something I find myself resenting.

Who Would Draw the Water?

Soon I spot a few tents and a *ger* set up beside a series of hills. There's no water out here, says Billy. That's why base camp is so far away. Each night we leave the place looking pretty bare-bones, he says, adding that in the past the expedition loses equipment to scavengers and profiteers, so they learn the hard way that it's better to take everything with them at day's end.

We spend the first hour unpacking what each team needs. Already the teams are at work for more than a month, racing against time to get whatever specimens they discover free of the rock. Stevie and Jess move between teams offering advice and encouragement as well as scouting future digs. Tömör trails along. The two scientists often stop to shoot infrared images of the bare ground. If things look promising, they perform a preliminary dig to hit whatever might be there. Then they try to identify what the stone might hold to see if it is worth the hundreds of hours it can take to bring it up into the light.

When I think of western scientists, I picture men in spotless white lab coats the color of snow. Stevie and Jess look nothing like what I imagine. Earlier Billy explains to me that they're a married couple. So when I see two women cresting a hill where Billy is pointing, I keep scanning the landscape. No, them, says Billy. Right there. I look again. How can they be the world-renowned dinosaur hunters?

Mun senses my confusion. They're lesbians, dummy, he thinks. In Mongolia, the idea of two women or two men making a life together is a concept I cannot imagine. In such a household, who would draw the water? Who would slaughter the animals? I am surprised my brother seems so comfortable with it, but then again, he has many more interactions with westerners than I have. Get with the times, Mun thinks.

The women are deeply tanned, wrinkles like rays shooting from the corners of their eyes, noses slathered with zinc. Both wear their hair in long braids. In some ways, they look more like mother and daughter. Stevie's hair is blond where Jess's is a pale silvery color. Billy whispers that Stevie is Jess's former student, but that's more than twenty years ago. This early in the morning, the women roll the sleeves and legs of their khaki shirts and pants all the way up, but later when the sun is broiling the earth, they unroll them for protection. There is something of the intrepid adventurer about each of them. I can easily imagine these women rolling across the landscape a hundred years ago as part of Roy Chapman Andrews's expedition.

Tömör seems nonplussed by two married women who Billy says spoil him rotten. I watch as the little boy swaddled in clothes takes Uncle's hand and begins to scramble up an embankment. I cannot help but think they look like playmates.

Billy asks why we're here. I give a nebulous answer. There's much to see in our country, I say.

I get it, Billy says. You're here for the kid.

Why do you say that, I ask.

He's something else, Billy says. An old soul. Nothing can stop him. He shakes his head. I mean, the way he finds dinosaurs out here—it's totally crazy. Billy gestures at the landscape. You dig what I'm saying, he says. It's like he's one of them. Like he's been here before.

Our Progress Hardly Discernible

Tömör and Uncle spend the morning scampering among the deep-red rocks. The two like partners in crime, the one egging the other on to new heights. I find myself shadowing Billy and a redheaded woman out to their dig site, a nondescript patch of earth covered by a blue tarp. Cindy, a fellow graduate student, rolls back the tarp to reveal a pit about one meter by three meters across. Ain't she a beauty, says Billy. He shines a flashlight in the hole.

I peer in but can't see anything. Billy seems to sense my difficulty. Yeah, at this point she's basically the same color as the rock, he says, running the light back and forth.

I get down on my hands and knees. I see something glint, a hint of bone. We call her Sally, says Cindy. She's a female adolescent. We're hoping she's the most intact protoceratops ever unearthed.

In the pit the great smile gleams. Teeth that can rip flesh to shreds with a single bite, each tooth a blade. She's probably seventy million years old, says Billy. Not that she looks a day over sixty million.

Because of the fossil's position, they choose to excavate her in this pit manner. Our biggest enemy out here, besides the sun, says Cindy, is the sand. A good sandstorm can erase days, weeks, of work. It can also wear down the fossil. It's like sandblasting, she says. What took millions and millions of years to form gets eroded in a couple of hours.

Plus it can kill you, adds Billy.

Yeah, there's that, Cindy concedes.

I spend the morning helping in any way I can. Billy and Cindy work in close quarters down in the hole while I stay aboveground, carrying away the excess dirt. Because they already excavate the earth that doesn't directly touch the specimen, the only thing left to do is the tough work of freeing the creature.

It's slow going, our progress hardly discernible. From where we are situated on the hillside I cannot see the other teams. It's like we're the only three beings in existence. Within minutes of their crawling into the hole, I sense that there is something between Billy and Cindy, an energy that has yet to express itself. The way they bicker without looking at each other. Cindy telling Billy to watch the tenth rib, Billy reminding Cindy not to hog all the light. I scan the landscape for Saran and Mun, but the earth is deserted. I imagine the pleasure and the agony of spending so many hours so close to the one you secretly love, their shadow on you at all times.

By nine o'clock it's hot. By ten it's unbearable. Billy crawls out of the hole and erects a canopy on a set of aluminum poles. It helps, though the air is superheated and unmoving, like wet wool that clings to the skin.

At eleven we stop work. We plan to return to our dig later this afternoon when the sun is not so angry. For now, we head back to the base camp where many of the others are already gathered. There's a buzz in the air, the camp blazing with excitement. What is it, asks Billy.

Uncle finds something of great interest. A mother dinosaur sitting on an intact nest of eggs. An image on a digital screen is passed around. The mother's eye socket visible in the dirt.

Impressive, says Stevie.

Uncle places a hand on Tömör's shoulder. It's all thanks to my teacher, he says. Even under his numerous protective layers, the child's happiness is evident.

Moving the Earth and Uncovering What Is

The break lasts until two. I spread my robe on the tent floor, a carpet of bright green artificial grass someone unrolls over the sand. I am not sure where our belongings are, where the Machine is. It feels good to be unencumbered. I feel like I can go anywhere, like the earth is made for my exploration.

Our journey is at its end, and from the look of things, we are successful. From the serenity of Uncle's demeanor, Tömör is indeed the One for Whom the Sky Never Darkens. What more is there to say?

Tömör rises from a nap. He is busy showing Uncle a small fossilized seashell that he discovers the previous summer. The shell is beautiful, the way it spirals like an ear. Just think, Tömör says, millions of years ago this spot is covered with water, and then millions of years later the dinosaurs roam. And now we're here.

Last night Uncle talks in depth to Stevie and Jess about the candidate. Tömör's family doesn't take refuge in the Triple Gem. They don't maintain an altar in their home. Tömör knows nothing about Buddhism. He knows more about dinosaurs and paleontology than he does about the Eternal Blue Sky.

The camp begins to scatter. People head back out to their digs. Moving the earth and uncovering what is. Bringing the geologic past to light. I watch as Mun and Saran go off with the scientist they befriend, a young assistant professor who chain-smokes and wears a ten-gallon hat despite the hat's inefficiency.

Back at our site, the sun sits in the sky like an open flame. I am thankful for the powerful SPF Cindy lends me. We work until five, taking a break to eat granola bars. Then it's back up on the camels and back to base camp. I wish I could say that I can see the difference a day's work makes, but I can barely see the specimen nestled in the darkness that holds her for eons.

In base camp it takes an hour to unpack everything. Uncle's discovery kindles a fire in the expedition. People move about, smiles on their faces, their eyes soft yet sparkling. Then the world changes.

The Sky a Dark Red

Tömör gives a sharp whistle. I look up from the crate I'm organizing filled with brushes of various sizes. With a gloved finger he points to the blue sky. In a small voice he says in English: sandstorm. There is a moment like when a flock of birds seems to hang in the air before radically shifting direction. A moment of complete stillness. Outside a camel is moaning. A pen rolls off a table.

I glance up the sky. Nothing, not so much as a cloud, the whole canopy a brilliant blue like something you can swim in. I am raised on the steppes hundreds of kilometers from here. I know nothing of the tides of the desert. Mun and Saran are also standing around confused. Then the world lurches into motion.

Little Bat hustles past, carrying a large footlocker and making for a truck. Everywhere researchers trying to batten down what needs battening, storing what can be stored. I hurry over to where Uncle is helping Tömör zipper on a series of heavy canvas panels that effectively close off the main tent. I grab a panel and get to work.

After five minutes the sky is a pale shade of lilac. To my eyes it doesn't look like anything out of the ordinary. Billy is busy wrapping up computer cables and putting them in a black hard-sided case. He works quickly though I sense a growing panic within him that he tries to keep in check.

Then I feel it. Sand gently brushing my skin. The sky still a soft pastel color, but growing darker by the minute. The panels are all zipped on, the trucks parked together, shovels at the ready for the first moments afterward.

Though I am not from here, I know that sandstorms in the Gobi can last days. Whole camps buried under mountains of sand. The sky a dark red as if filled with blood. This time of year, most storms last less than ten minutes, but for the expedition, ten minutes of sand whipping about at 150 kilometers per hour is enough to set them back for days. They can find themselves back at square one digging out a specimen—sometimes there is even more sand on the specimen than is originally the case. The red sands from the Gobi can blow all the way to Beijing, Tiananmen Square as if coated with rust.

The wind is howling like an animal. People are sitting evenly spaced around the edges of the tent with their backs to the canvas to help keep the wind from racing under the tent and lifting it into the air. The storm is not yet fully on us. One flap remains open as Stevie and Jess head out to one of the trucks to bring in the satellite phone just in case. The wind is screaming, sand whirling into the tent despite Billy and Little Bat trying to hold the flap closed with their hands. I hold my breath. Time passes. Stevie and Jess do not appear in the entrance. More time passes.

Soundless as a cloud Tömör slips out under Billy's arm. The love he feels for the two women is obvious. They are a family. He is their child.

When Tömör slips out, Uncle goes after him.

I am not really thinking of anything at the present moment. Just of the many different types of light in the world. How each one is precious. How each needs a hand to shelter it to keep it from blowing out.

And so in the ensuing chaos I am also out the door as if pulled by an invisible force. In a way, I suppose I am. Two weeks ago I vow myself to the cause of finding the One for Whom the Sky Never Darkens.

If you have attachment to this life,
You are not a religious person.
If you have attachment to existence,
You do not have transcendent renunciation.

If you have attachment to self-interest,
You do not have the spirit of enlightenment.
If grasping arises,
You do not have the authentic view.

I walk out to whatever may happen.

It Is Only an Illusion That I Am Trapped

The wind is a demon. I am within its roiling belly. I pull my robe over my head and stumble onward. It is like walking on an alien planet, a place that resists your existence. With only a few steps I have no sense of direction. The way ahead is a tunnel without walls, the noise deafening. I can't breathe. There is only heat and the burn of sand on skin, the stinging almost chemical, burning all the way through me.

I don't bother to yell. Maybe I ought to stop where I am. Perhaps by staying still, I can prevent myself from wandering out into the open desert where I would wander lost among the dunes. But I don't. The beating of my heart mirrors something in the wind, the thrum and urge. To stop would be to be smothered, to be buried like the dinosaurs, to succumb. I go on.

Quickly the sand is up to my knees. In a flash I am wading through it, the way a trapper plows a path through waist-high snow in order to find his traps. Soon it is as if I am swimming, my arms scooping desperately at the sand that is up to my chest. When I can no longer move my arms, I stop.

No. I don't stop. More accurately, the mental construct that I call my *self,* that I spend all these years projecting into the world, stops. Yes. I stop generating me. I stop being the story of someone named Chuluun, the Servant to the Redeemer Who Sounds the Conch in the Darkness. What use does life have for such illusions? No more Chuluun, no more journey. Nothing could be simpler. There is only ever this one moment. We are only ever this stillness, this silence.

And so it comes to me. The gateless gate. The deathless door.

Complete effortlessness. No dreams. No masks. From out of the annihilating sand a calmness descends, one I am only knowing for the first time. The beating of my heart fills my ears. As it is written in the Eight Verses on the Birth of the Mind:

To think "I will experience that"
Is a mistaken notion;
For the one who dies here
Is almost totally different from the one reborn.

Almost two weeks ago out on the grasslands a child aims his gun at me, and I want to live forever. Now it is as if I am shot with a diamond-tipped bullet. Clarity beyond clarity. All will be well because all *is* well, even now, in this moment at the end of all things. And suddenly the veracity of the Four Noble Truths courses through my blood: there is suffering. The cause of suffering is craving. There is an end to suffering. The end of suffering is the Eightfold Path. To finally know the Deathless now at the moment of death, to know it in the way the stars know their paths through the heavens—without thought. I become aware of a burning at the back of my throat, my lungs taking in sand, but in the same instant all I feel is gratitude. I take refuge in the Buddha, I take refuge in the Dharma, I take refuge in the *sangha*. May it never be otherwise. My being starting to fill with the foundational light of clear mind. The indestructible drop composed of the red drop from my father and the white drop from my mother, the drop quivering, on the brink of splitting.

And then he is there beside me, digging me out, his hands tearing at the sand like a machine. I feel my twin open his mind to me, clear as a mountain lake. The way we lie in each other's arms in our mother's belly, sharing this one existence between us. I am and am not the Servant to the Redeemer Who Sounds the Conch in the Darkness, and the Redeemer Who Sounds the Conch in the Darkness is and is not my brother, and there is no fire or ice between us, we are one, everything is one—one of us buried up to our neck in the sand and the other trying desperately to dig us out.

What I want to tell him in that forever moment: it's all right, leave me. It is only an illusion that I am trapped in the sand. I know now why the Buddha mandates that his monks walk the path of celibacy. I know it is not a path all can walk, but in doing so, I understand what I gain by living a dispassionate life. Renunciation is an act of liberation. It sets loose the light shining deeply within each of us, a light we can count on in the darkest dark. When you drop the world's bait, you see the world as it is. When you desire absolutely nothing, you become free.

Then my twin is pulling me up, and together through the blistering sands we are picking our way through the hills of Ulak Tolog where the dinosaurs walk tens of millions of years ago.

I take his hand in mine. There is no wall between us. There never is. The short winter days huddling together in the *ger* with Övöö and our father. The endless summer nights under the eternal blue sky. The early mornings at Yatuu Gol, first ablutions, the hours of chants performed for the enlightenment of every sentient being. And I feel his struggles of the past year. Making a life for himself in Ulaanbaatar, a place where he knows no one and no one knows him. The pain of his loneliness, of not wanting to come back, the pride, the determination. I see these past two weeks with my brother, and I know that the image I envision of him and Saran naked in each other's arms is a mental projection conjured from the darkness of my unbalanced heart, my jealousy as I stand on the edge of dedicating myself to a way of life that exists for millennia and demands that I never know the touch of a woman.

I feel my brother tighten his grip on my hand as together we stand in judgment under the merciless sands. I reach inside my robe and pull out the half-written letter.

Lust for existence chains all bodied beings.
Addiction is only cured by transcendent renunciation.

I am not sure which of us thinks these words. Perhaps my twin and I think them concurrently. I realize he knows all along of the letter girded at my heart, that even before I step foot in his small apartment in Ulaanbaatar, he knows of my struggle, and that he is consciously aiding me on my journey by not judging me for it.

I open my hand and let the winds take my doubt, the letter flying off into the storm. If I could open my eyes, I would see the world blown red as blood. This is not our first existence. If I listen hard enough, the gusting wind sounds like the distant heart that first powers the two of us into this world.

How the Great Cobra Shelters Him

Who can say how we find them? If we find them or they find us? Our hands tell us it is them. One with a robe pulled over his head. This is Uncle. The smaller form swaddled in cloth. Tömör. I sink down beside Uncle. Mun across from me. Together the four of us form a circle, our backs to the raging world. Let all be well. And just like that, all is well.

The first camel arrives, walking out of the flying sand, and lies down at our backs. I can feel the heat of the animal through my robe. Another arrives and positions herself perpendicular to the first. Then a third, then a fourth, and our shelter is complete, the animals like a pen around us. Is it my brother's ferocious deity Hayagrīva, the Horse-Necked One, that summons these animals to us from out of the roaring sands? At this moment are the pupils of Mun's eyes ablaze, each one ringed with a burning corona?

I think of the story of the Buddha and the Naga, how the great cobra shelters Him with her hood when it begins to rain, spreading it over Him as He waits for enlightenment to come. In such a moment there is time to think. The four of us in the lotus position. Every grain of sand, every drop of blood, every second on the earth and beyond. All contained in this one instant.

And so the great fires are extinguished in my brother. The one he has continually banked against me all these years. What I see is both dark and light. All his hopes, his fears, his dreams. His loneliness at Yatuu Gol. Sitting on his golden cushion at the head of the assembly. Ringing the bells. Chanting the prayers. Touching strangers with his forehead. Bestowing grace upon them. And the afternoon more than a year ago when my twin disrobes. The herder and his wife in the Rinpoche's office, their heads bowed, their daughter beside them. In Mongolia, an unexpected pregnancy is not looked down on if the man agrees to marriage. Because of the vastness of the grasslands, often there is not time for traditional courtship. If a girl falls pregnant after the chance meeting of a stranger, then the man is summoned and welcomed into the family, even if the man is a monk. Here among the burning sands my heart fills as I relive my brother's emotions one year ago when he disrobes after a brief encounter with a local girl. I watch as one week after disrobing, my twin leaves for the capital on the eve of his wedding when he learns it is a false alarm.

Then a great secret comes unmoored. Memories whipping about in the sand. In my brother's wayward life, there is only ever this girl and no other. The daughter of a poor herder living in the shadow of the volcano. I see my brother entering the home during an afternoon of *gurem,* I hear him murmur a prayer for the family, see them offer him what little they have. It's only now I realize the truth of it: he loves her. Theirs is not some sordid encounter. He loves her ever since walking through the door with his head bowed, the girl offering him a bowl of milk tea, their fingers touching, then the secret exchange of letters, their one and only meeting out on a hilltop at night among the grasslands—the human softness, the heat, the heartache when it is all a false alarm, and the resolve to go to the capital, to make a life, to establish himself, and, when he does, to bring her to be with him, her name Sarangerel, moonlight, not our Saran but another who lights up the earth, how I know now when he looks at our Saran he sees this other, nothing more, and I finally understand the great sacrifice he makes in giving up his job to come with us in our search as this journey significantly delays his plans for their reunion.

In turn my brother sees into me more deeply than ever before. The moment like standing naked on the surface of the sun. My reservations at taking my final vows. My sadness at never knowing the full pleasures of my body. My jealousy at his forging his own path forward.

Then out of the sand, a voice says: brother monks! Shed passion and aversion, as jasmine would its withered flowers. There is a door in every mountain, a secret drawer in every chest. Open it and enter into the place of emptiness.

As Jasmine Would Its Withered Flowers

We Should Look Upon All This as a Bubble

Now Saran sits in the back with Uncle. Her hair no longer finds its way into my mouth. The great mystery is solved, the reason why Saran floats above the earth, a dreamy smile playing across her face. Saran is in love! She is in love with neither me nor my twin. The man is a novice back at Gandan Tegchenling Monastery. Like Little Bat, he is also from Amdo Province in Tibet. This man is the reason Saran speaks Tibetan. The Abbot of Gandan Tegchenling sends her with us in the hopes of breaking up the happy couple. But after a few hours of sitting next to Uncle in the back seat, Saran confesses her secret. The old monk pats her hand kindly and tells her all is well. My favorite poet claims a lover has four streams inside, Uncle says, of water, wine, honey, and milk. Find them in yourself and pay no attention to so-and-so about such-and-such. There is so much kindness in his voice. Even in this moment of darkest dark.

Outside the landscape depresses. All day we are driving in Ikh Khorig, the Great Taboo. All day among the things the Russian army casts off decades ago. Shells of rusted-out trucks. Piles of empty crates, furniture, antiquated electronics. What from a distance looks like an *ovoo* is only a heap of boots. The earth is ugly, scarred, the trees cleared, the land as if mined for minerals, blasted by the artillery ranges we see every few minutes.

A hundred kilometers back we pass a herd of *takhi,* also known as Przewalski's horses. Twenty years ago *takhi* are all but extinct in the wild and found only in zoos and animal reserves, but recently scientists are reintroducing them to Mongolia. In other countries there are herds of horses that roam free, like the mustang in the American West, but such herds are feral horses that escape from domesticated stock. The *takhi* is the last true wild horse in existence—it is never domesticated.

The animals are short-legged and stout, most with brown heads and backs that gradually taper to a soft gray color on their underbellies the way color slowly changes on a fish. Their manes are short and bristly, like shorn grass. As we drive past, one raises its head from where it is feeding to stare at us. To descend from a lineage of pure freedom, to never know the bit in the mouth, the saddle. The image of this small herd stays with me even when it is well behind us. Perhaps someday a thousand years from now these horses may once again claim the land. A colt nuzzles its mother's belly. I think of the red horse that is born during the first *zud* of my youth. The Buddha says we should look upon all this as a bubble, that the visible world is only a dream. Species thrive and wither, thrive again. Universes are born and fall dead. We drive on.

Now a White Cord Stretches Between Us

We are driving to Burkhan Khaldun. Last year God Mountain is declared a UNESCO World Heritage Site. The Soviets establish the Forbidden Zone when they come to power through the puppet leader Choibalsan, but even before the Russians, there is a centuries-long prohibition banning Mongolians from this area, what Mongolians call the Great Taboo. Chinggis Khaan dies in 1227 presumably in his sixties. Historians claim he is surrounded by family and loved ones, that he has an easy passing. Conversely, the people he conquers tell vastly different tales of his demise. That he is poisoned. That he is stabbed. That a Tangut queen somehow hides a blade inside her body, and that when he copulates with her, his privates are shredded, leaving him to die in utter anguish, rendered completely manless.

In Mongolia, our first god is the Eternal Blue Sky. We never celebrate the dead the way other cultures do. Traditionally our leaders don't build mausoleums, pyramids, erecting great stones to remind the world that they exist. In the Mongolia of old, when a person dies, the body is either burned or left exposed for the animals. There is no other way. Our long winters mean that the earth is frozen solid for a third of the year. But in the Mongolia of today most bodies are buried, a few cremated in hospitals or modern funeral homes. Despite modern technology, nobody knows where the body of Chinggis Khaan is laid to rest except that it is somewhere here on God Mountain in the rolling green hills of Khentii *aimag,* the very place where he is born and what is subsequently named the Great Taboo, and which is off-limits for centuries.

It is said that when Chinggis Khaan is a young man, he passes a night on God Mountain and has a vision of his life to come. He declares that he wants to be buried here along with his descendants. Stories come down through the generations that a funeral cortege of more than a thousand warriors accompany the Khaan's body to its final resting place. Allegedly four hundred workers are used to cover the tracks made by this great host. In turn, these four hundred workers are killed in order to maintain the secret of where the Khaan is laid to rest. Legend has it that the killers of these four hundred are then themselves killed, and so on, ad nauseam, killers killing killers killing killers. An elite group of warriors named the Darkhad are charged with guarding the sacred site. Upon pain of death, only holy men or those burying a direct descendent of Chinggis Khaan are allowed to enter the Great Taboo.

More than seven hundred years after his death, the Soviets are still afraid of the Khaan and his lasting influence on his people. When they come to power, they take over the Great Taboo and rename it the Forbidden Zone. And so in 1937, at the height of Stalinist repression in Mongolia, the spirit of Chinggis Khaan goes missing, his spirit embodied in his *sulde,* the talisman a warrior-herder would erect each night outside his *ger*. A *sulde* is made by gathering hair from the tails of his swiftest horses and then tying them to a spear. Over time as it ages outside under the eternal blue sky, the *sulde* becomes saturated with the spirit of the elements, elements that are eventually channeled into the very spirit of the warrior himself. When he dies, it is said the warrior's spirit lives on in the *sulde.* For centuries the *sulde* of Chinggis Khaan is kept in a monastery along the River of the Moon. But in 1937, the Soviets destroy the monastery, and the *sulde* goes missing.

I remember one day out on the grasslands finding Mun plucking hairs from the tail of his horse. My twin tells me he is making his own *sulde.* I watch as he ties the hairs to an old radio antenna he's scavenged. The hairs hang limp. There are just a few strands, ten at most; most *sulde* are built over time and so become lush and full.

That is the first time I sense the fire in Mun, his ability to shut me out, though it is a skill he has yet to perfect. I follow him as he plants his *sulde* outside our *ger*. I cannot fathom the reason why he needs a *sulde*. When I try to access his thoughts, all I feel is a burning like holding my hand too long over a match.

Now my brother sits beside me in a world without fire or ice. As we drive along, we are connected by more than the caul that covers our face at birth. Now a white cord stretches between us, one earbud in my brother's ear, the other in mine. Earlier this morning as we break camp, I find my brother's MP3 player lying on a tarp. When I pick it up, it turns on. Something is amiss. I scroll through the screen. The only western album I find is one by the Beatles. Instead, packed on the little device are hundreds, thousands, of Buddhist chants in all languages. I press PLAY, and *Om tare tuttare ture svaha* fills my ears. This is the mantra of the Green Tara, the Mother of Buddhas.

> *May this mantra take root in my heart. May my mind, body, and speech be free of delusions and the eight fears. May I be liberated from duality. May I know ease.*

I don't know if my twin might ever come back to the faith. I know of stories of monks living monastic lives in the west, beings who are at once mindful and yet also completely of the world. Perhaps my brother is to be the one to fully bridge these two existences. As this journey teaches me, it is not my place to hope for an outcome. We must drop the world's bait. My brother is who he is. After the sandstorm as the four of us rise from the desert floor, my brother prostrates himself before Uncle. He remains a long time lying in the sand, his arms outstretched above his head, until Uncle finally pulls him up onto his feet.

May This Come to Pass

Even now Uncle is serene. As always, a calm light radiates from his face despite the plain white urn that sits between him and Saran.

During the terrible storm, Stevie and Jess wait out the sand in one of the trucks. They do not know that Tömör goes looking for them. They do not know what follows. When the sand stops, the landscape is different. Suddenly there are dunes where there are not dunes before. And the dunes that once exist are completely erased.

When Uncle goes out in search of Tömör, Little Bat follows. Somehow he never makes his way into our circle, the camels shielding us with their bodies. It takes several hours to find Little Bat. As is fitting, in the end, it is Uncle who finds him. Little Bat is his heart's disciple. The big monk is no more than a few meters from the tent's opening. We pull Little Bat's body from a five-meter mountain of sand.

Happily, he looks peaceful. There is no indication of pain, of the sand burning his lungs as he breathes it in. In his hands, he clutches a battered photograph, the figure in it barely visible, the photo more than thirty years old. You can only tell it is a picture of His Holiness by the way the figure is seated and His yellow-crested lama hat. I can still see Little Bat at break of day each morning praying for all sentient beings. The deep place he enters within minutes. May he find that as the sands are burying him. May he once again look upon his mother and his father and his brothers and baby Pema. May his spirit be a light to all those who wish to cross the mountains.

We are driving here to scatter a third of his ashes on God Mountain, in the place where the Great Khaan also lies and where even now only holy beings are allowed entrance. Another third of his ashes are to be scattered on a Bodhi tree back at the monastery in Dharamshala where the Dalai Lama presides over the Tibetan government-in-exile. And one day, perhaps in a life to come, Uncle might carry the remaining third to the mountain hermitage in Amdo province where Little Bat remembers playing as a boy in the land where he is born. May this come to pass in a world in which the Chinese no longer do such things as disappear a small child as they do to the Panchen Lama, the second-highest-ranking lama in Tibetan Buddhism who many years ago is disappeared along with His family and is not heard from since.

Listen Without Distraction

And what of the one whom we are seeking among the Reindeer People, the eagle hunters of the Altai Mountains, and the killing sands of the Gobi? Uncle does not say which is his old friend the One for Whom the Sky Never Darkens. First he must consult with His Holiness. Of the three children he only says when asked that all three are old friends—the boy shaman, the girl hunter, the ghostly dinosaur seer. Like mind, body, and speech, he says. It is then my brother silently reminds me that it is possible for a holy man to reincarnate his energy in several beings at once. It's true. In Sikkim there are two reincarnations of the one named the Benevolent Jewel. One is the reincarnation of actions, the other of compassion.

Then a thought bubbles up simultaneously in both our minds as if my twin and I are crafting the idea together. The Dharma is perfect, but men are the instrument through which it turns. Men are fallible in ways the Dharma is not. In the turning of the wheel, mistakes can be made. Perhaps it is why up until now my brother and I are in conflict all these years. Our true self knows no division. If one of us is the 5th Incarnation of the Paljor Jamgon lineage, the Redeemer Who Sounds the Conch in the Darkness, then we both are. If one of us is not the 5th Incarnation of the Paljor Jamgon lineage, then neither are. We are both servant and redeemer. There is no contradiction, only peace.

From the back seat Uncle taps me on the shoulder. For you, is the reincarnation the only objective of this journey, he asks. When I don't answer, he laughs, this man with one hand on the ashes of his heart's disciple. It is a weak faith that depends on the existence of a single being, he says.

And with that briefest of Dharma talks, my understanding is perfected, the wheel complete. Everywhere the world is raining flowers. Before me the way is paved with the yellow dung of good fortune. A woman lies down to sleep, and in the night a white elephant enters her womb holding a lotus blossom in its trunk. Twenty-five hundred years later, an interviewer asks the Dalai Lama: China is destroying your land, your people, your culture—how do you remain so joyful? His Holiness responds: I cannot let them destroy my happiness.

In this eon, a thousand Buddhas are said to rise and fall. Siddhartha Gautama, the Shakyamuni Buddha, is the fourth Buddha of our age. The next Buddha is named Maitreya. All sentient beings contain Buddhahood. Before this universe ends, every single being is to attain it.

Let me die tomorrow and never be reborn. I am ready to take my vows to renounce the world. My doubts remain, but now I recognize that they are part of the path. I must let my doubts enter me the way one might welcome a stranger into a hut on the edge of a forest. When the stranger arrives, one does not ask the guest why they exist, what their purpose is. One simply sits and listens without judgment or striving. I seek nothing. I am nothing. There is only refuge in the Buddha, in the Dharma, in the *sangha*. There is only refuge in wisdom, compassion, and goodness. There is only refuge in the way things are.

In all four schools of Tibetan Buddhism, there is the practice of reincarnation. Whole books are written on the mysteries of death. As we drive toward God Mountain, I ponder this. How long does it take the self to dissipate? How does one hold on to the heart's essence, the pure white light that shines in the center of the body after everything else is burned away? And do we come back to this earth in the same vessel, or is everything changed? Do we go back into the cosmic wellspring where each night is four billion years long, and at the end of it all, does the universe collapse on itself only to cycle into existence again? Or is it only metaphorical? Am I reborn each moment with each breath? Is each second of my life a choice? Does each instance take me down a different path? Does what I do from one minute to the next determine who I am and what energy I draw to myself? From my karma am I born and reborn thousands of times a day?

A few years back, His Holiness writes the following:

Therefore, as I have a responsibility to protect the Dharma and sentient beings and counter such detrimental schemes, I make the following declaration: When I am about ninety I will consult the high Lamas of the Tibetan Buddhist traditions, the Tibetan public, and other concerned people who follow Tibetan Buddhism, and reevaluate whether the institution of the Dalai Lama should continue or not. On that basis we will take a decision. If it is decided that the reincarnation of the Dalai Lama should continue and there is a need for the 15th Dalai Lama to be recognized, responsibility for doing so will primarily rest on the concerned officers of the Dalai Lama's Gaden Phodrang Trust. They should consult the various heads of the Tibetan Buddhist traditions and the reliable oath-bound Dharma Protectors who are linked inseparably to the lineage of the Dalai Lamas. They should seek advice and direction from these concerned beings and carry out the procedures of search and recognition in accordance with past tradition. I shall leave clear written instructions about this. Bear in mind that, apart from the reincarnation recognized through such legitimate methods, no recognition or acceptance should be given to a candidate chosen for political ends by anyone, including those in the People's Republic of China.

Listen without distraction: one day the light that is Little Bat may cycle back to this world, he who is well along the path toward mastering full-knowing. In turn, one day this light is to go in search of Uncle, just as one day someone is tasked with hunting for my brother, the Redeemer Who Sounds the Conch in the Darkness. Who knows what can be found if only one is open to seeing?

And now? Can you hear all the universes glimmering in your heart? Are you ready to drop the world's bait? What would happen if we each renounce the need for a grand narrative and simply vow to be present for each moment along the path? Yesterday I am an old man sitting in an ocean of grass. Tomorrow I am an infant growing in the billion-billion-armed cave of night. I am. I am not. I am again. Maybe one day someone might come seeking me.

Do Not Seek an Easy Victory
but Always Prefer a Defeat
That Advances Your Learning

DEFENDER: Sing, Bodhisattva of Heavenly Wisdom, in just this way on the subject of impermanence and nothingness.

QUESTIONER: And what would you claim on the topic of impermanence and nothingness?

DEFENDER: As my thesis, I state as given that whatever is produced is impermanent, just like a jar or a sound. I claim that my subject, Love, is not impermanent because it is not a product.

QUESTIONER: A clarification: if Love is not a product, then what is it?

DEFENDER: Love is not a product, like a jar or a sound. Love is a force.

QUESTIONER: The tides are a force. When they rise unexpectedly beyond the scope of human foresight, they sweep away entire civilizations. Yet the tides are a product of the moon's pull on the earth.

DEFENDER: There is no perversion. Love is neither created nor destroyed. It exists at all times and in all dimensions. Love is not something we create—it is something that wells up in us, like sap in a tree. It is an element in the fabric of the universe. Even on that distant day when sentient beings no longer exist, Love carries on. Perhaps our personal relationship to Love is impermanent, but Love itself is not.

QUESTIONER: The Buddha teaches us that nothing is permanent. All is impermanent. Human suffering arises in part from our craving for permanence.

DEFENDER: It is not established. If nothing is permanent, then that is a permanence. If nothing is absolute, then that is an absolute.

QUESTIONER: The cosmos itself is impermanent. If Love is an element in the fabric of the universe, then one day it too shall cease.

DEFENDER: The universe may cease to exist, but it does not follow that the fabric of which it is built should also cease. Love exists with or without us. Our purpose is to testify and witness its power, and in doing so we strengthen it. If a house is burned to the ground, the house and its effects still exist. True, the wood's material appearance is transformed into ash, but ash, like wood, is still elementally carbon. Love also changes over time and space. At times it can seem to disappear, as when one brother turns against his twin. But when this happens, it is because we close ourselves off to Love, like turning off a tap. Reopen the tap, and what always exists is known again, new and stronger. What the Buddha teaches us: when the only hope is a boat and there is no boat, we will be the boat. Time is irrelevant. There is only the present moment. Make of yourself a light that is unwavering.

ACKNOWLEDGMENTS

In researching this work, I owe many thanks to many individuals across the globe. Often after sharing with me their knowledge, guides, scholars, and religious figures would generously put me in contact with others, who in turn would introduce me to still others. It is with deep gratitude that I thank the following people for sharing their time and thoughts. Please note that all shortcomings or errors in depicting the life of a follower of the Dharma are strictly mine.

I spent one of my most memorable birthdays ever in the Gobi with "Jojo" Munkhzolboo Purev and Oogii of Tseren Tours—they introduced me to "The Whistle Song," which still brings me deep peace. Thanks also to the various guides and horsemen who showed me the regions where Chinggis Khaan was born.

Bhutan Travel was instrumental in helping me find my way in both northern India and Bhutan, and for introducing me to the knowledgeable and generous Karma Phuntsho, who chatted with me one afternoon; years later I ran into him in India, because it is indeed a small world. He is the founder of the Loden Organization, which supports social entrepreneurship and Bhutan's cultures and traditions. See www.loden.org for more information or to make a donation.

Early in the process, Anne Hansen introduced me to John Dunne, who in turn led me to Michael Jerryson, who then suggested I contact ErdeneBaatar Erdene-Ochir—thanks to all for their expertise and for elucidating the more complicated aspects of Tibetan Buddhism.

Similarly, Isadora Wagner at West Point led to Richard K. Wagner, who in turn directed me to the American Center for Mongolian Studies in Ulaanbaatar, where I encountered Temple MFA grad and jack-of-all-trades Narantsogt "Natso" Baatarkhuu, who then identified

Davaapurev Sainkhuu, a lama at the Gandan Tegchenling Monastery, as someone I should indeed contact. Natso in particular was a tremendous resource and an amazing reader of the work. Additionally I am indebted to him for his translations of various Mongolian idioms scattered through the text.

Fellow seeker Kelly Parks Snider put me in touch with Richard Davidson, who led to Dr. Barry Kerzin, whose thoughts on various sutras were tremendously inspiring.

Another early reader of the work was my friend and colleague Ron Kuka, who teaches at the University of Wisconsin–Madison, where several of the folks listed above also make their homes. I thank UW-Madison for funding that made possible many of my travels and interviews.

And a special thanks to my first teacher, Jan Sheppard, whose knowledge, grace, and energy are a blessing to the Madison area and beyond.

Finally, here are some Mongolian organizations that support Mongolian scholars, arts, and literature. Please see their websites for more information or to donate to their causes:

American Center for Mongolian Studies (www.mongoliacenter.org)
Mongol American Cultural Association (www.maca-usa.org)
The Mongolian Society (www.mongoliasociety.org)

Again, I thank these individuals and organizations for their help. To them, the various *sanghas* of which I am a member, and to anyone I may have overlooked—wishing auspiciousness to all!

BIBLIOGRAPHY

Dreyfus, Georges B. J. *The Sound of One Hand Clapping.* University of California Press, 2003.

Fremantle, Francesca, and Chögyam Trungpa. *The Tibetan Book of the Dead.* Shambhala Publications, 2000.

Kahn, Paul, tr. *The Secret History of the Mongols.* Cheng & Tsui, 1998.

Miles, Jack, ed. *The Norton Anthology of World Religions.* Norton, 2015.

Ajahn Munindo, tr. *A Dhammapada for Contemplation.* Aruna Publications, 2010.

Powers, John. *Introduction to Tibetan Buddhism.* Snow Lion Publications, 1995.

Reeves, Gene. *The Stories of the Lotus Sutra.* Wisdom Publications, 2010.

Stewart, Stanley. *In the Empire of Genghis Khan.* Lyons Press, 2002.

Thanissaro Bhikkhu, tr. *Dhammapada: A Translation.* Dhamma Dana Publications, 1998.

Thurman, Robert A. F. *Essential Tibetan Buddhism.* HarperSanFrancisco, 1995.

Weatherford, Jack. *Genghis Khan and the Making of the Modern World.* Broadway Books, 2004. Much of the description of Chinggis Khaan on pages 250–252 comes from this source.

FILMS

Cave of the Yellow Dog, 2005, dir. Byambasuren Davaa

The Eagle Huntress, 2016, dir. Otto Bell

The Little Buddha, 1993, dir. Bernardo Bertolucci

My Reincarnation, 2011, dir. Jennifer Fox

The Story of the Weeping Camel, 2003, dir. Byambasuren Davaa and Luigi Falomi

Unmistaken Child, 2008, dir. Nati Baratz

On page 279, Uncle's "favorite poet" is Rumi. The excerpts are from *Rumi: The Big Red Book,* translated by Coleman Barks (New York: HarperOne, 2011).

A handful of images (*e.g.,* page 6: "rising up rooted like a tree") were inspired by *Rilke's Book of Hours: Love Poems to God,* translated by Anita Barrows and Joanna Macy.

ALSO BY

Quan Barry

SHE WEEPS EACH TIME YOU'RE BORN

Vietnam, 1972: under a full moon, on the banks of the Song Ma River, a baby girl is pulled out of her dead mother's grave. This is Rabbit, who is born with the ability to speak with the dead. She will flee from her destroyed village with a makeshift family thrown together by war. As Rabbit channels the voices of the dead, their chorus reconstructs the turbulent history of a nation, from the days of French Indochina and the World War II rubber plantations to the chaos of postwar reunification. Radiant, lyrical, and deeply moving, this is the unforgettable story of one woman's struggle to unearth the true history of Vietnam while also carving out a place for herself within it.

Fiction

WE RIDE UPON STICKS

In the town of Danvers, Massachusetts, home of the original 1692 witch trials, the 1989 Danvers Falcons will do anything to make it to the state finals—even if it means tapping into some devilishly dark powers. Quan Barry expertly weaves together the individual and collective progress of this enchanted team as they storm their way through an unforgettable season. Helmed by good-girl captain Abby Putnam (a descendant of the infamous Salem accuser Ann Putnam) and her co-captain, Jen Fiorenza (whose bleached blond "Claw" sees and knows all), the Falcons prove to be wily, original, and bold, flaunting society's stale notions of femininity.

Fiction

VINTAGE CONTEMPORARIES
Available wherever books are sold.
vintagebooks.com